DATE
WITH A
ROCKSTAR

SARAH GAGNON

Spencer Hill Contemporary / Spencer Hill Press

Please visit our website at www.spencerhillpress.com

First Edition: June 2015
Sarah Gagnon
Date With a Rockstar/ by Sarah Gagnon – 1st ed.
p. cm.

Summary: Girl enters reality TV show dating contest
with a rockstar so she can win the prize money to
cure her illness and ends up falling for him.

The author acknowledges the copyrighted or
trademarked status and trademark owners of the
following wordmarks mentioned in this fiction: Boston
University, Chase, Jaguar, Macy's, Sheridan Luxury

Cover Design: Christa Holland
Interior layout: Jenny Perinovic

978-1-93939-258-9 (paperback)
978-1-93939-265-7 (e-book)

Printed in the United States of America

To Letta and Violet
for making me want to be more.

ONE

J EREMY BANE IS the most attractive guy on the planet. I once watched a documentary about his face. They had these charts mapping the symmetry of each of his features. According to the show, his lips are perfectly colored and proportioned to the size of his head. His strong jaw is masculine without being intimidating. His warm brown eyes seduce *and* comfort. There was even a medical explanation for why girls love him, but for me, it's all about his music. The eerie, haunting tones of his songs have been downloaded by billions.

But I'm not one of those lust-struck minions. I have another reason for being in this line. Two words: Prize. Money.

"What size shoe does he wear?" a girl behind me asks loudly, pulling me out of my thoughts.

"Eleven," a voice answers. She sounds shocked that the girl didn't already know.

Rain slides down my back. Jeremy Bane trivia is fun and all, but after three days of suffering in line, I just want silence. I'm so wet, the skin around my nails is beginning to peel. I lightly touch my tongue to my lips. The rain tastes metallic. Does pollution have a flavor?

I'm one of thousands in this line, which extends along the side of the building to the corner, wraps around the side and disappears. It's hard to imagine so many girls in one place—all of those families choosing their one allocated child to be female. With the child limits, Mom thought they might bring back welfare or free medical services, but the population boom that started in 2034 shows no sign of slowing twenty years later, and no government is that wealthy.

"No, I'm not going to give him your picture. I'm the one waiting." The girl in front of me clicks off her phone and presses her forehead against the cement wall.

I know her name is Susan because she keeps her phone volume on max and makes calls every hour. In front of her a plump, pink-complexioned girl huddles under an umbrella. I don't know her name, but I almost wish she'd pass out so I could snatch her damn umbrella. Asking one of them to hold my place in line while I go back home to get dry clothes is unthinkable. The other girls would rip me apart if I tried to get back in line. This is a competition. No one's my friend. Still, I feel a sense of familiarity with the people closest to me. I know the noises they make in their sleep and for the past few days, I've tolerated all their impatient fidgeting. All for a chance. Not a guarantee, just a chance.

My wet jeans chafe my waist, driving me crazy. I want to be dry. I close my eyes and slip into a daydream of basking on a warm, dry beach. Jeremy sits up and nudges my shoulder, quirking his lip in his famous smile. I try to feel the heat of the day, the heat of his smile. Instead, the rain intensifies, ruining my fantasy.

Okay, maybe part of me is one of those lust-sick minions. Jeremy Bane is beautiful, but I need money a hell of a lot more than a date. Until I'm disease free, nothing else matters.

TWO

A WHISTLE BLOWS. I jump to my feet, stagger with stiffness, and stand out from the wall, trying to catch a glimpse of what's going on. The studio door opens and a bald man steps out. Rain slides off his scalp as he adjusts the neck of his sports jacket. He's big all over. His shoes sink through the puddles as he moves farther away, glancing up and down the line. He shakes his head like we all disgust him.

Switching on the mic near his chin, he begins, "Listen up, girls. This is how we're going to proceed."

I lean forward, trying to hear, but everyone else does the same. All of us are straining against the invisible tether lashing us to the line.

"I'm going to hand out numbers in groups of two hundred and fifty. The first group will begin auditioning now. The second will come back tomorrow at seven a.m., and so on. Think you can handle that?" He stops and wipes the rain off his face with a rough hand. "When the top ten are selected, an announcement will be made on the general air waves, so don't be chatting on your phones or you'll miss it."

I glance down at my black T-shirt. I'm dirty and I'm in the first group. Others will have the chance to clean up and go home for the night, but I'll be ushered in. A day early. The strands of hair plastered to my neck flow like an oil slick.

"Pay attention, girls."

The other girls stop their nervous giggling.

"I'm only giving out a thousand numbers." Two reporters pop out of the back of one of the news vans. Channels seventy-five and thirteen have been camped out with us, gathering footage of the line. A guy in jeans balances a mini-cam on his knee, trying to keep the frame perfectly still for broadcast. I keep my head down. Right now nothing about me is TV worthy.

The reporters scramble around, pointing out what to film. I guess no one tipped them off about the auditions beginning a day early. A girl runs past the news crew and darts into the line right in front of me. The camera swings toward me, following her run. I freeze. The girl can't be more than fourteen. She bounces up and down on her toes, then goes still. I have to say something. Susan spins on the girl.

"What the hell do you think you're doing?" She pushes her and the girl stumbles into me. I catch her gently by the elbow. I don't want to be seen fighting. Susan curls back her lips in a snarl. "No. Line. Cutters." She punches the girl in the stomach and she collapses onto my feet. Susan turns away.

I reach down to help the girl up. "You can't cut like this." I try to step away.

Her hand clings to mine, nails scratching into my skin. "Please. I need to see Jeremy. Let me stay. Just pretend I've been here all along." She stares up at me, begging.

"Sorry." I shake my head. "I've been waiting too long. All of these girls have been." Then I point out the camera to her. "They have you on film, anyway, and besides, you're too young." I wrench my arm out of her grip. She sniffles and then starts a wailing cry. Susan keeps staring ahead as though nothing is happening. A team of bodyguards emerge from the door and follow the pointing. I press against the wall while they scoop her up and carry her off.

"Enough," the man in charge announces. The line quiets. With security right in our faces, it's all becoming so real.

"As I was saying. The numbers will be handed out in groups of two hundred and fifty. After that, the rest of you need to get out of here. No hanging around trying to get a glimpse of the winners."

A young guy in a suit steps out of the doorway with a clipboard. I focus on his serious face rather than his words. "...first names."

Ah, crap. I missed something. "What did he say?" I ask Susan. She squints her eyes at me like I'm too stupid to be any competition. She doesn't answer. At the front of the line, the first girl slips into the open door. She smiles back at us and gives a half-wave. "She's been here for two weeks," whispers through the line.

Jeremy Bane makes girls psychotic, and even some guys, too. In a recent interview he told the reporter that, though he has no current girlfriend, he is definitely hetero. Which accounts for why the equally infatuated guys who tried to enter the line had been promptly removed. With so many girls to choose from, I need to stand out. Jeremy controls who receives the prize money, and I need him to pick me.

Twenty minutes pass before the guy with the clipboard reaches me. "Proof of identity," he mumbles. I hand him my ID card. "Do you speak English?"

"Yes, sir." *Are they cutting the non-English speaking girls before the auditions?*

He makes a quick mark on the paper. "Name?"

"Monet O'Neal," I respond, even though he can see it printed on my card.

He grunts in response and stares sharply at me before handing me a number. *Probably making sure*

I'm a girl. He moves to the next girl in line. I slump back against the wall, cradling the number forty-two in my hand.

I take a comb out of my pack and work the snarls out of my long, brown hair. My cheeks are clammy and numb. Susan takes out a box of make-up and leans down to protect it from the rain. I try to see myself in her mirror, but she angles it away. A general melancholy over ruined appearances replaces the excitement of the line moving. I must look like shit. I'm shivering and I haven't slept much. What kind of impression will this first two hundred and fifty make? Maybe since we look so horrible, Jeremy will feel sorry for one of us. I need to balance between sympathetic and attractive. Gross, but not too gross. I let my breath out, mildly comforted by the logic.

Each time the line moves, I'm hit with a new rush of adrenaline and doubt. I've never tried to do anything so public. Hiding at home, keeping my disease a secret was the easy part. Now I have the chance to fail...or win. A large group gets ushered in together and then the line stalls. After that it takes a few minutes before each individual girl is let in. I clench my toes inside my sneakers.

The man handing out numbers disappears around the side of the building. There can't be many left. I hear screaming in the distance and then more security runs past. A group of girls circle back around the building and walk past us. Their hands are clenched and their faces are streaked with mascara tears.

"You don't deserve Jeremy. None of you do!" one of them yells. Another kicks a rock at us. I grip my number in my fist. If there's a fight, I'm never letting go. I might be quiet, but I'm not weak. I need this chance to change my life. The news crew walks closer to the girls and they switch from taunting to waving at the viewers at home. Security comes back and ushers them away.

An empty sickness fills me. Susan is at the front of the line. A pair of bodyguards step out, call her name and number, then she's gone. I stare at the closed door in front of me—a plain steel door with no handle on the outside. I'm wearing black ballet flats, sage jeans, and a T-shirt. This is the most attractive outfit I own. Nothing high-tech and figure enhancing for me. Three days ago, I looked cute. Now I'm drenched and dirty.

"Forty-two, Monet," clipboard guy calls out. He doesn't bother to glance up from his list.

I step through the door.

THREE

THE DOOR SLAMS shut behind me, closing out the rain and the chatter of the line. The big guys lead me down the hallway. Florescent lights flicker overhead and my feet squelch on the tile floor. The closer I get, the more I focus on my reasons and goals. I recite the flyer from the health clinic in my head. The words have been seared into my mind for two years.

Fluxem is a disease spread through saliva. The symptoms range from skin lesions, to red banding around the center of the body. As the disease progresses, a strong iodine smell may accompany the marks. Twenty-five percent of the world population reports symptoms of infection with the highest concentration being in poor communities.

Luckily or unluckily, the disease is completely curable for the bargain price of twenty thousand dollars—about the same as two months' rent in the nice part of town. Way too much frigging money for me and Mom. A private company developed the cure and they set the price. The government won't stand up to them, no matter how many Internet petitions I sign. The messed up part is that, in ten percent of Fluxem cases, complications occur and can lead to death. People are dying. Maybe even me, and still they won't give it away. And there's no way with Mom's credit rating that anyone will loan us money, especially not for medical reasons because there'd be nothing to repossess.

When Fluxem first showed up in the populous thirty years ago, there were all these charities devoted to finding the cure and helping people. We watched the old videos in class. Everyone focused on the terrible new disease. Then five years later some big company found a cure, and just like that everyone stopped talking about it. The cure was found, so the rich people were safe. Never mind that most of the world can't afford it. Every few years it pops up on the political agenda of someone who's running for office, but so far nothing has changed. Too many people, not enough resources.

There's even a vaccine, but obviously that would be too late for me.

I'm a carrier, and I don't have 20K. But the producers of the show do. They're offering thirty thousand to the winner of the competition, and a "chance at love!"– whatever that means. I used the tax calculator on the government website and based on my earnings and the winnings, I'll get to keep about 19K. Almost exactly the amount I need. The money's a big enough sum that most of the eligible population in Boston is probably in line, and who knows how many others flew in. Based on all the company logos on the advertisements, the producers have tons of corporate sponsors. It would be fitting if one of the drug companies paid for the prize money that would allow me to get the cure.

I suck my lips in, embarrassed to be contagious. I don't have outward signs yet, but I know that could change. Just like I knew every day of high school that if just one of my classmates found out, everyone in the school would know within seconds. The government might not provide medical treatment, but they'll sure buy TVs and computers for the populous if they think it will buy them votes. Most of the kids with money make smear videos for fun. As soon as they catch a student at their worst, the footage is repeated, then music and cruel titles are added. Wham, immortalized in the worst way. I just want to be left alone. I don't want anyone to have a reason to focus on me. And I'm a frigging idiot for auditioning for a TV show, but I really need the money. The alternative is years of saving for me and Mom. If there's even the slightest chance that Jeremy might pick me, then I have to try.

"In here." One of the big guys opens the door and I step into a waiting room. The chairs are full of girls. I turn in a slow circle, not sure what I'm supposed to do next.

"You sign in at the front window," the girl sitting closest to the door instructs.

"Thanks." I nod at her, surprised anyone would bother to help me.

"I'm Cheyenne," she says.

"Monet." I think about shaking her hand, but don't. "Good luck."

She smiles at me before I walk away. Her smile is better than mine—all glistening white teeth and radiating goodwill. I automatically like her and Jeremy probably will, too. I sigh as I sign my name on the clipboard at the front. I wish I'd taken drama classes and could play the part of someone more confident. I've seen pictures and interviews with Jeremy's ex-girlfriends, but I have no hope of pulling off that act. I'm going to be me. I set the pen back on the clipboard and pull my black T-shirt away from my body, trying to air dry it. Exhaust soot covers my butt from where I sat on the ground. Another black smear runs the length of one arm from where I fell asleep. Nice.

A shrill voice yells my name. She pronounces it wrong, emphasizing the "et," and I cringe. A packet of papers waits for me on the counter.

"Read these over and sign the bottom of each form."

I shuffle the papers around, trying to make sense of them. "What are they?"

"Legal releases."

"Oh, right. Okay." I take the stack and a pen from the dish. I find a seat near Cheyenne, but I don't want to break the quiet in the room by saying anything to her. The papers are weird. The overly formal language distorts the sentences. I think the studio execs are asking me and my family not to sue them for any reason, and for anything I say and do to be recorded. Well, it's reality TV; I can't expect them to do anything other than exploit every second.

Cheyenne leans in close to me. "I heard one of the girls who already went home say that she thought Jeremy is in the building. Like maybe watching the auditions through a secret window."

"Oh." Jumpy electricity flows through my legs. "Oh," I say again like an idiot. I could find him now. I sign my name to the bottom of the first page and then on each subsequent page without bothering to read anymore. People flow in and out of the room. New girls are ushered in, and the girls who've gone in for their auditions walk back out after fifteen minutes. Has anyone been chosen yet?

The door to the left of the window opens. "Number forty-two," a woman calls. The anonymous number reminds me of the health clinic again. Mom had insisted I go in and get checked out after Webber and her crew jumped me after school. My jaw was so swollen that Mom was furious enough to press charges. Then we found out one of them had infected me. Maybe my attacker didn't know she was contagious, or maybe she thought it'd be funny to cost me 20K. I convinced Mom not to make it public, but ever since she's been working her ass off to pay for the cure.

I tuck my lips in again and hurry over to the woman.

"Put your phone and computer along with any other com devices in the bin here." She points to a gray tray with a sticker with my number on it.

"I didn't bring any of those with me."

She looks like she doesn't believe me and might call for a strip search.

"You know the rain? It always voids warranties."

She narrows her eyes. "Just so that you know, if you're caught recording any portion of the proceedings, legal action will be brought against you."

"I understand." I follow her into another room where an older man in a tan suit lounges behind a desk. His nametag reads "Bill." The top button of his shirt is open and his thinning blond hair flops forward. A chair, my chair, sits five feet away. Black one-way glass lines the wall behind the man and I feel people staring. Why did I think I could do this?

"Please, sit."

I take the chair and stuff my backpack underneath. I'm so exposed, but I hold my head up regardless.

"You're seventeen?"

"Yes, sir."

"Still in school?"

"I graduated a few months ago." As I answer the questions, I stare into the glass. Is Jeremy back there watching the proceedings?

Bill tips his head and I notice a tiny black ear bud. How many people are on the other side of that glass? He scratches the side of his face before continuing. "How do you feel about dating?"

"I'm not sure what you mean, sir."

"Do you like dating, do it often, that type of thing?"

I bite the edge of my fingernail. I need a good lie. Um. Yes, no, I don't know. I force my hands back into my lap. "No, sir."

"No, you don't like it, or no, you don't do it?"

My mind is a befuddled mess. Why does he need to know this? Even if I wasn't contagious, most of the guys at school are drugged-out losers. "I haven't been on many dates, so I'm not sure I can judge how much I enjoy it yet."

He nods. "Are you sexually active?"

I glare at him, then at the glass. He listens to his ear bud and then writes more. "Sorry, we're just trying to cut out the overly eager girls. Jeremy doesn't want to be mauled."

He writes down more on his pad of paper and I want to leap up and read whatever the hell it is. My answers suck so far. I shuffle my feet together and try to sit up straighter. My socks are itchy wet. Come on, confidence. Don't fail.

"How about personal upkeep?"

"What exactly are you asking me here?" I try to subtly wipe the smudge off my arm. Am I not clean enough for the show? Give me a shower and a hair dryer. I could look better tomorrow. I force my lips into a pleasant smile. Damn nosy questions, but since I've been in line for days, I suppose they have no way of knowing whether or not I normally bathe.

"Hobbies?"

I should've thought this out ahead of time. I have a hobby. I work for the Metal Preservation Society. I'm not high up. I've only met my one contact, but the society's been around my whole life. The year I was born, China demanded our country pay back the debt we owed them and bam, the government came together to confiscate all the precious metals. I'm not sure how much they made, but China didn't declare war. Since that moment, the Society has been hiding everything they can before the government melts it. They hide it, and me and a bunch of other artists make it into new jewelry. All highly illegal and not a hobby I can mention.

I smile and tuck my hair back, trying to think of a good lie. There is my rough-edged design on the back of the concrete foundation in the bank cafeteria. I had to dig my knife in so hard to make marks. I can't think of any other hobby to make up. "Graffiti-style scratching...uh, but not anywhere illegal. Oh, and I draw."

He raises his eyebrows and I shift nervously. When the state joined with private companies to install graffiti-proof panels ten years ago, most street artists turned to chiseling designs right into the walls, but it's not exactly a socially acceptable hobby. His head tips, listening to something I can't hear. He's probably about to end the interview. I'm fairly sure he won't bother to mention my name to the authorities.

"Are there any particular buildings where your work is displayed?"

"Not right now." He looks slightly bored and I get the impression the question didn't come from him.

"How about cancer?"

"Huh?"

He narrows his eyes in irritation. "You are aware that a quarter of the proceeds are being donated to the Global Skin Cancer Initiative, located right here in the heart of Boston."

Wow. He sounds a little pissed about that. I wonder if that's how they bribed Jeremy into doing the show. Skin cancer's common with the depleted ozone, but I don't think much about it. "I remember Jeremy speaking about his family's struggle with melanoma, but I personally haven't been affected." Would I stand a better chance if I had a friend with cancer?

He shrugs a shoulder. "Uh, huh. Well, you sound pretty good and rate high in overall appearance. Let me get you a few more forms to sign."

What does he mean? Am I in? I try to finger comb the snarls out of my hair. Maybe whoever's behind the glass feels bad for me. Which is fine by me. Whatever it takes to get on the show.

"We're going to start filming the interview now in case you're selected later on. These papers are just your agreement to be filmed and other formalities."

I nod. I'm doing well. Cameras are good. Even if they're right in my face, exposing me to the entire world. I can do this. No big deal. I glance down. The word disease is written on the bottom of the sheet of paper right next to the line for my name. Shit. I'm signing a declaration that I'm disease free. Sweat coats the back of my neck. I sign and hand the papers back. I realize I'm biting the inside of my cheek and relax my jaw. A hiccup pops into the back of my throat, tasting like bile. Being nervous is normal and so what if I lied. A tripod on wheels rolls through the door.

"What would you do with the prize money?"

"I would use it to help fund my college education." I knew they'd ask that. Lucky I was prepared for that one. I mean, donating to charity might be a better response, but that might sound more like a lie.

The interviewer nods along. "What do you like about Jeremy Bane's music?"

"The quiet," I answer without thinking. The desk guy frowns at my answer, likely wondering if he made a mistake putting me on camera. My hands tremble as I grip them together in my lap. *You can do this.* "I mean the mental quiet. When I listen, everything else in my life shuts off. I only hear the beat, the strange noises weaving with Jeremy's voice. Nothing more. No worries, no desires. Just quiet." I glance up and the cameraman wheels closer. The lens whirs as he zooms in on my face. How many people are behind the glass?

"How long have you liked Jeremy?"

The obvious answer is forever, but I don't say that. Every girl will say a variation of *that*. "Well, I don't know if I like him yet. I've never spent any time with him. So I only know that he's attractive and talented." Ha, I sound good.

"When you imagine kissing Jeremy Bane, what location do you envision?"

The swimsuit cover photo of *Riffs and Reefs* magazine pops into my head. Smooth and bare-chested Jeremy, kneeling in the water, holding a guitar over his head. Memorable. He's definitely cute enough to kiss, but as soon as I imagine my lips on his perfect skin, I remember I'm contagious.

The interviewer clears his throat. "Um, a vacation spot."

I tuck my hair behind my ears. The idea of kissing Jeremy Bane chokes me. Spreading my diseased saliva all over my favorite musician is a definite no. I fold my lips in. My heart beats in my ears. I've never kissed anyone, and unless I come up with a bunch of money, I never will. The guys in my social class can't afford the vaccine any more than I can afford the cure. If I chance the results, I might mark them for life, or lead them to their death. Then I'd feel so guilty I'd have to try to come up with even more money for medical treatment for them. I couldn't live with that guilt. Kissing's not worth it. The whole thing makes me sick. Maybe Jeremy's had the vaccine. But it isn't one hundred percent effective, and how would I be able to ask if he's gotten it without tipping him off to my diseased status?

"You do want to kiss him, don't you?" The guy chuckles a little.

I can't speak. What lie do I tell to make him stop asking me this question? The camera wheels closer. Please leave me alone. Another hiccup hits me. I try to swallow and say something, but I gag instead. Shit. I jump up and spots float in front of my face. "I'm going to be sick," I try to mumble as I snatch up my bag and bury my face in it as I run to the door.

"Down the hall to the right!" the interviewer yells as the door closes behind me. I bang into the bathroom and barely make it into one of the stalls. My stomach empties and tears plop down into the mess. It takes a minute for the disaster my interview just became to sink in. I flush away the evidence of my failure and sit back on my heels in front of the disgusting toilet. I ruined my one chance. After all that waiting in line, I blow it in front of the camera. Minutes pass as I weep in disbelief. I suck. I dig in my bag for breath mints or some reminder of my real life. The stale crust of my vitamin spread sandwich makes me feel worse. Nice reminder.

There's a knock on the door. "Hey, are you all right in there?" Oh, great. They've sent someone to make sure I'm not dying.

"Yeah, I'll just be another minute."

The door opens and I see sneakers coming toward me from where I'm crouched by the toilet. "Do you want me to get you a glass of water?"

Wow, nice intern. "No, I'll be okay. I'm sorry I wasted everyone's time. I'll be out of here shortly." I wipe my mouth with toilet paper and swallow repeatedly to try and make the tears stop. I push the stall door open and smack Jeremy Bane.

My whole world freezes.

Jeremy Bane is in the bathroom. Jeremy Bane just asked if he could get me water. He's standing next to me. He heard me puke, and wow, he's just as pretty as the documentary said he was. Even better in person.

But I just puked. I need to just rewind this section of my life and clean up. His hand brushes my arm.

Holy crap, Jeremy Bane is in the ladies room because of me.

Dizziness hits me hard and the spots turn into a black wave. I stagger forward and his hand grips my arm to keep me from toppling over. My backpack drops to the floor and my stuff scatters.

"Whoa, you don't look so good." The blackness fringing my vision recedes when his hand touches me. I straighten up and cover my mouth in case I have puke breath or saliva on my face.

"You're fine," he says, taking in my self-conscious gestures. He's wearing a worn black T-shirt and jeans. We're standing so close together, and I look like shit, and I just threw up. My brain is malfunctioning.

"Thanks for catching me." I motion to the porcelain edge of the sink that I would've cracked my head on if he hadn't been standing in the way. We both crouch down and start picking up my things. I'm mortified when he hands me the crust from my vitamin spread sandwich that I ate in line days ago.

"What are you doing in here?" I ask.

"I, uh, wanted to make sure you were okay." He pushes his hair out of his eyes and glances at me. Whoa. The perfect angle of his cheek leads down to full lips. He blinks once and long lashes brush that gorgeous cheek. Dazzle effect. That's what the scientists named the hypnotic effect of his presence in the documentary I watched.

I shuffle my feet together and bite my lip. What do I say? We're both wearing black T-shirts. I'm crouching next to Jeremy Bane. I smell his shampoo. He's so close. I could just grab him. "Why would you check on me after I messed up my audition?"

"Who said you messed up? I liked everything you said."

"Really?" I pick my head up a few inches and watch him through the veil of my hair. The lines on his forehead show concern and he has a small, reassuring smile. He sweeps more of my stuff toward me and the open backpack. His long fingers are inches from me.

"Yeah. I'm glad my music means so much to someone."

If he only knew how much I counted on his songs to take me away after I found out I had Fluxem. "Well, this is only the beginning of the auditions. If you're watching them all, I'm sure you'll get to hear plenty of compliments."

"Eh, I hate all the gushing. It sounds so fake."

Right. Check. Don't sound fake. Should I ask about his music now? I want all the details that weren't in the specials. There has to be more. I'm about to ask a non-stop stream of questions, but I force my thoughts to slow. I need to win him over. Prize money first, indulging inner fangirl last.

I pick up my sports bottle and quickly slide it out of sight. It's then I notice the Metal Society's tiny piece of soon-to-be jewelry in his hand. How the hell did I forget that was in my bag? It's about the diameter of a golf ball and a fingernail thick. Small enough to slip under all the other junk I have with me. Jeremy turns it over in his hand. I've already scraped away enough of the black paint to reveal the gold. I freeze. I need an excuse. No way can I afford to get busted. Plus, if the authorities confiscate it, I'll owe the Society.

Jeremy flips the small chunk of metal over in his hand and raises his eyebrows. My illegal scratch-work covers the front. A crime punishable by a very heavy fine. How could I have forgotten to return it? I was so focused on the line and the audition. I clench my teeth, waiting for Jeremy's inevitable accusations.

I raise my head enough to meet his questioning stare. *Please don't turn me in.* The design on the piece is one of my best, and if I can get it back, the Society will make a lot of money from its sale. I might even get a small commission. I hold my breath, tabulating the fines and debt I'll incur if Jeremy follows the law. I don't want to have to beg him. He runs his thumb over the piece.

Then, without a word, he hands the evidence back. I slide it to the bottom of my bag. He continues to stare at me, but I can't meet his eyes.

"Here, I'll lead you back." He offers me his hand. His long fingers wrap around mine as he pulls me to my feet. Prickles shoot up my arm. There's seeing him on TV and then there's this. He's not putting on a performance. He's just helping me up, and the gesture is so real and so sweet. The prickles hit the center of my chest and whoosh to my head. He lets go of my hand and opens the bathroom door for me. A bodyguard nods at us as we step out. "This way," Jeremy says.

He walks a few paces, but I don't follow. "I can't answer any more questions on camera. At least, not right now."

"Oh, I didn't mean that I was taking you back to be interviewed. There's another waiting room that's more comfortable."

Good. I'll go anywhere as long as I don't have to be on camera again. I follow him down the hall, sneaking a glance over my shoulder at the guard following us.

"That's my friend, Derek," Jeremy says.

"Hey." I turn slightly and wave at the big military guy. How weird to be constantly shadowed. Does Jeremy like being famous? He opens the door at the end of the hall for me and I check out the new room. There are sandwiches arranged on platters. Fresh fruit. Holy crap, they have fresh fruit! I mean, I know people have fruit at home, but since Mom and I have been saving all our money for the cure, I haven't really had fresh produce for years. For a moment I forget even Jeremy and take a few quick steps toward the buffet. When I turn back to thank him, he's smiling at me.

The smile. His famous crooked smile. I melt.

"I'll talk to you later." He waves and softly closes the door.

There's no one else in the room. A camera sits in the corner, but I'm pretty sure it's off. I slam a strawberry in my mouth. The queasiness is gone. I grab a piece of watermelon, savoring the sweetness. Is this where the winners go?

I gorge on all the fruit and collapse into a fluffy armchair. Is this what it's like to be rich? I imagine Jeremy in the bathroom again. Play over every detail. The shine of his brown eyes, the one wave in his auburn hair. Up close he seems younger than I expected. Kinder. I concentrate on the way his hand felt on my arm, willing the sensation to exist again. This time, when he catches me, I lean into him and we kiss.

I'm still happily daydreaming when the door opens and the competition strolls in.

FOUR

I STRAIGHTEN UP from my slouch in the armchair. The girl steps into the room and swivels her head back and forth. She's a shark. Her black hair, sleek and dry, shows zero signs of suffering in line for days. Her subtle makeup highlights perfect features. With her light tan skin and slightly slanted eyes, she's gorgeous. Ugh. I feel like crap. I can't control the other girls Jeremy has picked to compete against me and I don't know how to stand out against someone like this. If I want to win, I need that control.

"Hey," I say.

"Hi." She looks me over. "Why didn't you change your clothes before the interview?"

I clench my teeth. I could lie and say my backpack isn't waterproof. But why frigging bother? I dealt with enough of these girls in school.

"Do you know anything about why we're here or what's going to happen next?" Maybe she has something useful to offer. I swear I see sharp eyeteeth as she opens her mouth to answer.

"We wait." She brushes her nails along her arm, straightening the tiny hairs. "They keep us around the rest of the day and if they don't find too many of us that are cute enough for TV," she pauses and flicks imaginary dirt in my direction, "we move on. Not until they're done interviewing the rest of the first group, though. So we may still be cut."

"Oh." I drop my head. I'm so frustrated and so sick of being contagious. I cannot spend another year watching Mom work herself to death for me.

I move back to the buffet table and pile a bowl high with tiny squares of a yellow fruit I've never seen before. The tart flavor bursts over my tongue and I'm suddenly glad I waited in line all those days. This is worth it. I met Jeremy and I got fruit.

"My name is Monet," I tell the girl.

"Jasmine." She walks over to me and picks through the fruit medley. She must be wealthy. Probably has a solar hair dryer. Her white frosted fingernail spears a raspberry, and she turns to face me. "So, why do you think they picked you? Do you have a special talent or something?"

I don't like what she's implying. "Nope," I say cheerfully. "I did throw up, though."

"So they felt bad for you." She wrinkles her pert nose and glances around the room like I'm not worth her full attention.

"I think Jeremy did."

"What? You think he was actually watching you?" She laughs. "Don't believe the rumors."

I could tell her I met him in the bathroom, but I don't want to give anything away. After our exchange, she sits down on the opposite side of the room and doesn't say anything. I almost wish another girl would show up, just so that I could ask what she thinks our chances are.

Every hour that passes by on my watch is a victory. I'm invigorated by all the food I keep nibbling. When I'm sure Jasmine isn't paying attention, I stash a few berries in my pocket for later. At five p.m. an official-looking older man comes in with more paperwork. The stripes in his suit emphasize his tall lines.

"Okay, you two are in for tomorrow." He takes a clipboard out from under his arm and flips through the pages.

"Do you mean we're going to be on the show for sure?" My hands tremble. Say yes.

He shrugs. "Guess it depends on what the producers do tomorrow."

Damn. I shrug like I expected that response. I've seen a lot of reality shows and I get how they work, but this initial casting phase isn't usually aired. Jasmine stares at the man. His hair is the fake kind of gray guys use when they're trying to appear more distinguished. She doesn't say anything, but the skin around her eyes tightens.

He hands us each a paper to sign. "General consent forms." He doesn't give us time to read. "For now, I don't want you to say anything to anyone about the proceedings you've been through today. If you give an interview to reporters you will be instantly disqualified. If you tell your parents, and they leak information about the contestants to reporters, you will be disqualified. Got it?"

"Yes, sir," we both say simultaneously. He waits for each of us to make eye contact with him. I feel awkward looking at him. I think he wants us to be uncomfortable.

"Good." He shifts his gaze back to the paperwork. "Now, we've been getting a positive response from this scheme, more than we originally hoped, so the broadcast is expanding. Remember, what you're hearing now is confidential. Starting tomorrow, this waiting room will be filmed as more girls are selected. I can't guarantee that you're going to be part of the show just yet. The producers will be checking over the potential contestants and making sure we have the right mix of girls." He stops to scratch his head and check a piece of paper sitting on the stack. I try to read upside down, but he moves it before I can. "We're planning dates for each of you in various locations— that is, if you're selected, so you'll need to sign these forms."

He hands us a new set and my legs start bouncing uncontrollably. "In your case, Monet, you'll need to take these home for your mother to sign and then bring them back tomorrow. I expect you girls to be here at seven a.m." I guess that means Jasmine is eighteen.

"Do you have any dress suggestions for us?" Jasmine asks.

"No, we want you to be yourselves. But I'll say this: keep your breasts and ass covered. This is for network TV, and nudity won't win you any air time." He gives her an awkwardly long stare and I have to turn away.

"Will we be provided with a personal stylist?" Jasmine sounds so composed as she asks questions. Like she professionally dates rockstars on TV all the time. Part of me wants to punch her, hard.

"Do your own damn hair." The wrinkles on his face draw in as he scowls.

Jasmine tucks her chin in and sits up straight, affronted.

"You're dismissed." He points to a lady standing by the door. She's in her forties, wearing a wine-colored suit. "Eleanor will show you out the back entrance."

"Hi, girls," she says. She lifts her eyes to mine like I'm vaguely interesting, or maybe disgustingly dirty. "I'll be along for the duration of the show, so if you need anything, I might be able to help."

The guy starts to walk away, but yells back, "Remember what I said about reporters." I nod. Eleanor mumbles under her breath. "Well, come on, then. The back exit is this way." Jasmine steps in front of me as we follow along. Judging by Eleanor's purposeful walk, she's in good shape. We're released back out into the real world. The door slams behind us and I'm left in the rain again.

Jasmine huffs and pulls out her cell. "Yes." She pauses. "Yes, no, send the car to pick me up." I pretend to adjust the heel of my flats as I eavesdrop.

In less than a minute a gray Jag picks her up at the curb. I hope all the other girls aren't as wealthy as she is. It seems like an unfair advantage.

I step over the cracks in the sidewalk as I walk home. Our apartment is two miles away on the thirty-fifth floor of a massive brick building. The crumbling façade gives glimpses of the steel structure beneath, which keeps the thing from caving in. China wasn't interested in old reclaimed industrial steel, lucky for us. On the bottom floors, bars cover the windows for security. One good thing about living up so high, if someone wanted to rob us, there are hundreds of easier apartments to choose from.

The rain stops, but the smog cuts the sun down to nothing. I avoid the wire pigeon traps a few blocks away. I can't take their feathers and desperate squawking. The poor birds overpopulate the streets almost as quickly as humans do. According to the city, they taste delicious—a new money-making crop requiring no maintenance. I'll take vitamin spread over flying rats any day.

My trail crosses through the park between the bank buildings. The Chase skyscraper is the nicest. A projection of a rainforest fills the mirrored glass, giving the illusion of a better world. The other banks have chosen different environmental themes. I love them all. If I stand close enough, I can pretend I'm there, in the wilderness, instead of this filthy city. Today, I keep walking.

When I reach our place, I try to pick our window out from the ground. I painted a design on the inside of the glass, but from this distance, all the windows on my floor look the same. I can't believe I'm coming home to this place after all of the extraordinary occurrences of the last few days. I never truly believed I'd be picked. Of course, I fantasized; I had to. To have a future in which I'm disease free, with a boyfriend that gets what's important to me—now that would be amazing. Maybe another artist. This show could give me those opportunities. With this prize money, my whole life could change. Now, to be back home as though none of it happened. No line, no room of fruit. But it did happen. I met Jeremy Bane. A small part of my brain adds, *and he touched your arm and held your hand for a second.*

A speck of rust falls on my head as I walk through the doorway and start up the stairs. I laugh at the building, daring it to fall down. My legs flex and push off each step. I don't even care that the elevator only works intermittently. At least my calf muscles are well defined. My climbing time is down to fifteen minutes. Not a bad cardio workout and cheaper than a gym membership. Of course, the elderly residents aren't as lucky as I am. If the supermarket didn't deliver, they'd be in a bad position. Still, to have to pay a delivery fee on top of vitamin spread costs must suck. The hollow echo of my feet on the stairs mixes with a crying child behind one of the doors. The floors speed by with the memory of Jeremy touching my arm.

I pause in front of our apartment. I slowly blow the air out of my lungs before swinging the door open. Mom waits on the couch a few feet from the door. She slaps her magazine closed and clasps her hands in anticipation. I know she wanted to check on me while I was in line, but there were no visitors allowed. "How was the audition?" She smiles at me, waiting for good news. Mom, the optimist.

I told her I have a crush on Bane to explain why I wanted to audition. I don't want her to know I'm doing this for the money. She'd think it was her fault for not coming up with the cure money quickly enough. Which would be stupid, because she's done everything she can. Besides, Jeremy Bane is an easy guy to imagine having a crush on.

She waves her hand in the air. "Are you going to tell me?"

"They picked me. I'm going back tomorrow."

She squeals in delight. "I knew they'd love you, honey. You're so beautiful." She reaches out and picks my wet, dirty hair off my shoulder.

"Ick." I twist away from her. "My hair is nasty, and you only think that because I'm your daughter."

"Bah, clearly *Jeremy Bane* does, too." She drags out his name, teasing me. "So, what are you wearing tomorrow?" She cocks her hip to the side and doesn't mention the brown smear on her hand from where she touched my hair.

Ugh. I hang my head and fall back onto the couch. My wardrobe is pathetic. "I have no idea."

"Well, give me that outfit, and I'll rinse it out in the sink." She retreats to the next room to give me enough privacy to change. Our coffee table opens up into a storage bin, which is where I keep my clothes. I move Mom's coffee and magazine to the floor as I search my belongings. Our apartment is small and efficient. Everything folds up and down in the two rooms. My bed is inside of the kitchen wall right now. Mom's is behind the TV. She and I have made the space homey. We painted flowers around the door and got peach curtains.

"Throw your clothes in," Mom says. The walls are thin between the rooms, and I hear her perfectly. I sit in my bra and underwear for a minute, then discreetly smell my arm. I always feel like a hidden camera could be watching me. Once I found out about Fluxem, I've been waiting for the symptoms—wondering if

I'll suddenly smell like a lizard some morning. I've never been around a steaming cup of iodine, but I read online that it smells like a crocodile and I can't get that description out of my head. So far, I'm good. No open sores marring my skin, or worse, yellow pus oozing from the scabs while my body tries to flush the disease out of my system. If I can win the prize money, I can put Fluxem behind me before it scars my life even more.

I sort through my clothes and pull out my other pair of jeans. I have a few skirts, too, those are easy to make and Mom is good at stitching things out of remnants. What will Jasmine wear tomorrow? Do I even want to know? Getting caught up comparing myself with other girls used to be something I avoided. Now I can't stop wishing I had paid more attention. This competition goes against every bit of common sense I have, and I've spent too long trying to be content with what I have. But then I see Mom coming home from the restaurant way after dark, exhausted. All because of me. Because I couldn't protect myself in a fight two years ago. Now we're even more broke. Not for long. If I can win the money, she can stop working so hard. Maybe then we can have a buffet like the one the TV show provided.

The buffet...oh, crap. That fruit is still in my pocket. I quickly slip on an old T-shirt and fumble in my jeans for the strawberries. "I've got a surprise for you." I step into the kitchen. "Which hand?" I ask, holding both behind my back.

Mom grins at me. "That one." She pokes my arm.

"Nope, the other one." I pull out the napkin and let it fall open. The berries are squashed, but she doesn't care.

"Oh, sweetheart." She pops one in her mouth, savoring the flavor the same way I had. I love her so much. I'm proud all of a sudden. I brought home food and I made it to the next round. "I have papers I need you to sign."

"Oh?"

I go back out to the living room and grab them. She finishes with my jeans and drapes them over the rack by the window. Then we settle down on the two-seater couch with the papers on our laps. She tips her head back and her eyes close.

"You're tired, aren't you?"

She sighs. "No. I'm only resting for a second."

There are lines around her mouth from smiling so much and dark circles under her eyes. I know she's tired even if she won't admit it.

She straightens back up. "I'm ready to sign. What do you have for me?"

I sigh. I'm going to win that prize money. I glance over the first page and then hand it to her. She squints at the small print and holds the page closer.

"You do realize they're asking my permission to let you fly all over the place?"

My smile widens. "I know. I had no idea the dates were going to be so...exotic."

"Monet, think this through. I want you to be safe and every city has its problems. Only the biggest local crimes end up in the news. It's not like the federal laws are enforced all that well anymore. If they're not gathering up metal or tax evaders, all of a sudden they don't have enough resources."

Ugh, the safety lecture again. Ever since I got Fluxem, she's been trying to protect me from everything else. "I can handle a trip. Besides, the TV show isn't going to let anything too horrific happen to the contestants."

She sighs. "The government used to be able to afford more. Plus, there's all that pollution. You'll have to be careful of the water, the ground, the people—"

"I'll be fine. I'm smart." I scratch the back of my neck. I want to travel, but...

She smiles again. "You're right. I know you'll be okay and this is a wonderful opportunity."

I pick the document back up and continue reading. "This one talks about them filming our house and me. I'm sorry, Mom."

"No, no, it's okay. I'm not embarrassed, a lot of the population lives like we do." She tucks her hair behind her ears and then twists it into a bun. "You wouldn't believe all the changes I've witnessed in my life."

"You're not that old, Mom."

"Forty-seven."

"So the world has had forty years to change, right? So it's not that much worse."

"Maybe, but at least back then I would've been able to get you medical treatment even if I didn't have money." She stops and massages her lower back. Which is my fault. She's on her feet working too much. I wish there was a way to just rip Fluxem out of my body. Mom relaxes back, still thinking about her past.

"When I was born, companies would just give you credit to buy whatever you wanted. Then too many people stopped paying back the debt." She stops and yawns. I hate when she rambles about politics. "There are only so many resources in the world. Not like the wealth is going to get redistributed in this lifetime. And you know what? I bet we're happier than the social elite."

"Yeah," I say, but my thoughts are all shifting to Jeremy. What would make him choose me?

She takes the paper from me and signs. "It's about time TV shows stop glossing over the economic disparity. It's the people wasting space in those sprawling mansions that should be ashamed."

I nod, not wanting this discussion to go on any longer. I'd be happier with money. No one who's eaten vitamin spread sandwiches for more than a week in a row would question the superiority of wealth. Mom says they're delicious. Maybe her taste buds have dissolved.

"I'm so excited for you, honey. You're actually going to get out of this city for a week or two. Though, they're a little vague on how long you'll be gone."

"I'll ask about it tomorrow." I glance over at her face. She's still young. Her eyes barely crinkle, and she's good at being positive. I wish I could close myself off to the problems around me. Every time I have to hide in bed to bend metal into jewelry I'm reminded how limited my future is. I have no shot at a career, no money for college, and no boyfriend. I'm not pissed. I'm not depressed. I accepted the facts long ago, and while I'll do everything I can to make my life better, I'm realistic.

She nudges my arm. "Always so serious."

I shrug. "I'm excited."

"What are you going to wear?"

I hold up my jeans.

"Good choice. Wanna borrow one of my shirts?"

"The maroon one?" I ask.

"Ha. My favorite. You've been waiting for an excuse."

Too true. "Please?"

"All right, but that Jeremy Bane had better fall in love with you."

I shake my head. I don't need love. I just need to get rid of Fluxem so that I can have a regular life. I just need a miracle so I can win the show. "He probably won't even notice me with all the other girls."

"Of course he will." She pats my hand and then uncurls her fist to reveal the second squashed strawberry that she still hasn't eaten. "Want to split it?"

"No, Mom, you go for it."

She savors the berry and I fill with hope about tomorrow.

FIVE

I WALK ALONG the sidewalk, avoiding the doomed pigeons and beggars. Mom's maroon shirt feels silky on my skin, and despite the gut-clenching nerves, I'm in a good mood. An advertisement with Jeremy standing on a stage flashes on the side of the mall.

Date With a Rockstar, *featuring Jeremy Bane...One girl will win thirty thousand dollars and the possibility of true love.*

I could be that girl.

My positive attitude lasts until I reach the studio. Outside, the next two hundred and fifty girls fidget in a ragged line. They look amazing. They're all bright colors and symmetrical faces, each one more beautiful than the next. Jeremy will probably pick eight more girls in less than an hour.

I walk to the front of the line because I don't even know where I'm supposed to go to get inside.

"Hey, numbers have already been given out, idiot," a crisp voice yells. I keep walking.

"Didn't you hear her?" someone else asks.

"I know." My voice squeaks as I try to answer. The camera crew is filming me from the tailgate of their van.

"Then get out of here," two girls say in unison.

I know what they're thinking—that I'm not good enough, not pretty enough or dressed well enough.

I hate being judged. They don't know anything about me. I keep my back straight and stamp away the urge to run.

"I'm number forty-two, Monet," I tell the clipboard guy at the front of the line. "I'm not sure where I'm supposed to go this morning." I offer him my ID.

He checks his list. "Oh, yeah. You go in the other entrance. The coordinator should've made that clear." I shrug; maybe Eleanor forgot. A rock bounces off the back of my leg. I don't turn around. "But for today, I can just let you in here." He opens the door for me, and I whisper my thanks.

Inside, I notice Jeremy's bodyguard from yesterday standing in front of a door at the end of the hallway. I wave and he gives me a warm smile. I might as well ask him for directions. Who knows, maybe I'll run into Jeremy Bane again.

"Monet, right?" he asks, holding out his hand. I shake it. The guy's got a fierce grip.

"I'm sorry, I can't remember yours."

"Star struck," he says, laughing. "I'm Derek, and don't worry, Jeremy's fans always forget me."

I glance up at his strong jaw and masculine face. He's not very forgettable, either. "Do you know where I'm supposed to go this morning?"

He turns back down the hall, his snug T-shirt stretching with his bicep as he points me in the right direction. "The waiting room is around the corner, first door on the left." I bet he can crush skulls.

"Thanks, I guess if I'm selected I'll see you around." I bump into the wall as I turn around, but he doesn't notice my lack of grace.

He nods, the good-natured smile back in place. "As long as they keep you girls camped out with the breakfast buffet, you'll be seeing me when I get a break in an hour."

"Cool." I wave and walk around the corner. What an easy job watching Jeremy Bane all day must be. Or, scrap that, maybe I only think it would be easy because hanging out with such an awesome musician all the time would be cool. In reality, Derek probably has to be constantly on alert, waiting for danger. Still, if I had to stare at someone all day, Jeremy's the guy. I take a deep breath and push open the waiting room door.

Jasmine has spread out in the chair closest to the camera. Her legs are crossed and her back arches slightly to display her breasts. Quite the pose. A man works the settings, and I recognize the telltale whir of zooming in and out. Jasmine's aqua dress and sculpted calves must have him captivated. Instead of allowing her to intimidate me, I stride to the buffet and fill up a plate with granola and berries. If I only get one more day, I'm going to eat my fill.

"Hungry much?" Jasmine asks.

"Sure, aren't you?"

"I don't eat breakfast." She flicks the tips of her nails in my direction.

"Too bad for you," I say, keeping a cheery tone. Even she can't get me down.

She humphs and returns to posing for the camera.

The next girl through the door surprises us because, physically, she's the exact opposite of both Jasmine and I. With her blonde hair and curvy figure, she's attractive in a different way. "My name is Shelley Anne," she announces with her arm stretched out.

I stand to shake her hand. "I'm Monet." As long as I don't bleed on her or spit into her mouth, she won't catch Fluxem from me.

"Oh, this is so perfectly exciting." She checks out the rest of the room, nodding and smiling.

I wonder if there's a pattern in Jeremy's choices. His past girlfriends look more like Jasmine, but that doesn't mean that's the only type of girl he likes. In fact, I imagine he's more into personality than a set physical description. Shelley has enthusiasm.

She spins in a circle. "I'm so delighted to be here. Isn't this going to be so much fun?"

Jasmine grimaces.

"Absolutely," I tell her. "You should try the fruit."

"Yum, yum, yummy," Shelley says around a mouthful. The cameraman wheels closer to get a shot of her sucking her fingers. Ugh. I hope she's not doing it on purpose. All the girls haven't even been chosen yet.

The next girl through the door shares Jasmine's coloring, stylish clothing, and snotty attitude.

"I'm Mel." She cradles her slim waist with tan arms and her turquoise nails splay like she's a mannequin on display. Great, like the competition needs a Jasmine clone. Are they even asking these girls the entire questionnaire? With the speed they're arriving, I feel like they're selecting every other one. I gravitate to Shelley Anne, who is by far the friendliest in the group. I don't want these girls to be my enemies, but I can't help making comparisons. She's taller than me, has longer hair, bigger breasts. The lists continue in my head until I have a chunk of brain filled with inadequacies.

The new girl, Crystal, whistles an entire song of Jeremy's while the camera records. I'm sure her ash blonde hair glows on screen, and they probably can correct the tone of her notes.

Shelley Anne purses her lips in a sour expression. I try not to laugh. Poor Crystal. Good thing there isn't a talent portion to the competition. According to the papers, we're just going on dates. No pageant theatrics, we just need to impress the viewers and Jeremy.

As I consider this, a buxom redhead flows into the room. "Claire," she states. I nod. She has a salsa dancing outfit on. Not a minute later, a petite Latina girl slips into the room and hides on one of the back couches.

Number eight also looks like Jasmine, but with geometric lines tattooed around her eyebrows. Her name is Brie and I kind of want to ask how painful the procedure on her eyes was, but I keep my mouth shut. I'm a thin brunette like her, Jasmine, and Mel, but I think our similarities end there. *Celeb* magazine ran a story about Jeremy's break-up with porcelain, brunette actress Fiona Wilde about a year ago. Miss Wilde told reporters that Jeremy was too absorbed with his music and other women, and she was "done wasting her time." I bet *he* dumped her. Though I could be wrong. Maybe he dates and leaves tons of women and I'm just influenced by all the positive press about him. Still, in the bathroom he seemed like a good guy. Not that meeting him in the bathroom once qualifies me as an expert. All year, the tabloids have managed to snap a new shot of Jeremy standing next to a random girl almost every week, but they never turn out to be his girlfriend. No matter what the truth is, he's got a lot of women around to choose from. I wonder if he's really doing the show just for charity, or if there's some truth to him wanting to find the right girl.

I count the girls off on my fingers. Number nine, Erin, speaks with a southern accent. Number ten, Jaime, wears purple contacts, giving her eyes a creepy, mystical glow. That's ten.

Please, no more girls. If he picks one more, will Jasmine be asked to leave, or me? I take a deep breath. Jeremy's not having any trouble picking out a whole pile of girls. Jasmine has her fixed predator expression on. The door handle turns and we hold our breath.

Derek walks in and goes directly to the buffet. *Phew.* I take the opportunity to eat even more. "Hey," I say.

He nods with his mouth full and swallows. "So, this is all of them," he says, turning to face the room. He rubs the stubble on his chin and shrugs. "They're all polished and girly, nightmare dates. What is Bane thinking?" He laughs and then pauses for a minute. "The one with the boobs isn't bad."

I try not to laugh. "Okay, what type of girl would you have picked?"

"A tough one. Someone who can take care of herself and handle a weapon. Preferably with very large—"

I raise my hand before he continues. "I get it."

He turns back to the table and loads his plate up.

A muffled loudspeaker announcement echoes through the walls.

"Shhh," Jasmine yells.

I freeze, listening. "Girls number 500 through 750, follow the guards into the auditorium."

I turn back to Derek. "Do you think he'll pick more girls and make some of us go home?"

"Nah, he'll just sing the remaining girls a special song or some such shit. He's a sucker for his fans."

I relax and grab a piece of fruit.

"Back to work for me. Later." I wave at Derek as he lugs off his plate of food. Then I nod at Jasmine, who's been listening in. She lifts one corner of her mouth in a partial smile.

If they're dismissing the other girls, we're in.

I'll get time alone with Jeremy to convince him to pick me for the prize money. Relief bubbles through me. Phase one of my goal achieved. I'm just that much closer to getting rid of Fluxem. Ten percent odds are better than I had two days ago. Now I've got a whole week or more to figure out how to win Jeremy over. I might be able to do this.

After the ten of us are assembled, a large screen rolls down behind the buffet. Soon after, the guy who did the initial interviews strides into the room. He's rubbing his hands together in anticipation, which must mean the producers are pleased.

"Okay, ladies. Congratulations. Selections have been made and we're happy to welcome you to the show. For those who don't remember my name from the auditions, I'm Bill. I'll be along for the duration of the show to coordinate the producers' needs with your own. So, you'd better remember my name from here on out." He smiles at us, pleased at how important he's just made himself sound.

"Take a look around you, because these are going to be your friends and competition for the next few weeks. You'll all be able to go home tonight and pack, but tomorrow we'll be meeting at the Bellfonte airport and flying to our first location..." he pauses, trying to build our excitement. "...the beautiful city of Key West, Florida." He waits like he's expecting applause, but no one claps. "Tonight we'll be airing an advertisement showing views from the line montaged with Jeremy talking about the selection process."

"Excuse me, Bill? Did Jeremy watch our auditions?" I can barely hear the question. I turn around. It's the shy girl hidden at the back edge of the room. I struggle to remember her name. Pammy? Pollie? Praline, that's it.

"He surrrre did." Peppy doesn't match his chubby, stuffed goose demeanor. He acts differently without the ear bud in. Maybe he's more relaxed without people watching him through one-way glass.

"Oh, wow. Jeremy was watching *me*." She brings her hands to her cheeks. "I can't believe Jeremy was here. I'm just so excited." Her awed expression exudes extreme fangirl even more than the rest of us. She probably knows a lot more about Jeremy than I do. I'll have to watch her.

"Any other questions so far?" No one says anything. "Good. The studio will decide a date for each of you, highlighting different locations in Key West to promote tourism. After you've all been on one date with Jeremy, there will be two rounds of voting. The audience will select the best three and then those girls will continue on to the final round." He finishes up in his talk show host voice.

"Jeremy won't be the one deciding who he likes best?" Shelley Anne asks. "On the ad it said Jeremy gets to pick."

"In the final round he will, but until then, you girls need to impress the viewers. Though you never know, there might be a twist."

Yeah, there's always a twist. The only way reality TV programs can compete against each other anymore is to surprise the viewers, who are never surprised anyway, which makes them all the more ridiculous. Then it hits me. I'm a part of this. Oh, this is bad. Very bad. I'm not good on camera. Visions of throwing up on Jeremy Bane's feet pop into my head.

"As a special treat, we're letting you girls see the commercial before it airs." The producer's assistant from before, Eleanor, comes in and hits a few buttons before the screen lights up. "Get ready to be famous," Bill announces.

*Date with a Rockstar...*flashes across the black screen. *Only one girl will win a cash prize and a chance for love with Jeremy Bane.* The words fade into an image of the line. The camera starts at the front and girls are smiling and waving as the view loops around the building and then skyward. From the air the trail weaves through the buildings. I was right; there were thousands of girls in that line. Then Jeremy Bane comes on screen. His face is so flawless, my fingers itch to stroke his skin. A bio-chemical reaction, nothing more. His eyes appear to stare directly at me, but I know he's just looking into the camera.

"I don't know who I'll find in line, but I'm hoping to form a real connection. There are so many people in the world...I wonder how many of us never find the right one." All ten of us hold our breath when he speaks. He sounds so sincere, so sweet. Praline clutches her chest and fans her face with the other hand. I hope the studio picked her and not Jeremy. I can't imagine a girl more different from myself.

Then the commercial shows the line start to move. The first girl waves out at the audience as she enters the building. I'm glad she at least got her face on TV after waiting for two weeks. "Who will he choose and who will you? Which girl is after his heart and which girl is after the money?" a voice says. "Starting June 14, help Jeremy Bane find the right girl."

I gulp. That line could have been directed straight at me. I'm so guilty.

The screen fades to a commercial for the Global Skin Cancer Initiative. They use the same overhead footage of the line, but this time they zoom away from the girls and across the city to show the research building. The camera goes through the front doors, and the receptionist and patients wave. They're clearly actors. Then they show a swatch of skin growing in a petri dish. The voiceover comes on. "GSCI, continuing innovation and excellence to solve all your skin cancer needs. The ozone layer might be diminished, but we can help you stay safe. Support us on June 25 by attending Jeremy Bane's benefit concert at Madison Square Garden with the finalists from Date With a Rockstar."

Shelley Anne wanders over to me. "What did you think of the commercial?"

I tuck my hair behind my ears. Jeremy's so generous and I'm after money. Not much of a match. Shelley raises her eyebrows, waiting. Right. "I think it's awesome he's supporting such a great cause."

"Me, too. Cancer is the worst."

I nod, not sure what I can add. Cancer's worse than Fluxem because there's no cure and it affects a lot more of the population.

Jasmine stops Bill before he can leave the room. "How many days will we be gone? Should we be prepared for dressy dates or casual?"

I listen in, even though I don't have many clothing options. How am I even going to get to the airport? I fear the subways, but the shuttle costs a lot. I'd be better off scraping the last of my money together for a dress. I don't suppose they could pick us up?

"You'll be allowed two suitcases of clothes. No more than that, so pack carefully. You might end up hiking or at a fancy restaurant. The dates haven't been coordinated yet, so I can't give you any more information than that."

Two suitcases? I don't even own enough to fill one.

"That's an awfully small amount of luggage if y'all are expecting us to do our own hair and makeup," Jaime says. Her purple contacts gleam in the artificial light. Maybe Jeremy likes purple.

Bill shakes his head. "You'll manage."

I study Jaime, and she thrusts her chin out and returns my stare. She has a petite button nose and curly brown hair. I wish I could find a flaw in her appearance, but other than the fake eyes, I can't. Maybe she'll be a finalist.

All of the girls are complaining about the allotment. Who cares? I don't even own a suitcase.

Then Bill drops the second problem. No electronic devices on the trip. Another item I don't own. The girls yell over each other about how impossible that is, as though their phones are physically implanted in their heads.

As Bill wraps up our day, I'm freaking out enough to consider spending the money I've been saving for the cure on clothes. If I looked better, would I stand more of a chance at winning the prize? Maybe a new dress could be thought of as an investment in getting more funds.

Eleanor hands each of us a pamphlet on Key West and releases us out the back door, right into the waiting herd of press. With the rest of the line dismissed, they must have figured the final ten were inside. I keep my hand over my face, duck down, and block as much of myself with my arm as I can. None of the other girls stop, either. The threat of being disqualified looms over us.

As the others drive off in cars, I start off toward home at a brisk jog. A reporter follows me for a couple of blocks, yelling questions at my back. I'm in better shape than he is. I have to get home and to the mall. Discount shopping takes time and I need to find a killer outfit.

I'd feel safer if I had a chip in my arm like everyone else, but I don't have enough money to warrant a bank account. I rush up the stairs and into the apartment. I grab my meager savings from my bedside table. My backpack is still on the floor from yesterday. I bite my lip. The fact that I left property of the Society in an unsecure location for twenty-four hours just proves how insane this competition is already making me. I dig through the bottom. My fingers close around the small metal disc and I exhale my relief. I remember how Jeremy looked at me when he found the piece. Is it possible that he appreciates visual art, too? I tuck the gold chunk deep in my front pocket. I need to get it out of my possession before I leave.

I speed down the flights of stairs. Snatches of conversation follow me from floor to floor. I suspect rodents consumed all the insulation in the building years ago, because I hear everything. The faster I can descend, the less I have to learn about my neighbors.

From what I do catch, they're a miserable, creepy bunch. Still, this building is nicer than where Mom and I used to live. With the limited available housing, we were on a wait list even for this place.

Outside, the thick, oppressive air clogs my lungs. There isn't enough sun to bake off the humidity, so the moisture hovers in the air, trapped on this messed up planet just like me.

The Metal Society has an entrance on the bottom floor of the old public library. I walk the few blocks, trying not to draw attention to myself. The old library is wedged in between taller buildings. I start down the alleyway to the side entrance, but there's a street cleaner machine in the way and I have to wait.

The metal in my pocket has me shifting on my feet. I could be attacked, robbed, arrested. Would the show producers inquire about my disappearance or just pick another girl? Finally, the cleaner moves down the road. A guy across the road throws a plastic beer bottle against the front steps. When nothing happens he staggers forward and gives the brushes a kick.

A dumpster blocks a door with a scan panel. I palm the metal disk in my hand and run it underneath. The Society does something to the metal to make it traceable, which also works to open the door. I have a coin at home that works the same way. A few years ago a guy caught me doing scratch graffiti and gave me the first invite to work for the Society. So far I haven't seen the guy again, but if I do, I'll thank him.

I glance down at my work. It's a little sad not to be able to keep what I make. If I had a chain, my carving would be a complete and beautiful necklace. I love making jewelry, even knowing it's going to wealthy patrons. With the plastic knock-offs so convincing, they can get away with wearing the real thing. The door releases and I slip in. Horizontal strips of sun filter in from the barred windows far above. My feet leave prints in the dust as I cross the room to the metal cage of lockers. Mine is twenty boxes from the left and five up.

I punch in a long string of numbers and digits. The cage pops open. I reach around inside and pull out a finger-sized bit of silver. I push the intercom button at the top of my locker.

"Excuse me, there are no instructions with this piece."

There's a long pause. "Number 8723M1, no instructions on file. Let me check the system."

I squint at the back of my locker. The person on the intercom might be behind the wall or on the other side of the country.

"There's an accommodation for your last necklace, but nothing else."

I rub my sneaker through the dust. "How about payment? Any tips?"

"Not yet."

I didn't really expect anything, but it would've been nice. "Thank you." I leave both the gold and silver pieces behind and hurry out.

The air outside the old library has taken on a slightly sulfurous tinge as the wind shifts in my direction. I walk back out to the main street. Mall entrances are located all over the city. In some areas the mall is underground, and in others it stretches up above the street.

Heavy plastic doors flashing with advertisements welcome me to the mall. The corridors are enforced by remote security. I stop and wait while a couple in front of me is scanned for weapons. Two double green lights indicate that they are clean. I'm next.

The mall is one of the safest places to be. I wish they'd apply the same defenses in the subways. I tuck that thought away. There's no point in worrying about tomorrow morning. I thought about asking Shelley

Anne for a ride, or seeing if the studio could send a car to pick me up, but I don't want special treatment.

As I enter the mall, I press my money deeper into my pocket. Macy's flashes sales and product advertisements at me. A small perfume-spraying robot waits just inside to ambush shoppers. From the outside the white floors and walls give the store a brightness I envy.

Macy's isn't a store I can afford, but I go in anyway. The robot wheels up. "No. Thank. You." I announce the words slowly so that the voice software recognizes them. The damn thing sprays my leg anyway.

I stroll around the fountain and stare up at the fake sky ceiling. I'm wasting time. Maybe I shouldn't buy a dress. It's a stupid idea to spend money to stand out from the other contestants. Before I got Fluxem I was too young to have money of my own and by the time I actually started to earn a little from the Society, I needed to give it to Mom for the cure. I get it. I know what's important. I just occasionally wish I could shop. Maybe go on one of those sprees like you can win for signing up for all those magazines.

I drag my hand over the clothes. I pull a black dress out. Beautiful. I feel awkward walking into the mirrored dressing room. God, do people actually have closets like this? I pull off my pants and shirt, straightening up in front of the mirror. My legs look stronger. The dress slides easily over my head, pooling around my thighs. Such a pretty cut. Flattering.

I walk out and sit on the couch. The luxurious fabric matches the fake room. I'm like a different person. I'm about to get up when I hear a slightly familiar voice.

"No. No. This one won't work, either." Claire walks through the rows of formal dresses. She's changed out of her salsa outfit for a suit. I freeze. Shit. I quietly stand up and try to slip back to the dressing room to get my clothes.

"Monet."

I turn back around.

"Shopping for the trip, I see."

I shrug. "They, uh, didn't give me much time to pull together a suitable wardrobe."

"Exactly what I said. Can you imagine all of my clothes trapped in my closet a thousand miles away, and they expect us to leave in the morning like we have everything we need already? Ridiculous."

"Yeah," I say. She doesn't know anything about me. I could have money. I walk back through the closet to the dressing room and quickly change back into my clothes. I put the dress back on the hanger, letting the gorgeous fabric run over my fingers one last time. I gulp and take a deep breath before putting it back in its spot.

Claire looks up from the couch.

"Not going to buy the dress?" she asks.

"Eh, I'm still shopping. It didn't fit that well, anyway."

She raises her eyebrows and then her lip tilts up like she knows I'm lying.

"Good luck finding what you need," I say as I hurry away.

"Likewise," she says with a slight edge to her voice.

The robot sprays me again on my way out of the store. My jeans are going to stink for a week.

I don't have enough money to buy anything. It was silly to even come here.

Humidity coats me as I exit the mall and jog home. There's something so freeing about running, like I could escape my own limited future if I move fast enough. I tip my head up, letting the air blow my hair back from my face.

Mom's at home when I get back. I wonder what she would say about my plan to win the prize money. It's a bit manipulative on my part, even if it is for a good reason. Money, that's important. Most of the time I feel like if I can't buy opportunities I won't have any, and Jeremy is the key to the prize.

"I went to the mall," I say, slumping back on the couch. "All the clothes are too expensive."

She sighs. "I wish I had more money to give you."

Shit, now I feel guilty again. "You do more than enough for me."

She frowns and I know she's thinking about the cure she hasn't been able to provide. "How about you grab dinner out of the oven for me?"

I stand in front of the stove. "Mom, you forgot to turn it on again. What were you trying to make, anyway?" I open up the oven door. Oh! There's a package. A wrapped gift. I grab up the box and run to the other room.

"I got ya, didn't I? You thought I messed up another vitamin spread a' la casserole."

"Oh, Mom, you didn't have to." I tear into the paper. My hand meets green cloth. A dress. The leafy green fabric unfolds in my hands and I'm holding up a simple wrap dress. "I can't believe you got me this! Can we afford it?" *How much harder will you have to work because of this?*

She swats my words away with her hand. "Now, what else do you need to pack?"

At the end of the night, we catch the commercial for the dating show. I point to where I am in line and Mom *oohs* and *ahs* over the close-up of Jeremy. We read over the Key West pamphlet, marveling at the photos. On the cover in between high-rises, a swath of aquamarine beach surrounds a palm tree and a bar.

I wonder if the water really is that blue. I know the skies can't be that clear. They must have pumped up the images for print. Nowhere I've ever been is clean like that, not that I've ever been out of the city. In less than twenty-four hours I'll be there, at the hotel on the brochure. I squeal in delight.

SIX

MY BELONGINGS ARE packed in a tote bag, cinched tight with string and looped over my shoulders. I'm ready to run. Mom lifts her head up off the pillow and waves goodbye. Two hours should be more than enough to get to the airport by seven.

I pause at the exit of our building and take time to stretch my hamstrings. I flex onto the balls of my feet and lean over the front of my legs. Next I slide out a small metal cylinder from where I've hidden it in my waistband so Mom wouldn't notice. I grip it tight in one hand and then the other. Its weight in my fist comforts me as I do a few test punches. I don't have enough body mass to make my hits count without the added weight.

I'm as ready as I'm going to get. The stairs down to the subway station are covered in pigeon feces. I fold my hands close to my body, not touching the railings. Clean air is pumped down into the tunnels, but that doesn't keep disease off the surfaces. A man slumps over on the stairs. He opens his hand weakly as I pass. His shoe is on a step a few feet down, leaving his dry, cracked foot exposed.

At the bottom of the stairs the murmurs of pain crescendo. Why do the miserable always crawl down into the subways? They rest up against the walls, begging and moaning. Flies land on the face of an elderly woman who's spread out on her back. She might be dead. I pick up my pace. Smells of decay and vomit creep into my nose even though I breathe through my mouth. There's a map painted on the main wall by the platform. I check for the number car I need.

Eight.

I hope to hell it arrives soon. Trains come in fifteen-minute increments, but I have no way of knowing when the last one left. I don't want to spend a single second in this place.

"'Scuse me. Pretty lady? What's in the bag?"

I ignore the words and move along the platform. I'll run back to the yellow mark when I see the eight train.

"Come back here!" the voice commands in suddenly clear words. I glance back at the man curled on the ground. The sleeves are torn off his shirt, showing wiry muscles. There's a red, scabby mark on his face, probably Fluxem. I shudder. He stares, but makes no move to get up. What's wrong with his legs? They're bent at odd angles. Can Fluxem do that?

I bounce from foot to foot. Ready for anything. The number six arrives and leaves. A single person exits and no one boards. The trains continue along their circuit whether anyone uses them or not. The thought sends a shiver through my spine. I crack my knuckles around the steel in my fist and refuse to let the fear settle in.

The man with Fluxem crawls toward me. At least he's slow. When he's ten feet away I dart around behind him to the other end of the platform. Scratchy music starts playing over the intercom system. The number four pulls up and leaves. Screams echo off the tile walls. *God, I hate the subway.*

The number eight arrives from the other direction and the Fluxem guy blocks the door as it slides open. I have to make the train. The door starts to close. I dart around the reaching guy. His hand swipes at my foot, but I jump through the train door before he can latch on. I release my breath as he's shut out.

The car rocks back and forth, speeding toward the airport. A shrunken man with beady eyes follows my movements. I stand in the center of the aisle, trying not to touch the seats or handholds. Minutes pass slowly. I feel like the guy is staring at my bag. Brakes screech as we stop at another station. A middle-aged woman climbs on. She's normal and clean. Her presence makes me relax a bit. We watch each other balance as the train jerks back to speed.

One more stop, then it's me on my way to Key West. I let out a deep breath. Suddenly the train lurches. I stumble against a seat and fall to one knee. "Damn train," I mutter as I feel a pull on my shoulder.

I know the sensation and my elbow flies back fast and hard. I catch my assailant in the arm. I spin around, shocked to find the woman gripping my bag. I hesitate a second, then swing. My fist connects with her jaw, hard. She cries out and crab walks away from me. When I glance up, she cowers while the man smiles at me and claps his hands. His cackle sounds insane. The woman rubs her face and grinds her teeth, but the door opens and I leap out before she can move.

Ha! I made it. The modern airport terminal feels like a different world compared to the subway. I open my sack enough to slide the metal cylinder away. I check my hands. Elbowing attackers is safer, less chance of busting open a knuckle and catching whatever they might have.

As I walk through the sliding glass doors, my security scan is welcoming. My metal cylinder shows up as an exercise device. People stride by me with purpose, and I cut through them to find a bench to wait on. I'm more than an hour early. I use the time to replace the images of the subway with composed business people. I dig for my ear buds and tap on

Jeremy's latest release. The player was a gift from Mom the year before we had to start saving, and the song I borrowed from the library. I wait for the music to erase the stress.

The song starts with a moan that sounds more like trapped wind than a human. The title is "Ocean 65." I can pick out the sound of water crashing even though I've never been to a real sea. Boston Harbor, with its coal black tides, hardly qualifies. Wind and waves intersperse at the beginning of the song. Then the rhythm starts, matching the beat of my heart, then faster, bringing me with it. I tip my head back, close my eyes. I disappear into the spray of waves and thumping bass.

I'm startled by a tap on my shoulder. Praline stands next to my bench. Not my first choice, but I motion for her to sit down.

"You're early, too!" She's quivering with nerves and clearly not as shy as I first thought. "Tell me your name one more time."

"Monet O'Neal."

She has two magenta suitcases propped up against our bench. "I was a little excited, you know? So I came early."

"Yeah, me, too." Excited and trying not to get killed.

"I've been thinking all night and I'm pretty sure Jeremy will be on the plane with us."

She fans her face with her hand. Jeremy on the plane. I hadn't considered the possibility. I guess I need to be ready to stand out. Maybe just being real will be enough. "Even if he is on the plane, he'll probably be in a separate section."

"Oh, I thought of that, too, but I might get a glimpse." She raises her eyebrows, and I again wonder what Jeremy saw in this girl. "Hey, it's Eleanor." Praline hops off the bench and launches through the crowd to intercept her. After that, Praline stands on the bench to make it easier for the others to find us.

Eleanor sighs as she sits down next to me. "That girl has too much energy," she whispers. I nod. Praline seems like a different person from the shy girl in the back of the room.

The security sensor over the entrance sweeps a green light over the single file stream of people entering. I watch for the other contestants, surprised the studio didn't have a better system for gathering us up this morning. One of us could easily go in a different entrance and get lost. Hmm, would that mean a better chance at the prize money?

"Mel." Praline waves frantically. "Crystal." Then, unfortunately, the rest of the girls find us, and as a group we're lead through the airport to a private runway. Bill drives up to us in a luggage cart. The girls struggle to lift bursting suitcases onto the vehicle. Jasmine has a third bag on her back, but no one reprimands her. I opt to keep my tote bag with me. It's not heavy and since it contains every article of clothing I own, I'm not letting it out of my sight. I don't see Jeremy, but I don't think he'll be able to just walk through the airport without getting mobbed.

The big steel plane waiting for us intimidates me. My hands tremble as we cross the tarmac to the staircase. Hazy air sticks to my face and arms. I pull the strap of my bag tight and climb up. The aisles are smaller than they look on TV. We pass through a cabin of white leather couches, and then through a curtain to the back of the plane. I want to ask a ton of questions, but I don't want anyone to know this is my first time.

Shelley Anne sits next to me. "I've never flown before," she says under her breath. I clutch my hands together so that she doesn't notice I'm shaking.

The Jasmine clones, Brie and Mel, are sitting together one row back, frowning and jealous of each other, I suspect. One Jasmine is enough, three of them is ridiculous. Claire walks past wearing a sticker with her name on it. Where did she get a nametag? Did she make it herself, or are they handing them out and I missed getting mine? She's not sporting her dance clothes this morning. Maybe those were just for the interview.

Then the curtain parts and Jeremy is standing at the front of the cabin. All of my negative thoughts grind to a halt.

"Hey," he says. "I just wanted to say hi before we took off."

After a second of shock, all of the girls are talking over each other to say hi. The wave in his auburn hair flips to the left rather than the right today. Dark circles rim his eyes and his shoulders slump under a rumpled T-shirt. He doesn't have his stage presence this morning. He just seems normal and tired. I'm staring at the hint of stubble on his face when his eyes meet mine. Oh, my. The corner of his mouth twitches and I wonder if he's thinking about smiling at me. He looks like a real guy. Someone I could talk to.

"Can't wait to get to know you all on our dates," he says. His gaze flicks away from mine and the loss makes me sad. "Have a good flight."

Again the girls talk over each other. I don't even try to make myself heard. The curtain falls closed behind him and I wonder if there are seatbelts on the white leather couches. What position does he sleep in? I think back to all the articles I've read, but I don't know the answer. Will he be thinking about new song lyrics on the flight? I wish I prepared myself more to win.

"I think he was staring at me," Shelley Anne whispers.

I was pretty sure he was making eye contact with me. She crosses and uncrosses her legs repeatedly and I rub my knuckles. I already elbowed one person today and that was terrible. Why am I suddenly considering whacking Shelley Anne? She adds to the leg crossing by biting her fingernails and I try my damnedest to block her out. Was he really looking at her, and why do I care?

The roar of the plane's engine knocks me out of my thoughts. I sit on my trembling hands. Shelley Anne grips the armrest. I pretend to sleep so that she won't know I'm nervous, too.

In my daydream, Jeremy walks across the park and sits on my blanket. He pulls out a guitar, his long fingers wrapping around the neck of the instrument. There are big trees overhead, casting triangles over his features while he strums. He hums a line and I want to kiss him so bad. After the song is over, of course. Oh, and he's brought a picnic basket full of fruit.

Eleanor and Bill pass by and disappear into Jeremy's section, completely distracting me from imagining what types of fruit would be in the basket. Fifteen minutes later they come back through with a cameraman behind them.

Jeremy ruffles his hair and rubs his eyes. "They thought it would be good to have me ask you girls a few questions now in case they need filler for the show." He holds up a piece of paper. "Uh, I'll just go down the row and ask a question to each of you." Gosh, he looks tired.

Bill points out which girl to start filming—Shelley Anne, who is right next to me, and I'm strapped down with no way to escape, with a video camera two feet from my head. No pressure. "Question one: if you could have one wish in the world, what would it be?" Jeremy glances up from his sheet of paper and waits.

Shelley flips her hair one way and then the other. "There are a lot of things I would like for myself," she pauses and stares right at Jeremy, "but if I only have one wish, it would have to be for world peace."

Ahh, so cliché, and yet, what else could she have said to sound better? Bill points to me and Jeremy shifts his gaze. "If the world was ending and you could save one other person, who would it be?"

Oh, crap. This is one of *those* questions: if I say I'd save him, I'll sound like a loser. I don't really know him and I'd be essentially picking a complete stranger over people I've known my whole life. But then, I don't want him to think that I'm leaving him out there to die. "My mother," I say with a sigh.

He gives a tired laugh. "You don't sound so sure."

"I just don't want you to think I'm abandoning you in a field with fire and brimstone raining down on our heads as I grab someone else to save. I suppose I could trade you for me, but when it came down to it, I'd probably go for self-preservation."

"That's as honest of an answer as I've ever heard." He smiles again at me, but Bill points to the next girl. Claire. "What's your favorite food?"

"Butternut squash ravioli and cheesecake." Ugh. I recognize the food from an interview Jeremy gave about his favorite meal years ago. Like that's going to impress him.

Next up, Praline. Jeremy rubs his eyes again, poor guy. "How long can you hold your breath?" Huh? Guess my question wasn't so bad.

She doesn't say anything and then I realize she's holding her breath. I hope Eleanor or Bill started counting. An awkward sixty seconds of silence pass. Finally she sucks in air. "About a minute," she announces.

Bill shakes his head and points to a Jasmine clone, Mel, I think. Jeremy loses his place on the page and runs his fingers over the words while we all lean forward in our seats, watching him. "If you had to pick one tool to survive in a winter landscape, what would it be?"

"A thermo tent," she says. *I don't think that counts as a tool.*

Next clone, Brie. "If you had to pick one other contestant to throw off the plane, who would it be?" Jeremy laughs as he asks. He's merging into deliriously tired. I know the look.

Brie points to Jasmine and all of us try not to giggle. I think Jasmine whispers "bitch" to her, but I'm too far away to make out the words. Jeremy turns to Jasmine and she's all smiles. "If you had to be cursed with either big feet or big hands, which would you choose?"

"These are funny questions. Did you come up with them yourself?" She bats her eyelashes at him.

"Yeah, sorry."

"Oh, don't be. You're so much fun. I guess I'd pick big feet. They're easier to hide."

Jeremy nods and Bill points at the next girl, but the plane bumps up and down and the seatbelt sign pops back on. "Thank God," Jeremy mumbles.

Bill stands in front of us. "I guess that will be enough. Everyone make sure your seatbelts are buckled." I watch him and Eleanor return to their seats. They have a pile of paper between them and I wonder if they're assigning dates right now. Or maybe that's up to the producers. Did Jeremy like the answer to my question? Is honesty a good thing?

Outside of the plane window, dark and light clouds pepper the sky. I bet if they were a food they'd be sweet. Maybe like marshmallows. Lucky for me, processed sugar is almost as cheap as vitamin spread. We're too high up for a view of the landscape below. According to most environmentalists, the entire country is as overbuilt as Boston. I'd like to see that for myself.

The plane tilts and circles down to land. Before we reach the ground, I catch a glimpse of foliage and blue water that look just like the brochure. Key West. Palm trees decorate the edges of the airport terminal. I instantly love them. All the leaves are on top, like the trees have big, shaggy hair. The city buildings are circled in thin clouds, but appear to be close. The plane bumps to a stop.

"Girls, stick together." Bill stands in front of us, adjusting his suit jacket. "Our agenda for this morning is to check into the hotel and get situated in our rooms. The first date will be this evening, but we'll meet and discuss that along with our schedule in the hotel meeting room this afternoon."

I reach under the seat in front of me and pull out my bag. Shelley Anne fumbles with her lap belt so I demonstrate with my own. A big whoosh of warm air encircles me as I step off the plane and I wiggle my toes. Anything new and different is awesome.

Jeremy is already off the plane. A limo pulls up alongside and he turns, smiles, waves, and climbs in the back. I'm smiling so wide my face feels stiff. The air here even tastes sweet, or if not quite sweet, it doesn't taste like the tar exhaust of cars.

We board a compact white shuttle. I snag a window seat to watch every single thing. If Fluxem gets me, I'll have all of this to remember. I shake off the fatalism. I can do this. I can win enough for the cure. The shuttle whips through the street too quickly. A golden arch frames the hotel entrance. *Grand Escalatta*, the neon lights proclaim. A clean swath of green carpet leads in. This is so incredible. I turn back toward the shuttle and I'm rewarded with a glimpse of the ocean. The whole city hums. "What's that noise?" Eleanor asks the bellboy.

"The water purifier, ma'am."

Oh. I understand now. This section of ocean truly is aquamarine because they're cleaning it. Constantly, from the sound of it. I wonder how much that costs? Bill checks us in at the front counter and holds up five envelopes.

"Two to a room. Pair up now." Shelley Anne is still standing close to me, so I just slide a bit closer and she flares her nostrils in relief. She's such a strange girl. I'm just glad I'm not sharing a room with Jasmine.

We take the stainless steel elevator up to the seventh floor. The carpet is patterned in tropical colors and the theme continues inside, with a parrot-shaped lamp next to the first bed. The room is three times the size of my apartment. In the bathroom, I pull back an orange shower curtain to reveal a bathtub with a cyclone feature. I step back out into the main room and kick off my sneakers to slowly walk the perimeter. My toes sink deep in the plush carpeting. We have a window that overlooks half of another building, a parking garage, and a quarter inch of aqua water.

"What are you doing?" Shelley Anne asks.

"The carpet is really soft."

She raises her eyebrows at me. "Who do you think will have the first date tonight?"

"I have no idea," I say, pausing at the window again.

"I hope it's me. I can't wait to kiss Jeremy." Her voice is high with excitement and I'm glad I'm facing away so that she can't see my grimace. If the other contestants are going to be physically affectionate, it might hurt my chances to impress the viewers.

"How can you be so sure he wants to kiss you?"

She turns and huffs. "It's a TV show. There's always kissing." Hmm. Not an encouraging thought.

"He's a real person, you know. This isn't just some actor."

"Geez. I didn't mean anything by it." She narrows her eyes in my direction. "You don't have to be so mean. Isn't there a chance he'd want to kiss me?"

I lean against the window. "Sure." There's a chance of just about anything happening. I was only alone with him for a moment...in a bathroom. I'm not an expert, but in the interview they asked about whether or not I was sexually active because Jeremy doesn't want to be mauled. I don't know about the rest of the girls, but I'm going to apply that to my strategy.

The hotel meeting room is windowless and sterile with white-washed walls and a gray formica conference table. I feel like I've gotten one of those dreadful secretarial jobs, until the wave of perfume hits me. The mix of strange fragrances the other girls are wearing instantly gives me a headache. I hope Jeremy isn't smell-sensitive, because he's in for it.

"Bill isn't able to join us," Eleanor says. "I'll go over the important points with you and he can fill in anything I missed later." She drags her hand through her shoulder-length graying hair. "This room will be ours for the length of our stay. Consider it the viewing room." She pushes a button at the corner of the table and the wall behind her comes alive. "This screen will show views from the various cameras during the dates. Unfortunately, the audio from the personal mics will be dubbed in later, so you'll only have the visual. Of course, you don't have to watch, but as I said, the room will be open."

I stare at the blank screen and then across the table. All of us are staring, contemplating being watched every moment of our date. Not a romantic thought.

"Here is the list of dates." She sets a sheet of paper in the center of the table and everyone grabs for it. Praline wins, clutching the edge of the paper. The rest of us form a circle behind her, trying to see our names.

Claire—Dance Club
Monet—Beach
Praline—Emperor Exhibit

I can't read anymore. I'm number two and I'm going to the beach. My luck is gone. I don't own a bathing suit. I have practically no money and I can't swim. I don't have a chance.

Shelley Anne squeals. "I get to go canoeing!" She sways on her feet, a dreamy expression filling up her face. "Imagine me in a little boat with Jeremy."

Praline taps Eleanor on the shoulder, trying to figure out what hers means. Now that the list is free, I read over the rest. There it is, 4. *Shelley Anne—Canoeing.* I assume the formal names are restaurants. And because I can't help it, I scan for Jasmine's name. 10. *Jasmine—Snorkeling.* I wonder how she feels about that. From her snotty expression, it's hard to tell whether she's considering herself superior or is just plain pissed off. The dates are arranged for both daytime and nighttime. The producers must be packing them together so that the finalists are chosen before the benefit concert.

I can't believe they signed me up for a beach date. A dinner date would've been so much easier.

"Don't pout, Monet. The expression is unbecoming." My jaw tightens. Thanks a lot, Jasmine. And I wasn't pouting. She sashays over to the table. "Eleanor, will meals be provided for us?"

"Yes, yes, of course. I forgot to mention that. Thanks for the reminder. Our assigned dining room table is L27. The restaurant opens for a period of two hours surrounding meal times and you girls are welcome to order anything you want. With the exception of alcoholic beverages, of course. I know some of you may be accustomed to drinking at home, but that behavior is not something the show wants to promote."

No one argues the rule and I wish they'd all hurry up and leave so that I can talk to Eleanor about my date.

"Also, each of you needs to remember to leave your prints on the elevator panel. The floor is secure for Jeremy, and we need a record of who's coming and going. Do not forget or you will lose your date privileges and be excluded from the competition. I'm sure you girls can appreciate the absolute necessity of keeping Jeremy safe."

We all nod in unison. I think Shelley Anne scanned her thumb to open the elevator door; I don't even remember if I did afterward or not. From the shifting about in chairs, everyone is wondering the same thing.

"Um, since we didn't know, can we just go scan in now? I mean, I would've if I'd known, but no one told us when we checked in and—"

"Yes, that's fine, Praline. You can scan in after the meeting." Eleanor goes back to her checklist and continues reading to us. "Time of day for each date will be finalized with the contestant twenty-four hours in advance. Claire, sorry for the short notice, but you'll be collected from your room at six-thirty this evening. Monet, be ready by ten a.m."

Wow, this is really happening fast. First I get interviewed a day early, and now my date is one of the first ones. After years of trying to save money, this chance is so close.

"Any other questions?"

The mumble of voices fades out and all I can think of is the time ticking away. Seconds closer to my date with Jeremy. A minute. Two minutes. I'm going to the beach with Jeremy Bane! The most amazing musician I've ever heard and the most attractive man on the planet. And I'm doing it tomorrow. Unfathomable. I've been plugged in, amped up. I'm all adrenaline and anticipation. I just need a damn bathing suit.

I wait for the others to leave for the restaurant before I approach Eleanor. "Hey," I say, shy all of a sudden. "I'm scheduled for a beach date tomorrow."

"Uh, huh." She straightens her pile of documents and stands by the door, ready to leave.

"I don't have a bathing suit with me."

"Oh," she says, considering my problem. "You're allowed to go shopping within the hotel."

"I'm not sure if I have enough money." I flip over my wrist, displaying my lack of a chip.

"Oh." Her tone of voice changes and I wonder what she thinks of me now. "Uh, I guess the studio can buy you one. I mean, they want good ratings and all, so you in a bathing suit is important."

The studio thinks people want to see me scantily clad? All those people ogling me on their TVs. The thought makes me feel grimy.

"We can stop in the hotel gift shop on our way to lunch."

I'm such a loser. "Thanks."

The hotel gift shop has a total of three bathing suits hanging on the wall. All bikinis with "Key West" written on them. Oh, boy. I get to advertise as well.

Eleanor wrinkles her nose at the selection. "The locals will love it," she promises. "Bright purple, lime green, or yellow?"

Oh, so many choices. "Purple," I say in my best attempt at enthusiasm. "Thank you so much. I'm so embarrassed not to have packed one." *Not to own one.*

She scans her own chip at the register and pushes a button for a paper receipt, which she sticks in between the stack of papers. "Thanks again," I tell her. She hands me the bag and I see the extremely vibrant purple glowing at the bottom. Maybe the color will attract Jeremy's attention.

Eleanor and I leave the gift shop and walk down the hall into the restaurant. The ceiling is vaulted.

Fake parrots dip and swoop overhead. They must be robotic, which is good since I don't want anything falling on my plate. She knows the way to our table and I follow along gratefully. I flick through the menu screen on the table. I want to try everything. I will not miss a single meal.

Claire is already at the table along with Jaime and Crystal. Claire has the first date and judging from her dancing outfit after the interview, she must have a plan to impress Jeremy. They probably picked the dance club location to showcase her talent. Across the table, the pores in her skin stand out even with foundation. "Are you nervous about tonight?" I ask.

"No way. I know I'll have a blast. I just hope Jeremy can keep up with me on the dance floor. I like to move." Her lips bulge as she slides her tongue along her teeth.

"Maybe he doesn't even like dancing," Jaime says. I wish she would change out the purple contacts for something less distracting.

Crystal clinks her glass on the table. "He's a musician. Of course he likes dancing, duh."

Claire straightens up, pushing her breasts out. "Well, he'll like grinding with me."

I take a sip of my water. Jaime stares at me. "You're date number two."

I nod.

She sips her water, still staring. "Do you think you're lucky to have the beach date?"

"Uh, no. Not really." I glance down at the tabletop and then up at the fake parrot.

Jaime's expression softens. She rubs her finger along the rim of her glass. "Am I the only one here who just wants to find out what the real Jeremy is like?" I wish I could say yes, but I'm here for the prize. Hanging out with Jeremy will be cool, but I have a very real disease.

Crystal swallows a mouthful and sets down her fork. "Yeah, getting to know the real Jeremy would be nice, but be serious. There'll be a camera constantly on, this could be nothing more than another performance for him."

"For me the dance club date is a definite advantage. Even if I'm not chosen, being on screen could help my dance career. Who knows, maybe Jeremy and I will have some real chemistry." Claire sits back in her seat.

Jaime rolls her eyes. A Jasmine clone arrives at the table and snags a chair from the one next to ours. "Hey, I caught the tail end of the convo. I'm Mel, in case anyone forgot. It's so hard to remember all the names."

I nod. No one shakes hands. It's weird being friendly, but not too friendly.

"I figure my advantage is looking like his ex-girlfriend." She laughs. Hmmm, I share the same coloring as the three clones. I've never compared myself to his ex, Fiona Wilde, before. Even if I did have that going for me, it wouldn't really set me apart because of the others.

"Unless the tabloids were wrong and they had a bad break-up," Crystal says.

"Ouch." Mel taps in a selection on her menu. "I'll win him over with my personality, then."

I need a plan. These girls are big competition. I don't even know how to stand out. A hotel bikini isn't going to impress anyone. Still, I wish I had Mel's confidence. At least these girls are here for Jeremy. I'm the one that came for money. I press my fingers against my eyes. This sucks.

———

Five minutes to seven, I open the door of the viewing room to watch Jeremy on the first date. All of the other girls are already there, waiting for the feed to start. Part of me wanted to stay in my room and give Jeremy a small amount of privacy, but I've never seen him live on a date and I might be able to use the information to win.

Black static in four segments light up the screen and then fill in with images. Will I have to contend with four cameras following me tomorrow? Claire and Jeremy are in line in front of the club. He's wearing jeans and a T-shirt and leaning heavily on a brick wall. I think he must be even more tired than he was on the plane. They should've given him a day of rest before starting the filming.

The nine of us sit in rolling chairs pushed up against the U-shaped table in front of the screen. Shelley Anne concentrates on the scene with a neutral expression. Jasmine taps her nails on the table. The others fidget. Being a voyeur to someone else's date feels wrong, but I can't look away. So much for private moments.

In front of the dance club, advertisements play over the brick walls. Wet pavement reflects the flashing, colored sign onto Jeremy's black sneakers. Claire has a band of blue silk wrapped around her breasts and a short, flowy skirt. She hooks her arm through Jeremy's as they walk into the club. I gnaw on my thumbnail.

The camera pans to take in the dancers. Their swaying is creepy without hearing the song playing in the club. Claire spins at the corner of the dance floor. Her skirt flares high and it's all skin and strobe lights. Jeremy's mouth opens in what I think is a laugh. Claire dances backward, sliding her hand down his arm and twining her fingers with his.

Praline gags. I'm with her, but make a mental note that Jeremy appears to like dancing. All of the shots of him on stage usually just show him surrounded by computers and long keyboards while he mixes in instrumentals and sound effects over his own voice.

He's not one of those guys that runs around doing choreographed steps.

Claire's red hair bounces in time with her hips. Jeremy follows her lead, smiling while she twirls around him. She raises her hands above her head, shimmying her shoulders, and even I am impressed with her muscle tone. They stop dancing and stand close together, mouths moving. Presumably the song ended. Jeremy leads her to the bar. I guess he doesn't know about the no alcohol rule, but it's not technically illegal. He's over eighteen and I think Claire is, too. They clink beer bottles and I wonder what they toasted to.

The rest of the date continues with more of the same. Claire is beautiful on the dance floor. I count Jeremy's smiles. Fourteen. Shelley Anne cries and wipes at her face with the sleeve of her shirt. I expected that from Praline, and I'm surprised about the depth of emotion my roommate has for a man she hasn't spent any time with. I wish I had my scratch pad to distract me from the drama.

After two hours of hell for us, the date moves back out to the street in front of the club. They lean against the wall, bodies turned toward each other. He definitely likes her. All the physical signs are there. The limo pulls up. Jeremy opens the door for Claire and she sits on the edge of the seat, her legs splayed out, preventing him from closing the door. He leans down and kisses her cheek. One of the camera displays zooms closer. She turns her head slightly, and then they're really kissing. Huh. I wonder if he's thought this through. How many girls does he kiss? There are a lot of diseases out there. Fluxem's only one of them. He steps back away from the limo and gives Claire an intense stare. Then he closes the door and waves goodbye as the limo pulls away. The screen flicks off. There's a moment of silence, like someone important has died. Then one at a time we push away from the table and leave the room.

Kissing to impress isn't something I can do. I'm just going to have to hope conversation is enough on my date. I gaze down at the square pattern in the carpet as I make my way back through the hotel. Shelley Anne falls in step beside me, but doesn't say anything. Her face is puffy from crying. I bet there was a secret camera in the viewing room. They'll probably intersperse shots of her crying while Jeremy dances. I'm not going to show any emotion in that room.

Inside our hotel room, I try and put the memory of Claire's twirling out of my head. It would be helpful if I could go to the hotel gym and work out, but I have my own date in the morning. I can't let her get to me. I have other problems. I pull open the bag from the hotel gift shop and bring the purple bikini into the bathroom. I've never been this naked in public in my entire life. Air touches parts of my body that are always covered. I gulp. And this will be televised.

I turn in front of the mirror, adjusting the ties.

That's when I notice it.

A big, pinkish-red mark spreads over my back. The skin's puffed up and darkening fast. I can't pull air in and out of my lungs fast enough.

Fluxem.

The spot is about three inches wide and five inches long, in a grim diagonal across my lower back. I've never been marked by the disease before. Stress probably finally triggered it in my system. Two years of lying dormant, and then I join a frigging reality TV show and I'm covered in sores. It's only going to get worse. I've seen the pictures. This will turn into a crusty, scabby mess. Oh. My. God.

Now, right before my frigging beach date, I get this.

I touch the wound gently with my fingertips. It doesn't hurt, and I'm pretty sure it wasn't there yesterday. I would have noticed. I push on the red part and a bit of puss squeezes out of the center. I gag and try to wipe it off with toilet paper. Any other frigging time. Any time but now. A shirt would hide this. A one-piece bathing suit. But no, I have a neon purple bikini. I put my head between my knees and try to concentrate on breathing. Jeremy is going to think I'm disgusting.

I sit for a long time. Eventually, the horror morphs into grim acceptance, and the tightness in my chest lessens. I stand in front of the mirror again. From the front, the mark isn't visible. I tighten my stomach muscles and flip my hair to the front, covering the words scrawled across my breasts. One side says "Key" and the other "West." Maybe I can wear a T-shirt the entire date. Nervously I peek my head out of the bathroom door. God, I can't even walk across my hotel room in this thing. "Hey, Shelley Anne? Do you think I can get your opinion?"

"Yeah, sure." I can hear the sulk in her voice.

I step out of the bathroom and pause. Head back, standing straight, I can do this. "How bad is this suit?" *Do you notice anything diseased about me?* I turn slightly to the left and then right.

She bursts into tears. *Oh, shit.* "Sorry," I say and duck back out of sight. She must have seen the red spot. I crack the door enough to talk to her. "Do I look that bad?"

"You know how pretty you are," she snaps through sniffles. "You're the prettiest one of the group and you don't have to show off."

Me? Is she crazy? She thinks I'm pretty and she didn't see the mark! I stand by the cracked door, stunned. I pace back to the mirror and tuck my hair behind my ears. I don't know. Dark hair, dark gray eyes, smattering of freckles. It's the same face I've been staring at my whole life. But this time when I stare, I can't help my grin. I've never had another girl call me pretty and Shelley's anger is oddly...confidence building.

But being considered pretty quickly loses its rush. I think about Fluxem dissolving my bones and disfiguring me. I lift my arm to my face and sniff. I still smell like me. Is this the beginning of the end, or will my symptoms be mild? How long will my appearance last if I don't come up with that money?

SEVEN

TODAY IS THE day. My date with Jeremy Bane. My body hovers between having a heart attack and ecstasy. I run to the bathroom first thing, but the mark is still there, slightly darker but with no crust.

I slip a gray T-shirt over my head, letting out my breath as the material covers all evidence of Fluxem. Next, I tie a knee-length wrap skirt around my waist. Apple blossoms and branches twine together on a neutral gray background. Two years ago, Mom made the skirt for me out of a Japanese tablecloth. I've only called her once since arriving. Her optimism and my anxiety about the competition don't mix. I just want to shake the well-wishing out of her.

Shelley Anne sits up in her bed.

"Are you going to watch my date today?" I ask her.

"Yes, duh."

"I didn't know after last night with Claire." *You cried for hours.* "Maybe you shouldn't watch any more dates. I might not, either. I don't want to psych myself out." That, and there won't be much point. I'll have already had my chance to win him over.

"I bet you'll feel differently tonight," she says.

There's a knock on the door before Shelley Anne's sulk can depress me. A cameraman stands directly behind Eleanor. I freeze.

"You're going to have to get used to it," Eleanor says, leaning in. "Now, let me fasten your mic to your back."

I stand still while she reaches through the neck of my shirt and tapes the tiny device under my shoulder blade. I don't think there's any way she can see the mark on my lower back. I hope. I try on a sincere-looking smile for the TV audience and follow her down the hall. "When are we meeting up with Jeremy?" I ask her.

"Right now." She turns to face me, widening her eyes and raising her eyebrows. I feel like there should be a drumroll in the background. She stops and knocks on another door at the end of the hallway. Holy shit, we're picking him up at his room? I'm going to know the location of Jeremy's room. Eleanor must secretly want me to win, or maybe she feels bad about the bathing suit. I hope the other girls aren't watching the feed yet, otherwise there'll be a stampede.

Jeremy opens the door and he looks...wow. Smoldering hot. His light green T-shirt makes the auburn highlights in his hair pop. His long lashes blink down and I realize I'm staring directly at him and not saying a damn thing.

"Hey, Monet." He offers me his hand and we shake in greeting.

"Hey, Jeremy." His hand is warm in mine. I struggle not to be clingy and release his touch after the appropriate amount of time.

He gives me his crooked grin. "Now, I can't forget that name. In a good way, of course."

Eleanor motions us out the door without breaking our dialogue. Oh, right. The cameras. I sigh and follow her down the hall again.

Jeremy falls in step beside me. "Don't worry, the cameras creep me out a bit, too. It's like I spend my whole life trying to dodge them, and then the studio makes me an offer I can't refuse. It's not like I could say no when the money helps cancer patients."

"Of course." Walking next to Jeremy Bane is so surreal. He's so famous, but he's just striding along next to me like a normal guy. On stage he's more a supernatural character than someone I could be near, and now he's just right here. I almost want to poke my finger into his side.

He brushes his hair back from his forehead and stuffs his hands in his pockets. "I mean, I'm not implying that I don't want to be here. But I'd rather be dating you in the normal way, without the tail."

He'd like to be dating me. Be cool. "I understand." And I do. I don't want to think about how every one of my actions right now will be analyzed by the viewers. "Is the cancer foundation the only reason you decided to do the show?"

"Well, you never know who you might meet." He smiles at me again, but the answer sounds too much like the one from the commercial. I want to ask him more, off camera. I want to know everything about him.

We both scan in at the elevator and I recognize his bodyguard, Derek, when we step off. His snug black T-shirt stretches over his muscles, giving him that tough guy look, but he still has that repressed smile at the corner of his lips. In comparison, Jeremy's not as bulky and has mysterious eyes. Derek's are a harder slate blue, more badass than artistic. Despite our entourage, I can't stop staring at Jeremy. He's so tall standing next to me. There has to be a way to relax around him. I'm not going to be able to impress anyone this wound up.

Eleanor opens the hotel doors and hands us off to another assistant. A chauffeur comes around the side of the limo and ushers us in. Cameras point over the front seat of the limo. I sigh again and Jeremy pats my back lightly as he settles in. "You'll get used to it," he whispers.

"Do you know what beach we're going to?" I ask even though all I'm thinking about is the deep, breathy quality of his whisper.

The assistant hands back a brochure. Jeremy holds it out between the two of us and I scoot a few inches closer.

Coconut Beach on the outskirts of the beautiful city of Key West is known for its snorkeling, crystal blue waters, and drinks served out of coconuts. Ranked one of the top ten cleanest vacation spots.

The limo slides through the narrow streets without a bump or jolt. I've never been in a car that doesn't make noise. Maybe the wheels don't touch the ground. Jeremy pulls a bottle of sunscreen from the pocket behind the seat. "Did you already put on yours?"

"No. I didn't even think of it."

He nods and hands me the bottle. I spread the lotion over my face, but I can't think of anything brilliant to say. *Be calm. Pretend he's an average nineteen-year-old guy.* The assistant narrows his eyes at me, probably irritated that I'm not doing anything worth filming.

Jeremy seems content not to talk. He sits close enough to me that our arms are touching. The warmth from the contact sends a quiver through my spine. Does he feel even a tenth of the excitement I do? The city landscape tapers off abruptly and palm trees replace buildings. Foliage springs up in tight masses, taking advantage of the small amount of open space. I shift in the seat to try and see every bit of it. I want to slip out of the car and breathe in the air. I wonder if the taste will be like I imagine when I lose myself in the projections in front of the bank buildings. Jeremy leans over my shoulder. Geesh, I'm up on my knees, face pressed to the glass like a five-year-old.

"I grew up by the ocean." His lips brush my hair and a portion of his chest presses against my back as he peers out the window. "We had so many trees. I miss it." He reclines back in the seat.

"Can't you go back?" With all of that money, couldn't he live wherever he wanted?

"No. I was still young when the whole area was developed. You know how it goes, not enough space in the world for undeveloped green space."

"Oh."

"Don't look so sad. It's not apartment buildings or anything. Just a vertical crop farm. The technology's cool and at least the nature is preserved, even if no visitors are allowed."

"Still, it's sad that you can't go home anymore."

He sits quietly for a moment, staring out the window. "I have other houses. But you're right. That place always did feel special to me."

The limo pulls to a stop and the assistant tells us to sit still while he unloads the cameras and sets up for us to exit. I just want to climb out of the car.

"This is idiotic," Jeremy says to me. "I wish we could ditch these guys."

Me too. They tap on the glass and we clamber out of the limo on cue. Jeremy offers me his hand and I let him pull me up and out. Every time his skin brushes mine, my head heats up.

The air is warm and green. I lick my lips. "This is so—"

The assistant steps in front of me. "Slowly walk down the trail to the beach bar and lounge chairs." Way to ruin my moment. The cameras are dragged onto the sand while the operator mutters about the damage being done to the equipment.

Jeremy flexes his jaw like he wants to kill these guys. As it is, they have us walking so slowly we might as well be doing a bridal march. Derek stays at a discreet distance, but I catch his muffled laugh as he watches the processional. The path to the beach splits and Jeremy quickly takes my hand and cuts off to the side. "Let's get a drink."

It's only ten a.m., but I don't argue. I need a drink. "Two coconuts," Jeremy says and holds up his wrist for them to scan. I pull my hands behind my back, rubbing the empty spot where my chip would be embedded if I had one.

The bartender tilts the coconuts under the spigot and then puts a scoop of fruit in each, just as I imagined on the plane. The cameras have caught up with us, but we ignore them. We sit at a table under the shade of a thatch umbrella. Sweet coconut liquor fills my mouth and muffles my nerves.

"Thank you for the drink," I say. He clunks his coconut against mine and takes a gulp. "What did we toast to?" I ask.

He leans into me. "To escaping the crew. I have a plan."

"Good," I mouth. He's drinking fast, so I try to follow his lead. I'm not buzzed, just tingly, but that could also be from being near Jeremy. I don't know what he has in mind, but spending time away from the cameras would be perfect.

"We'll have to play along for a while," he whispers.

I nod and smile, taking another sip. I'm on my first ever date, and it's televised. I'm so nervous I can barely speak, but he spoke last so I have to say something. "How do you pick the background noise for your songs?" I hope that doesn't sound like a magazine interview question.

He looks around at the people on the beach. "What do you see out there?"

"People covering themselves with sunblock, talking on their phones, and enjoying the beautiful scenery all around them."

"Okay, good. Now close your eyes and tell me what you hear."

"Yelling kids, splashing water. The camera crew shuffling around the table."

He laughs. "I like your perspective. So, if I were writing a song from your viewpoint, I'd pick those three pieces of noise and mimic them. Take a few yelling kids, draw out the notes, and repeat the sound until it's more instrumental rather than noisy."

I take a gulp of my drink. I'm stunned. He really is an artist. "That's amazing to think about. How would your perspective be different?"

He grins at me. "I'd probably focus on you and the sound your coconut makes on the table, like a drumbeat. Then I'd pick a few key lines for you to say."

"And what would you have me say?" I ask, leaning closer.

"Uh-oh, now I'm on the spot." He takes a big drink.

I drape my hair over one shoulder, giving him a second to think. "You don't have to answer."

"Eh, my lyrics sometimes cut to the emotional center of an idea. But...okay. How about this: 'Coconut liquor heating my tongue. What does heat taste like? What do you?'" He pauses and flushes. "Uh, then I'd play the noise your lips make when you lick them."

My face is burning. "I'm speechless."

"Damn, our first date and I've already scared you." He glances down quickly and swirls the liquor and juice around in his coconut.

"No, nothing like that." I drag my finger through the condensation under my drink. "I think your song would be much more romantic than mine. Yelling kids aren't that melodic."

He looks back up at me and I have to bite the inside of my cheek to prevent succumbing to the dazzle effect.

"I think that's why I got so popular with my last few recordings. I'm trying to find the sexy parts of the natural world." He flips his hair back.

My brain flutters. Jeremy Bane sitting inches from me, talking about music. Dream come true. But now I need to pull it together, because I need that prize money and I can't lose my ability to reason. "You do a great job composing. I wish people connected with visual art the same way they do with music."

"I remember you said you do scratching in your interview. I want to see your work sometime."

I nod. Any excuse for more time. "I'm sure it's amateurish compared to what you produce."

"Hey, don't undercut yourself. I'm sure it's incredible."

I shrug. I don't think I'm any better at taking a compliment than he is.

"Let's see if we can get a moment alone." He takes my hand. I push my drink back and stand up. I wish I could keep the coconut. I'll never be able to see one again without thinking of his lyrics. My feet sink into the hot sand and we take quick steps together toward the water. "Do you swim?" He asks the question as though he expects me to say, "Of course I can swim."

"No."

He stops his brisk steps and turns to me. "You can't swim?"

"Sorry, this is my first time at the beach."

"You didn't learn when you were growing up?" His eyebrows lift and I find the expression particularly endearing.

He must have grown up with a lot of rich kids. "I'm from Boston and they don't let people swim in the harbor."

"Huh. I can't imagine not swimming. But don't worry, I'll teach you. It's not hard."

"Okay." *I can't do this. I'll sink like a stone.*

He pauses by a lounge chair close to the water's edge and strips off his T-shirt. The bottom drops out of my stomach. *Oh. My. God.* He ripples with muscle in the bright sunshine. He's so real and so sculpted, and his chest is better than any of my fantasies. "Are you swimming in your T-shirt?" he asks.

My T-shirt. Crap. I choke and glance at the camera. Jeremy follows my gaze and steps in front of the lens. "I'll walk behind you into the water."

Oh, God. He just thinks I'm shy. "It's not that. Well, it is, but also—" I try to swallow, but my throat tightens and damn...I'm so nervous. He's watching me, silently asking me what my problem is. I don't want to be this girl. I want to be confident, pretty. And I really don't want to admit I'm diseased. I slide my T-shirt over my head and toss it on the chair next to his. I keep my back turned away from him and the cameras.

"Purple," he whispers.

I drop the wrap skirt. The cameraman edges around Jeremy to get a clean shot of me. "What the hell, man?" He puts his hand over the lens. "Show a little bit of respect."

"She's agreed to be filmed."

"I doubt she agreed to have every guy in the world watch her undress."

The assistant holds his hand up for us to give him a minute as he opens his briefcase. I wonder if I actually did agree to that very thing.

"Come on." Jeremy turns his back to them and I stay in front of him, walking backward until my heels hit the cool water.

"Oh!" I freeze. "The water's not warm."

He laughs at me. "Don't worry. Your body will get used to the temperature." I rub my hands over my goose bumps.

"Did you think it would be like an indoor swim center?"

I bite my lip. "I'm not sure what I expected." I shiver and step quickly into deeper water. We face each other. My balance would be better if I walked the other way, but Jeremy would see my back. I stumble and he grabs my arm to support me.

"The waves will knock you around if you let them." He keeps one hand on my arm to stabilize me.

I'm up to my thighs in the cold water and the sand slips away under my feet. I stare down. My legs are obscured by the sediment I kick up as I try to move.

"Hey, focus on me." He tilts my chin up. "You don't have to look so scared. I'm not going to let you drown."

His fingers on my chin are gentle. Water weaves between my legs and I'm unsteady on my feet. He drops his hand away from my face, but continues to watch me.

"The sensation is so weird. The waves keep trying to push—" A wave cracks against my back and I'm flung forward, past Jeremy, and all of a sudden I'm underwater. I thrash back and forth, trying to find the bottom or the air—anything to figure out which way to push. I'm drowning. I'm sure of it. Then I feel Jeremy's grip tight on my wrist, yanking me back up.

"Just put your feet underneath you," he's saying. I cough and sputter. There's sand in my mouth and I think my head hit the bottom. "Deep breath, you're fine."

I do what he says and plant my feet on the ground. I pat my back. The mic is still attached. "I thought you said you weren't going to let me drown!" I push the hair out of my eyes and cough out more sand. "You could've caught me."

"I tried, but you were pin-wheeling your arms all over the place, and then you just sat down."

"I didn't do that." I blink the water out of my eyes and glance down at my top to make sure the purple triangles are still in place. Then I'm laughing. "I just sat down?"

"Pretty much."

"Then how did I get sand in my mouth?"

"I have no idea." He takes my hand and pulls me to his side. "I think you'd better risk the camera and let me go first to protect you from the waves." I hope the camera is far enough away to not have a clear shot of my back. If only my hair was four inches longer, my entire lower back would be covered. Jeremy takes my hand and kisses my knuckles. The gesture knocks the need for self-preservation right out of me and I follow along meekly.

"It's easier once we're past the wave breaking point," he explains.

I try to smile, but the deeper we get, the more my body tries to float away. The water laps at my neck by the time he finally stops.

"Mission accomplished." Did I miss something? "They won't be able to hear us now." He touches my shoulder blade where the mic is submerged. "Water distorts the sound too much. This may be as much privacy as we're getting today."

"Oh." What now? Should I tell him about Fluxem? If I want the sympathy vote, confessing that might do it. And ruin our date, too.

"Tell me something real, that you don't want the world to know."

I gulp. This is it. Tell him. I swallow my contagious saliva back down again. "I, uh, can answer the one-wish question you asked on the plane."

He pushes his wet hair back out of his face. "Nice, I love hearing how people respond to that question."

No pressure. "I'd make all the water in the world clean and—"

"Hey, that's my wish." He splashes me.

Argh, what am I doing? He gave me the perfect opportunity. "Well, I wasn't finished. I was going to add more."

"No double wishing."

"So I can't add the ability to breathe underwater so that I can collect treasure?"

"Nope."

"Well, crap."

He narrows his eyes at me. "How am I supposed to believe that's really your wish? You might be using my ocean series of songs as inspiration?"

"Fine." I raise my chin high above the water. "I take it back. Dump the pollution in, I only want the treasure at the bottom of the ocean."

"Selfish, huh?" he asks, laughing.

"Only when it comes to treasure," I say, smiling. "Your turn, answer the same question."

"I told you, you stole *my* answer."

The water laps at my face and I bounce on my toes. "Pick a different wish."

"All right, I'll re-grow that huge section of redwood forest that they cut down. I love the old pictures of that place."

"Oh, me, too. I have this black and white picture of the tree branches weaving together, kind of chaotic, like life." A wave pushes me forward and I stretch to try and reach the ground. My head dips and water goes up my nose. I try to cover my face and blow it out in a ladylike fashion, but the salt burns. Jeremy touches my shoulder to steady me.

"Do you want me to teach you how to swim?"

"Yes."

How do I bring up Fluxem? I should have wished for the cure. Though maybe there's a chance he might pick me just because.

"You're going to have to pay attention if you want to learn."

"I'm with ya. I was just thinking up more wishes."

He smirks at me. "You're certainly a person with a lot of desires." His voice deepens at the end.

"Nah, I'm a simple girl."

"Yeah, right."

"Hey, you're the mysterious and romantic musician."

"Oh, the flattery." He fans his face, which splashes water in my direction.

"Better watch that, or I'll start gushing. And I remember how much you said you hate that."

He plugs his ears and floats on his back, humming a song I've never heard. I want to chase after him, but his chest floating on the top of the water is so real. He's not wearing many clothes and he's–*wow*–toned. I try to walk deeper after him, but a wave goes right over my head. My fingers graze his side as I duck under.

"I think I'd better teach you how to swim for your own good." His forehead wrinkles with concern while he holds my arm.

I love the way his hand feels. "What do I do first?" I ask.

"Let your feet float up from the bottom."

I do and my head dips below the surface for a second, then Jeremy firmly grasps me by the shoulders. "Did you sit down again?" He shakes his head at me. "Okay, let's try a more direct approach. I'm going to put my hand on your back and you lean into me. Your head stays *above* the surface of the water."

"Got it." His hand slides to the center of my back. *Please don't move your hand any lower.* He's about ten inches away from hitting the Fluxem mark. I don't want him to find out like this. I bite my lip and try to relax my body. My feet leave the ground and I let him tip me back. My body floats to the surface and his other hand supports my upper back.

I open my eyes. I'm doing it. I'm swimming...or, well, floating. I smile up at him and he has a strange expression on his face. His head is close to my body and I think he's trying not to look at me. He focuses off to one side, then the other, and finally up at the sky.

"What's wrong?" I ask.

"I, uh..." He seems suddenly off balance.

He's not answering and I turn in his grasp. His hands trail to my front as I struggle to plant my feet. "What is it?"

"Nothing." He clears his throat. "You're just a really pretty girl." *Huh? Jeremy Bane thinks I'm pretty! Oh, wait, I get it. He's physically excited. His hands are still on my arms. What do I say?*

"Thank you. I think you're amazing, but I guess everyone does."

He glances off to the side. *Maybe I shouldn't have reminded him about all those other girls who think he's hot. What do I say now?* His hands are warm on my arms and the silence stretches into awkward territory. He turns back to me and there's a scary intensity to his gaze.

And here it is. He leans in closer to me. His hands tighten a fraction, then his lips. His face tenses, his eyes check mine for permission. Then I realize. He's going to kiss me.

I drop my feet out from underneath me and sit down hard. My butt bounces off the sand and my hair waves above me in the water. *Jeremy Bane almost kissed me and I almost gave him Fluxem. My chest is caving in.* He hauls me out of the water.

"Jeez, you don't have to kill yourself not to kiss me." He sounds hurt and exasperated.

"I, uh–" I suck in air and wipe at my eyes. *I don't want to tell you that I have a disease.*

"Hey, it's all right," he says, steadying me as I cough. His smile is gone and I'm an idiot. He steps a few feet back from me, releasing my arm. So clearly it is not all right.

"I didn't mean to fall down."

He raises his eyebrows at me and wades toward shore. He stops when we're half out. He turns to face me and I'm stricken. I've ruined our date. His hand reaches around behind me and covers the mic on my shoulder blade. "I didn't mean to rush you or anything. I'm used to girls being–anyway, I am sorry. Forgive me?" He runs his hand through his hair and water drips down his arm. His eyes shift down to the water.

Forgive him. How can he even ask that? Everyone wants to kiss Jeremy Bane. It's just that I'm diseased. "Of course, but you have nothing to be sorry for. I'm sorry, too." *What did he mean by "girls being–"? Eager to kiss?*

He takes his hand away and our conversation is being recorded again. I have to tell him about Fluxem. But how can I now? We wade out of the water. He cocks a grin at me, but keeps his distance, and I feel those two feet between us like a blow. The easy touching is gone.

The assistant waits at the edge of the dry sand. "We could barely film anything with you up to your necks in cloudy water. What were you thinking?" I scratch a design into the sand with my foot while Jeremy gets yelled at. "Your heads bobbing up and down aren't what I consider interesting television." I take a closer appraisal of our warden for the day. I didn't think a small man could turn such a shade of red. He's like a tomato ready to burst at the bulges.

"I couldn't give a crap what you think is interesting for TV." Jeremy brushes past him and I follow.

"Wait, we need you to do something worth recording."

Jeremy picks up his pace and I stride along next to him. He's focused forward, fists clenched. I stop at the lawn chair to get my T-shirt and slip it over my head as I run to catch up.

"It's okay if I tag along, right?" My question lightens his expression and he slows his pace.

He looks at me through lowered lashes. "Yeah, I'm sorry. I shouldn't be taking it out on you. I get frustrated easily."

Apologetic Jeremy is so damn cute my chest constricts. "Where are we going?"

"I thought we'd go check out the trees outside of the resort. They're not redwoods, but they're cool. You seemed interested when we were in the car."

"Yeah, that would be awesome." Even when he's angry he's thinking about me.

I probably shouldn't have said "awesome." I'm definitely not impressing him. I pull my T-shirt lower to cover my butt. At least my mark is covered now.

"Your shirt is getting all wet." He stares at me for a minute and then back at the road.

I look down and my bathing suit has made two wet triangles on my shirt; lucky it's not white or the red mark would show right through. "Eh, it'll dry."

"I probably have an extra shirt in the car if you need to change."

"I'll be fine." I'm not exposing myself anymore than I have to around the show staff. He shrugs. The camera crew follows as we walk along the side of the road, staring off into the foliage. This place is beautiful. Jeremy pauses next to a huge tree; the wide base curves outward in a giant U-shape.

He crouches down, examining the exposed roots. "I'm not sure what type of tree this is."

I stop next to him. "I wonder how old it is?"

"Who knows with all the growth hormones they're pumping into the soil these days. They might've grown a tree this size in a year."

"Wow, that's crazy technology."

"Too bad there's not enough green space to capitalize on it. Might help clean up some of this pollution."

He stands back up. I wish I knew more about trees so that I could say something scientific and impressive. We start walking again. I brush my free hand against his, palm to palm. His fingers twine with mine and he glances at me in question. I can imagine his thoughts. *She wants to hold hands with me, but won't kiss me?* I love the way his fingers fold around mine. And I love the sound of the leaves rustling and birds chirping. Real sounds, not pre-recorded animals from decades past.

"You look happy."

"I am. I've always wanted to be in a real forest."

He nods. He might be starting to understand that I haven't had a lot of opportunities in my life.

"You're beautiful when you smile." He keeps his head forward, and the comment makes me smile even harder. His thumb traces a circle on the back of my hand as we walk. I'm in heaven. "I can't figure you out, Monet."

I wish I could've just kissed him in the water. "I'm no mystery."

"Hmmm." His gaze flicks over my body before turning back to the forest. He thinks I'm attractive. I want to spin in a circle. He even seems to like the purple bikini. But will that be enough for him to choose me to win?

"We'd better head back. I think our allotted time is up."

Bam, happiness doused with ice water.

We wander back toward the resort. The cameras film us coming toward them. Jeremy might help me get the cure if I just tell him. He might be disgusted, but once I'm Fluxem-free I could get over the embarrassment. He'll probably realize I'm here for the money. That would suck, but I'd accomplish what I came on the show for.

Jeremy's thumb draws another circle on my hand. Oh. I'm ruined for other guys. This date will haunt me forever.

The assistant waits by the car. "Well, at least we have footage of the natural attractions and you two walking. Nice swimsuit, by the way, Monet. Do you mind taking the T-shirt off and posing for a few still shots?"

I fold one arm over my breasts, horrified. "I, uh—"

"She's not doing that." Jeremy scowls and places his hand on my shoulder.

The assistant humphs and narrows his eyes at me. "If you're not going to take off your shirt, hurry up. Date time is over. I'm sure Jeremy wants to eat and have a few hours of downtime before his next date tonight."

I imagine my steel cylinder in my fist as I punch this asshole. Doesn't he care at all what this date means to me? How important a few simple hours are to all of the contestants? This is one of the biggest moments of my life and he disregards the significance. Blood surges in my muscles. I'm strong enough to take him down, or at least I am now. After getting infected I needed to be able to protect myself. Maybe I should punch this guy. My mixed martial arts training is just going to waste.

"No hurry," Jeremy tells him. "Monet and I are going to lunch together." *We are?*

The assistant snorts and the action balloons his belly in and out. Jeremy has his lips pressed tight, holding in a smile. I wonder if he noticed my kill expression.

"I'll be right back." Jeremy runs off across the beach. He jogs back with my wrap skirt and sandals in his hands, all sculpted chest and perfect abs. I'm suddenly breathless. He passes me my wrap before slipping into his T-shirt.

"Thank you so much," I whisper. "Are we really going to lunch?"

"Yeah, why not? You got a date with someone else?" he asks jokingly, then looks ashamed when he realizes his own words. He does in fact have a date with someone else tonight.

I ignore the cataclysm of jealousy. "I'd love to go to lunch with you."

EIGHT

W E SLIDE INTO the car and the cameras point at the backseat again. This time, instead of the assistant issuing directions to the driver, Jeremy leans forward, and in an authoritative voice, takes over. I don't know any of the street names or restaurants so the conversation is all gibberish to me. I try to relax in my seat, but the difference between Jeremy's life and mine is stark. He's so comfortable giving orders, and I can't imagine having authority. Still, I'm relieved that my date isn't quite over.

The driver pulls up in front of a tall, mirrored building. A few stories up the reflective glass changes to clear. Letters flash on the outside: *Blue Moon Café.* Cool. I wonder what they serve? I hope Jeremy offers to pay because I don't want to admit to not having a chip. Only a few pedestrians meander by along the scrubbed clean sidewalk. How many people have enough money to vacation here?

"What are you thinking about?" Jeremy asks.

I turn away from the limo window. "Sorry, I'm just taking in all the differences."

Derek, the cameramen, and the assistant climb out of the vehicle. Jeremy pulls the assistant aside. "We don't need the film crew." I glance at Derek and he grins back. I don't know what it is about that guy that puts me at ease. He raises his eyebrows as he watches

Jeremy and then shakes his head. Jeremy must be so sick of being followed, it makes sense that he'd have a friend for a bodyguard. I try not to notice Jeremy's increasing hand gestures and agitation.

The assistant stumbles back. "Look, you might think you don't have to answer for your actions, but you have signed a legally binding contract, and I *will* be filming this."

From the hard edge to Jeremy's jaw, I can tell he wants to say more to the assistant and is holding himself back. Instead he removes the mic from his shoulder and throws it back into the limo. I quickly do the same with my own and his frown lessens. I slip my hand inside his and his shoulders relax. "The air here smells so much cleaner than Boston. But I guess you're used to this?"

He shifts his focus away from the assistant. "Nah, I'm not used to it at all. I travel a lot when I'm on tour. You'd be amazed at the shitty air quality all over the world. There are very few places that can afford a clean air dome."

"I didn't realize there's one here." I look at the sky, but I can't detect any barrier. "It must be amazing to get to travel so much."

"Not really. A lot of tiny hotels and people like this." He hooks his thumb back in the direction of the assistant who's giving directions to the cameraman about what to film. The door slides open in front of us and we step through together, his hand still holding my own. An escalator zigzags up the floors, and it's one of the clear ones. I hate being suspended on a single pane of glass. With a gulp, I don't even pause as I follow Jeremy on. The ground beneath my feet gets farther away and the railing hums through my fingertips. I just can't accept the safety of this technology. I quickly step off at the top. Thank God, the floors aren't clear, too.

The entrance to the café is in the shape of a sparkly, blue crescent moon. I bend my body into the curve as I walk in. Jeremy smirks at me. "You're not that big, I don't think you were going to bump into anything."

I shrug. "I'm fitting in with the environment."

He shakes his head at me. "Table for two." His fingers slide along my hand, brushing my wrist as we follow the host to our table. He seats us at the edge where we can overlook the street below. From the inside, stars lightly frost the glass, giving the impression of the night sky. It's beautiful.

"You don't have a chip?" Jeremy asks when the host leaves.

My wrist. Shit. "Nope. I don't have any money." I try to sound like I don't care and I think it works.

He laughs. "Well, I think I have enough to cover lunch, so don't worry." Enough to cover lunch for a million years. I exhale and the tension in my back releases. My being poor isn't a big deal.

I tap on the menu. Whoa, they even have seafood and steak. Meat is expensive.

"You should get the steak," Jeremy says. "Since I'm paying and all." His tone is light and joking.

"Very funny. Maybe I will."

"Do you like beef?" he asks seriously.

"I've never tried it."

He reaches across my side of the table and punches the selection button for me. "I insist."

"What else should I order?"

He leans over again and hits a few more buttons. I smell ocean water in his hair and I want to touch him so badly. "Do you want to approve my choices before I send them to the kitchen?"

"No, I trust you."

He punches in his own selection and then focuses back on me. "So, you already know all about me. Tell me about the mysterious Monet."

"Hey, I only know you from interviews. That's not exactly a deep understanding."

He shrugs. "Okay, we'll trade questions. But, uh—" He narrows his eyes. "You're not one of those girls who's going to sell every word I say to the tabloids are you?"

"Oh, God. I would never. Do girls do that to you?"

He quirks a half-smile. "Can I count that as your first question?"

"Sure, but I want more."

He raises his eyebrow like "more" could mean anything. "I've had a girl hide a mic on her and sell the recording to *Celeb*. It's not so much anything that I said was private, but man, she was with me just to score a payout. It was insulting."

Ah, so I guess now would not be a good time to mention needing money for the cure to Fluxem. "I'm sorry that happened. The girl was a complete idiot."

He shrugs. "I've met a lot of nice girls since I became famous, and also a lot of shallow ones. People definitely treat me differently now."

"What do you think of the girls in the competition?"

"You do realize that's another question."

Damn. "So, I'll owe you two?"

"I'm keeping count." He taps his fingers on the table. Short nails, long fingers. All of a sudden I can't believe how close I am to him. "I don't know enough about the girls in the competition until I go on more dates, but what I said on the commercial for the show wasn't all crap. I wouldn't mind meeting a nice girl, but after my sister's brush with skin cancer when she was younger, I'd do the show just to help other kids like her. Skin cancer is no joke."

"Did your sister get diagnosed when she was young?"

"She was six. Most of my childhood was overshadowed by her treatments and trips to the doctors."

"Hmmm. That must have been hard. Not as much time for you, I would assume."

He shrugs. "I think that's why I took up music initially. I just wanted to excel at something. Sounds so stupid to be jealous of my sister with cancer, but in my little kid mind I just wanted a reason for people to think I was special, too."

"I don't think that sounds stupid at all. Now that you're so famous, I doubt anyone will ever ignore you." At a table behind us a man and woman stare at Jeremy's back, talking in hushed voices. When the woman realizes I noticed, she pretends to look out the window and drink her coffee.

Jeremy ruffles his fingers through his hair. "Which is the funny thing. Now that I've been getting all this attention for the last few years, I'm done with it. I'd rather work behind the scenes. Find a nice, quiet girl that doesn't want to just be with me *because* I'm a rockstar."

I stare down at the table. *I'm a nice, quiet girl.* "Is your sister okay now?"

"Yeah, she's fine. But it makes me pay attention to how much time I spend outside, especially when I travel." He sits back in his chair, relaxing.

I try to follow his lead and recline in my chair, but my legs bounce and I'm too amped up.

"I'm glad she's better. Did she go to the facility in Boston?"

"Yeah, that's why I really want to give back, you know?" He glances at my foot sticking out from under the table and smiles.

I nod.

"At least Key West has a dome. Clean air and sun protection. Cities like this are the best. But enough serious talk. I believe you owe me a few questions." He lifts an eyebrow and leans into the table.

I wipe my sweaty palms on my skirt. "What do you want to know about me?"

"Everything?" he suggests.

"That would be pretty boring," I tease.

"I doubt that."

I don't know what ideas he has about me, but I'm neither exciting nor mysterious. "I'm average." Wait, I'm trying to win a competition. I should've been less honest.

"No one's average, not really. How about work? What do you do?" His eyes wrinkle at the corners slightly, like he's figuring out everything about me and remembering it. I pin my legs together and force them still.

"I just graduated. The last job I had was sorting database files for the library, but they ran out of funding for the project." That was over three months ago. I should've gotten a new job by now. "But I haven't found a new job yet."

"What do you want to do?"

"There's a difference between what I want to do and what I can do, you know?"

"Well, what do you want?"

"In a perfect world, I'd go to college and study art."

"And in this world?"

"Get an entry-level job until I can save up enough money to get my bartender's license." He frowns. I don't have many choices. "It's an okay job and there are still plenty of people who want a person to hand them their drinks rather than a machine." I smooth my hair back self-consciously.

"I'm sure you'd be good at it. But I think you should go for art if that's what you want."

I frown. I agree, and maybe that's why I haven't been doing anything for months and latched onto this contest as the answer to my problems rather than getting out there and working. But then I never would've gotten to meet Jeremy.

"I didn't mean to make you sad." He reaches over the table to touch my hand. The sound of the camera zooming in shakes me out of my reverie. Crap. I hope they don't broadcast the fact that I don't have a job. I thought I was safe with the microphone gone, but the camera probably records sound, too.

"How about you? Do you want to spend your whole life making music?"

He laughs and flips his hair back. "I don't know. I'd like to at least keep composing, but I've been thinking about going to school for a real job."

"Music's a real job. You certainly get paid for it."

He shrugs.

"What else do you think you'd be good at?" I ask.

"I thought maybe I'd go for medicine." He shrugs again and shifts around in his chair.

It's strange to see him unsure of himself. He's always so confident on stage.

"I bet you'd be great at that."

He smiles at me and his warm brown eyes drag me in. He'd be the most popular doctor ever. The waiter arrives with our food. Steak, with...an unknown vegetable and...a pretty pink drink. Jeremy has the same thing on his side of the table.

"What are they?" I ask, poking at the green circles.

"Fiddleheads. They're the tender top part of a new fern."

I point at the drink.

"Sparkling lemonade."

I try the green circles first. The flavor is light, buttery, salty, and fresh. Next I cut into the steak. Disturbing juice leaks out, but the texture is completely unique. I chew hard. Vegetable spread only requires swallowing. This is so much better.

"You're so easy to please," Jeremy says, watching me as he takes a big bite.

"Thanks?"

"Absolutely. It's a nice change."

A change from what? An ex-girlfriend? Fiona Wilde? I keep eating even though Jeremy is watching me.

"I'm trying to think of a good second question." He props his head on his hand. A mannerism I've never seen on TV or anywhere. I'm truly having lunch with Jeremy. Crazy. I hope he doesn't ask about other guys or sex. Oh, crap, what if he asks what my favorite sexual position is, like they always do in *Celeb*? I swallow my steak and wash it down with the lemonade.

"What do you do in your free time?" *Phew.*

"Well, you already know about graffiti-style scratching from my interview." As opposed to the illegal stuff I do for The Metal Society. "Other than that, not too much. I like mixed martial arts."

"Watching or practicing?"

"Both."

"Are you any good?" I like how his voice gets a little cocky.

"Want to find out?" I lean closer to the table in mock challenge.

He smiles and narrows his eyes. He's about to speak when a screech fills the restaurant.

"Jeeeereeeemy! Are you filming the show now?" Then—*bam*—there's a girl at his side. Then another. They're lining up. Derek races across the restaurant from his perch at the front entrance. He pushes himself between the girls, but they squirm around him, reaching for Jeremy. I clutch the edge of the table to keep from being thrust out of the way.

"Will you sign my lower back?"

She leans across my food, giving me a view of Jeremy's name tattooed just above her butt before presenting him with the image. Her face is even with mine while she waits for him to sign. We glare at each other.

"I don't have a pen on me."

There's some shuffling around while one of them comes up with a marker. I take a sip of my lemonade even though the girl stays in my face. Then Derek slaps her on the back. "You're all done. Move along."

Thank you, I mouth.

Jeremy scrawls his name on a few other magazine clippings. They step a few feet back, but they're not retreating.

"I guess that's the end of our relaxing lunch." The few waiters and waitresses stand off to the side, watching the fans. All they have to do for a tip is set the food on the tables. They're clearly not going to help with crowd control. Jeremy scans his chip as the bill displays on our table. "I'm sorry, Monet."

"It's okay," I mumble as I stand up from the table. The girls are blatantly staring at me. "She's a contestant," one of them whispers. Another shakes her head and smirks like I have no chance. Derek corrals them on one side of our table while we slip out. I keep my head down and follow Jeremy's feet out of the restaurant. I step through the moon. I wish our lunch hadn't been interrupted. I peek at Jeremy through my lashes, and from the sullen look on his face, I think he does, too. I guess the girl's tattoo wasn't that impressive.

"Is this what it's like being you?"

"Sometimes." His face has no hint of expression, but the corners of his eyes are sad. We walk back out to the street and I wonder if he would talk to me more if we had kissed in the water.

The cameraman pulls his gear onto the escalator behind us. The camera's pointed down, so I assume the recording has stopped. The assistant waits for us by the limo. "About time. You need to get ready to go to the museum."

I wish I could go to the museum. Jeremy holds open the door while I slide in. He sits next to me, tracing the lines on the palm of his hand. I want his good mood to come back.

"I don't mind about the autograph scene. I know that's part of your job." I nudge him with my shoulder.

He looks over at me. "It's just that I have no control over shit like that. We were talking, and those girls didn't even realize they were being rude."

I set my hand on his arm. I'm shaking with nerves. "I know you're more than just a guy on stage."

He covers my hand with his. "Yeah?"

"Of course. I mean, you're putting up with a dating show to help cancer patients. I've only known you for a little while, but I think even without the fame, you'd be a pretty awesome guy."

"Thanks." He breathes deep and gives me a partial smile. On stage he always seems so confident; sitting here next to me he's still gorgeous, but I know the other Jeremy is just a show.

He traces my knuckles with his finger and tingles dance up my arm. I want to say more, but the silence feels right. Comfortable.

We arrive at the hotel entrance all too quickly.

"Thanks for the day," I say, not letting my sadness show in my words. My date is over. I climb out of the limo, reluctantly letting go of his hand. He slides out after me and closes the door. "And thank you for almost teaching me to swim."

"Hey, anytime. Just as long as you don't sit down next time." His eyes tip down to mine for a second and he pauses like he might say something. He looks at my lips and I tuck them in.

"I had a great time. Thank you," I say.

His hand brushes mine and then he squeezes gently. Not a handshake, but not holding hands, either. My fingers flex toward his as he pulls back. He gives me his crooked half-smile before Derek and the production crew step in between us. They start filling him in on his schedule for the rest of the night while I walk into the hotel.

I stand in the hotel lobby for a minute, glancing out the window, waiting for another smile, but I know he's busy. I go back to my room to change.

Shelley Anne waits on her bed in a meditative pose. "How did the date go?"

"You were watching, what did you think?" I kick my shoes off and sink my toes into the plush carpet.

"Honestly, it was kinda hard to tell. Maybe if we'd had the dialogue—"

"Oh." She's not even crying, so my date must not have been too heart-wrenching. I hope that doesn't mean the viewers at home aren't going to like me.

Shelley picks a lock of hair off her shoulder and runs it across her lips. "Your bathing suit really stood out, though." *Is she being mean? Did she see my back?* "I forgot to tell you last night how funny it was for your boobs to say 'Key West.' It's really nice of you to advertise the location. Did the studio talk you into it? 'Cause I sure don't want to wear a swimsuit they pick. I shopped forever to find mine. Oh, and what's that nasty mark on your back?"

My heart stops. Blood rushes up my neck and fills my head like a sewer. My brain throbs.

"Uh, what mark?"

"Looks like you got attacked by a jelly fish." The throbbing intensifies. She knows I'm diseased. She'll tell everyone. Maybe the other girls saw the mark, too, and know what it is. Shit. Keep it together.

"Oh, I didn't notice. That sucks." My voice stays level like I'm not concerned, but I feel my face turning red.

"Well, for your sake I hope it goes away fast. 'Cause...ew, gross."

I blink my eyes rapidly. *Come on, don't cry. Hold it together.* I straighten the blanket on my bed, then fluff my pillow. Anything to keep my face turned away from Shelley. If I don't make a big deal about the mark, she'll forget. I just have to not let her see me react.

Did Jeremy see the Fluxem spot, too? Or the producers? Would they take me off the show or find a way to expose me on air? Great, the whole world will probably know I'm contagious. For the rest of my life I'll be branded as the diseased girl that tried to win a date with a rockstar, because most people won't think about the fact that someone on TV might not have enough money to get the cure. I've seen it on other shows: the stereotype that Fluxem's a dirty poverty thing is everywhere. Never mind that people are dying, or that I could potentially be developing life-threatening complications this very second. I muddle through my thoughts enough to find a sentence for Shelley Anne that doesn't make me sound upset. "You must be really excited about your date. You're up next, right?"

"Yeah, he's going out with the short girl tonight and then it's me and him."

"He's really nice in person. I'm sure you'll have a great time." I keep my tone optimistic and she appears vaguely disappointed that her comments didn't hurt me.

"Yeah, well, since we'll be canoeing we'll be very close together." She stands up off her bed, straightening the front of her sundress. "I'm heading to the restaurant before the viewing room, do you want to come?"

"Sure, why not?" I change out of my swimsuit and back into my regular pair of jeans. I clench my fists once and roll my fingers. I'm still shaky. I thought I could get through this show without anyone knowing about Fluxem, but now there may be video evidence of the mark on my back. If it's not that noticeable, I'm okay, but if the other contestants figure it out...

We walk down the hall together. Shelley talks about a designer I've never heard of while I nod along, watching my feet. At the restaurant, we sit in silence and wait for the food to arrive. I need a new plan. I can't count on a win. If I told Jeremy, would he give me the money?

Shelley picks at her food, only eating a few leaves at the edge of her salad plate. I eat mechanically as I analyze everything I said and did. There are seven more dates and no way to know if I did enough. After Shelley Anne's comments, who knows how they'll edit the footage together for TV? I need the viewers to like me. I'd been so focused on Jeremy that I wasn't playing it up for the screen. I should've smiled at the camera more, showed more cleavage, or acted more confident. Too late now. I massage my temples. I'm being stupid. I finish my fajita. I'm not going to waste food, no matter how insane this contest makes me.

Shelley Anne and I are the first ones to arrive in the viewing room. I'm done talking to her for the night. If she wants to be competitive, that's fine by me. Jasmine and the others file in. Claire keeps her head lifted higher than mine, like an invisible string pulls her chin up to the ceiling. I don't know why she thinks her date was so much better than mine. Oh, right, because Jeremy kissed her.

One of the Jasmine clones focuses in on me. "It looked like you had a fun date." No hint of sarcasm.

"Thanks, Brie."

Jasmine shakes her head and turns toward her. "You thought that about the other one, too."

Brie lifts a shoulder and swivels her chair around. "I'm just surprised Jeremy's so generous with his time. He even took Monet to lunch after, and that wasn't scheduled."

Claire stares at me. "I would've liked more time with Jeremy, too." I wait for more accusations, but she lets the conversation go.

Brie turns away from Jasmine to address me again. "So, what did you think? What's the man behind the music like?"

"He's a good guy."

Crystal sighs and drops her chin onto her cupped hand. "I wish we could have more dates."

Claire doesn't say anything. I wonder what her impression of Jeremy was. It's possible one of us might not want to win after spending time with him. *Ha. Yeah, right.* I drop my head into my hands, letting the weight off my neck. What am I doing? Have I lost my mind? This whole thing is supposed to be about me getting treatment for Fluxem.

The wall flickers on and Praline's door swings open. My jaw drops. She's wearing a dress that looks like it's made from black diamonds. The fit and cut are perfect for her body. Breasts accentuated, hips minimized, bell sleeves conservatively cupping her arms. She twists slightly coming out of the door and the camera shows a slit up the side of her knee-length skirt. The gap reaches all the way up to her panty line, and as she walks the play of black diamonds against tan thigh is captivating. The camera stays pinned on her, and so does Jeremy's gaze.

"That's a very pretty dress," I say. A few murmurs of agreement meet my statement. I want to cry. Jeremy opens the limo door for her and she flashes the camera again as she climbs in. Inside the limo, he pulls a small gift box out of his pocket.

"What the hell?" Claire slams back into her seat. "I didn't get a gift."

"Me, neither." A souvenir would've been nice. I might have been able to sell it.

Brie shrugs. "I'm sure it's just product placement, but we can ask Eleanor about it."

Jeremy's mouth moves and Praline puts her hand over her heart before taking the box. The camera zooms in as she unwraps the gift. A black bracelet to match her dress.

Shelley Anne's lip quivers, and then the sobbing starts. I'm so overloaded from my date and the thought of being discovered, I just want to cry, too. Instead I leave the room.

NINE

I STARE OUT the hotel room window. I'm part of a competition. A performance for ratings. Studio execs with money are taking advantage of obsessive girls to make more money. And I have to play this game to win, which is just twisted logic all around.

And I'm stupid because I think the date was worth it—that a moment with Jeremy is worth an incomparable amount of money. I shake my head, disgusted with my lack of strength. Like in the water, I'm letting everyone push me around.

Enough of that.

I open up my tote bag and take out my best denim jeans, then I stalk into the bathroom. The mark on my back hurts. I ball up tissue and try to seep the pus out of the center. I turn back and forth in the mirror, letting the light hit it from different angles. I feel disgusting. The salt water made some of the redness fade. At least I have that.

I need to tell Jeremy. That's the new plan. I nod at myself in the mirror. If he doesn't want to pick me as the winner, maybe he can still figure out a way to help me.

I can't keep fumbling around with my future just because I have feelings for him. There, I admit it. Feelings or not, there's no future with Jeremy, and without money there's no future for me. Maybe he already saw the mark, anyway. I wash the salt out of my hair and spend a long time blow drying the strands into a perfectly smooth mass of dark waves.

When I hear the door to the room open, I know Shelley Anne has returned and Jeremy's date with the other girl is over. I stay in the bathroom, giving Jeremy enough time to get back to his room, and Shelley Anne enough time to cry herself to sleep.

My black tank top scoops low over my breasts. I think I look good. This is my power outfit. I continue the pep talk in my head as I walk down the hall to Jeremy's room. I can tell the truth.

Clenching my fist tight, I rap on his door. I wait sixty seconds and then more tentatively knock again. He should be back in the room by now. I gave him half an hour. On my second knock the door opens a crack.

"Monet?" He opens the door wide and I'm struck by his low-hanging pajama bottoms and lack of shirt. His smooth chest is only an arm's length away. "Do you want to come in?"

I'm so disarmed by his appearance I almost forget my purpose. *In? Right? Telling the truth.* "I wanted to talk to you off camera for a bit, if that's okay?"

"Sure, come on in." A sheen of sweat covers his skin and a small electrode shows on the side of his forehead.

"Did I interrupt something?"

"*Combat Junkie.*" He drops his head in a slightly embarrassed manner. "Do you play?"

"No, I've never been able to afford the system." I step past him to check out the tiny box next to the projection platform in the corner of the room. "Is it true what the government says about all the precious metal in the console?"

"No. I still can't believe they actually tried to pass a bill to reclaim video game systems. Like that was ever going to happen. There's probably the equivalent of a thousandth of a gram of gold inside the CPU. They wanted to sell the systems as a whole to other countries."

"Wow, you know a lot about metal and video game systems."

"Eh, it's a hobby of mine. Actually, that reminds me. What was that little piece that fell out of your bag in the bathroom?"

"I don't know what you're talking about."

He holds his fingers up in a circle approximating the size. *I am so busted.* "Oh, just some metallic-looking plastic."

"Uh, huh." He grabs a gray T-shirt off the couch and slips it over his head.

"No, really."

He walks over, waiting for a better answer. "You don't have to lie to me. I don't care if you kept a piece of gold rather than turned it in. You'd better believe I wasn't going to give them anything of mine. It's not like I decided to borrow all that money from China."

"Non-conformist?"

He quirks a half-smile. "You're not answering my question, and don't you still owe me one from the restaurant?"

"I do not."

He nudges my arm. I suppose the likelihood of Jeremy turning me in to the Feds is slim, but the idea of talking openly about anything illegal has me looking over my shoulder for the cameras. "All right, yes, it was a piece of metal, but it wasn't mine."

"Oh, a criminal enterprise?"

"I keep telling you I'm not that mysterious or interesting."

"Uh, huh. I'll ease your fears of incarceration. Have you heard of The Metal Preservation Society?"

My breath huffs out in a big whoosh. "Maybe."

"You're not much of a liar. I saw your reaction. Don't worry. I give them money and commission pieces now and then."

"How do you know I'm not going to turn *you* in?"

"I could tie you up and keep you hostage in my hotel room."

Please? I force myself to laugh and not think anything spicy. "The piece you found was actually for the society. I do work for them now and then. Helping them reshape raw materials into jewelry they can resell to patrons. I think the opportunity for artists to still craft jewelry and sculpture with precious metal is important."

"Absolutely." He pushes his hair back from his face. "And cool that you donate your time. I'm surprised we're both members."

"Totally." *Oh, man, did I just say that?* "I still think melting down the Statue of Liberty was a huge mistake."

"Huge." He tightens his jaw and presses his lips flat. "Do you still have the piece? From what I recall, it was very detailed."

"I gave it back before I left home. It's probably back with the patron who commissioned it already."

"How did you make it?"

"I scratch into bits of aluminum and then dab adhesive into the grooves and rub gold shavings in."

"You'll have to do a secret metal work for me some time."

"Okay. Anytime." If there will ever be another time. If I'm chosen. He looks at my face and the moment of silence starts to make me nervous. I'm supposed to be telling him about Fluxem. "So, *Combat Junkie*? Can I watch a round?"

"Uh. It's pretty boring if you're not in the action."

"Can I anyway?"

He shrugs and steps up to the projection platform in the corner of the room. A holographic image overlays his body, showing his points, areas of weakness, guns and ammo. He taps his foot and the game starts again. Trees and vines spring up around him, and even though they're semi-transparent, the effect is amazing. A small machine on the floor pumps smells and moist jungle air into the room. He pulls the gun from his shoulder, and I wonder if there is an illusion to make it feel heavy. His muscles are taut as he bobs under a branch, crouches low, and fires at an enemy I didn't even notice hidden in the canopy.

"I heard the military uses this game for training," he tells me. "Derek played a similar version in basic training."

I can believe it with the realistic environment. A green grid of lines overlays his perfect body. I'm fascinated by the way he moves. Weaving up and down, gun ready. He fires again and another enemy falls out of an overhanging tree and hits the ground with a thud before fading out of the projection.

He taps forward and the game pauses. "You want to try a round?"

"I don't want to ruin your score or anything. I'd probably get killed right away."

"Here, I have another memory chip you can use." He steps down from the platform and pushes a button at the back of the device.

A cool girl would play this game and do well, but I have no experience. I don't want to mess up while he's watching. But when he motions me forward onto the platform, I take his place. He peels the tiny electrode off his forehead and sticks it on me.

"How do I start?"

"Here, I'll tap the button for you. Get your gun ready." I grasp the transparent gun and my brain interprets the object as real. I have no idea how any of this technology works.

"Pay attention," he says and the game flickers to life.

Branches come at me as I walk. Twigs snap behind me and I run. The floor under my feet moves as I move. As the scenery changes, I believe the landscape. The green grid hits my eyes occasionally, but it's not blinding. I'm breathing hard, scanning the bushes for attackers. An animal screeches and I take a shot. Just then I feel a dart of pain in my shoulder blade, then the retort of another rifle.

"What the hell was that?" I let the gun swing down on the strap.

Jeremy jumps up. "Sorry, I have the pain setting on. I completely forgot. Are you okay?"

I rub my shoulder, not entirely sure. "The pain setting?"

"Yeah, I keep it on high. I find I play harder if I'm afraid of getting hurt."

"I don't doubt it. My shoulder really hurts." I rub the muscle, trying to understand. "But how can a game make real pain? I don't get it."

"It's the electrode. Your brain believes."

I stare into the jungle in front of me. The trees are both beautiful and scary now that I know the enemy can hurt me. He double taps the platform and the game starts to shut down.

"No, not yet. I want to try one more time."

"Let me change the settings first." He grabs the game controller off the arm of the couch.

"Just leave the pain on for now."

I tap the game on myself and pump the barrel of my gun to reload. A snake slithers over my foot, but I shake it away, not losing focus. I scan everywhere, crouching low as I move through the trees. A glint above me, then I whip my gun up and fire. The image of a man falls through me and disappears from around my feet. Two more pop out of nowhere. I shoot one in the head, but the other hits me in the stomach. I cradle my injury for a moment and then start to move on. I'm concentrating so hard, Jeremy stepping in front of me is a shock. I'm startled enough that I fire my transparent gun at him.

He double taps the platform. Game over. "I can't watch this," he says.

"Hey, I wasn't doing that bad!"

"It's not that. I just can't watch you getting hurt. It's different when I play. Seeing you get shot is just... wrong. If I witness you getting hit one more time, I'll have to dive in and knock you off the platform."

"That would probably hurt more than what the game delivers."

He laughs, but he still sounds bothered. "I've got medicine," he says, disappearing into the bathroom.

He returns with the tube and motions me to the couch. I sit facing away from him and he lowers the edge of my tank-top. My lower back is still covered. "This is where the first one hit you, right?"

"Yeah, I didn't dodge very well. It still really hurts. Amazing."

"I'm sorry." He sounds unhappy.

"Why? I like the game. Thanks for letting me play a round."

"Next time, no pain setting for you."

"I thought you said it makes you play harder."

I glance at him over my shoulder and he shrugs. "I've changed my mind." He touches my injury gently with the cream and in an instant the pain is replaced with a fuzzy, warm sensation. Good stuff.

"Wait a second. If the pain is all in my head, why does the medicine work?"

He turns the tube over and shows me. It's just a warming lotion. "But you feel better, right?"

"Give me that." I read the ingredients and there's nothing special. "Huh. I feel like I should've just been able to think myself out of that."

"Well, next time you can try imagining the pain setting is on." I shove his arm and he leans back, laughing. "Okay, okay. But I can't promise the game system will be set up next time you stop by."

The coffee table has a fake wood diagonal pattern. I trace the edge with my finger.

"What are you thinking about?" he asks.

"I wanted to talk to you about the date," I say, gathering my courage.

"I had a great time with you, Monet. You don't have to say anything."

Oh, God, this is hard. I want him to like me so bad, but— "I, uh, dropped down in the water bec—"

"Hey, I didn't mean to rush you."

"Jeremy, I have Fluxem." My heart stops, waiting for his reaction. Dreading the next words out of his mouth. This is the end. I'll never see Jeremy again.

"Fluxem?" He pauses for a long second. "Like, the open sores and stuff?"

I want to be able to say no. But. "Yeah, I have symptoms."

"Oh." He scratches the back of his neck and looks over at the video game platform.

I hold my breath and concentrate on the pounding in my ears. I don't know what to say. "I can go now. I just, uh..." *wanted your money.*

"So that's why you didn't let me kiss you?"

"Yeah."

"I mean, you didn't have to stop. I've been vaccinated."

"Those vaccines aren't a hundred percent. You're not supposed to risk infection." I look down at my lap.

He pauses for a few seconds. "But it is curable, and so far the cases of Fluxem coming back are rare."

"Yeah." I don't look up.

Another long pause. "So, where are these sores?" He looks me over, focusing on my exposed skin.

I'm shaking all over, embarrassed. "I've got one on my back."

"Can I see it?"

"I'd rather not show you."

"Okay."

The silence stretches. I'm the most awkward person in the world. Why did I come into a rockstar's room and confess that I'm diseased? *Great plan, Monet.* We're sitting facing each other on the couch, both looking down.

"Well, you don't smell," he says in a lighter tone of voice.

"Thanks." I blink my eyes rapidly to keep from crying.

Then he touches my hand lightly. "I'm not disgusted or anything."

But you said it, so you had to be thinking it.

"You should probably get the cure really soon. Did you read that new study they put out? The disease mutates when left inside the host for too long. After a while the cure is less effective."

My throat closes up and all of a sudden every bone in my body aches from the sores that I am now convinced are eating away at me. "What do you mean by less effective?"

"Sorry, didn't mean to scare you."

"Too late, I'm freaking out here."

He pats my shoulder. "Just go get the cure after the show is over. I'm sure another week won't matter." He shifts back away from me on the couch. "So, tell me what you're looking for in a guy?"

"Don't even bother, Jeremy. I know I just freaked you out."

"I was just surprised. Not many people I know get to the point of having symptoms."

In other words, he doesn't know anyone as poor as me. I swallow down my thoughts of impending death and try to re-find my strength.

He reclines back on the couch. "Let's just talk, okay?"

"Yeah, okay." I bite my lip and breathe deep through my nose. He didn't offer money. What am I supposed to do now?

He smiles. "The question was, what kind of guy do you like?"

I try to imagine my life without Fluxem. Hell, to answer this question I need to be a different person entirely. "Do you want honesty?"

"Always."

"Okay. I'll try here. But it's not a topic I spend a lot of time dwelling on. I've been focused on just surviving, making a niche for myself–"

"Are you stalling?" He pushes a wave of brown hair off his forehead.

"Yes."

"Uh, huh. Out with it. What are these mysterious qualities?"

"I want a guy who gets me and my art. Someone who's not afraid of the world and willing to stand up for people. There were these guys at my high school that were so jacked in all the time. Cell phone feed in one ear, music in another, and then they go to ask you out. Even when they're standing in front of me asking for a date, I'm half ignored. How can I be expected to want to make out, when they can't even pay attention?" My face feels hot and my teeth clench.

"Sounds like you knew a bunch of stupid guys."

"I was kind of beginning to think most people are more involved with their own lives than making relationships work. The contestants on the show are different, though. The girls are hyper-focused on you."

He flops his head back against the cushion. "Don't remind me. But seriously, Monet, there are real guys out there that will give you the attention you deserve."

I stare down at the carpet.

"Would you let me kiss you, now that I know about the Fluxem thing?"

"Uh, uh. You mean now?"

He drops his head. "Um. No. I mean anytime you wanted to."

"Oh." I think that was an offer, but how can I think about kissing right now? All I can think of is these symptoms that are probably getting worse while I sit here, and I need the money, and I can't bear to straight out ask him because I like him. Shit. I. Like. Him. "I've never been kissed."

He straightens up, eyebrows high with disbelief. "Never?"

"No." *I'm pathetic.*

"How the hell did you catch it in the first place?"

"Hey, it's not just a kissing disease."

"I didn't mean anything by the comment. Just most people report being infected through sexual contact."

"Well, that isn't me." I shake my head, defeated. A familiar wash of anger covers me. "A few years ago this girl and her friends jumped me outside of school. I don't even know what the hell I ever did to her. Looked at her wrong? Or maybe a guy she liked looked at me. Who knows? Her friends grabbed me and held me down while she beat the crap out of me. But it was her spitting on me in the end that gave me Fluxem. I don't even think she knew she was infecting me, because she never bothered to heckle me at school about it afterward."

"Holy shit. That's messed up."

"Yeah, that's when I took up mixed martial arts. I figure I need to be able to protect myself better if I'm going to survive this life."

I'm waiting for him to make the next logical jump. *If you caught Fluxem years ago, why do you still have it? Why didn't you get the trio of shots that cures the disease?* Then I would say, "I don't have the money or health insurance." Then he would offer to pay. If I ask, he'll think I'm using him. Is that what I'm trying to do? I told him the truth. Anything more is wrong. I know it. I dismiss the thoughts from my head. Or at least, try really hard. I'll find a way. I still have a chance to win the prize money. He knows I have Fluxem and he still wants to kiss me. That's a victory, isn't it? But will he feel the same when he sees the mark? When it spreads?

He ruffles his hand through his hair. "Do you want more 'medicine' for where the bullet hit your stomach?" His voice is light and joking, but he passes me the tube instead of rubbing any more cream on me. I guess he doesn't want to touch me now that he knows. I push the tube of cream away. I want to kick the wall in frustration. I cross the room quickly, trying to escape before I do anything stupid, like cry.

Jeremy rushes after me and places his hand on the door, holding it closed. "Will you wait a minute?"

I stand there clenching my jaw tight to keep any emotion from leaking out.

He stares down at me. I can see his face without lifting mine all the way up. "I meant to tell you during our date. What you said about my music in the interview...about the quiet. I wanted you to know that I feel exactly the same way. Like music blocks all the noise and stress of the world. But I could never phrase it like you did."

I raise my eyes slightly. "Your music is brilliant."

He looks off to the side and shifts back and forth on his feet. His hand caresses my jaw and he angles my face up. We're staring at each other and his eyes are a deep, warm brown. I'm in a daze. Then his fingers drop away. He takes a step back and shakes his head. "Good night, Monet."

"Good night, Jeremy." I close the door behind me, smiling.

TEN

B ACK IN THE room, I analyze every minute of the video game almost-date. The eye contact and the comment about the music must mean he likes me. But then there's the Fluxem confession. Did he not care because that's how a politically correct person is supposed to react? When he thinks more about the actual symptoms, will he be turned off? I rub the spot on my back, wincing at the pain and wetness on my fingertips. Disgusting.

I climb in bed. I'm not imagining this, right? There is a connection between Jeremy and me. I crush my pillow in my fists and flip back and forth. He wants to kiss me. Does he want to kiss all the contestants? Did the studio make him give Praline that bracelet? Maybe Brie was right and the designer paid for a spot on the show. I fall asleep with one thought repeating.

I *want to win.*

In my dream, Jeremy is poor like me. When he cups my chin in his hand, I feel calluses and smell motor oil. We lay together on a thin cot and the wall behind us shakes as a shuttle passes by. I place my hand over his heart and I feel his music radiating through my palm. I even hear the sounds of his voice and the ocean in my ears. "Do you like this song? I wrote it for you," he says, and then his lips touch mine. I smile through the kiss and press against him.

BAM! I'm on the floor. Shelley Anne looks down her nose at me. Morning light fills our room and she's playing Jeremy's "Ocean" compilation on the hotel room's sound system. Guess that explains the dream.

"You'd better get up if you plan on watching my date today."

Ugh. More dates with other girls. If it was just between Claire and me, my odds of winning would be excellent, but who knows what will happen on the other dates? I get up off the floor and climb back in bed. Shelley sorts through her suitcase with short, deliberate motions and power-walks back and forth between her bed and the bathroom. I sit in bed, just watching. I'm tired. I want to finish my dream.

Shelley Anne flops around in a big, white robe and appears ready from the neck up. She has on subtle brown eyeliner. Her lips are shiny pink and her blonde hair falls in a soft wave.

"You look nice," I tell her.

"Wait until you see my suit." Right, how could I forget? Shelley Anne and her victorious canoeing trip with Jeremy. But how good can she look? I mean, she's no Jasmine. I'm not worried. Until she opens the robe.

"What do you think? It's genius, isn't it?" She drops the robe to the floor and I'm speechless. Where did the weight go? How the hell—

"Promise not to tell how it works?" she asks. She rises up on tiptoes, eager.

"I promise."

"Good, 'cause I don't want Jeremy knowing I'm not perfect until he's already hooked on me." She rubs her hand over her bare belly. "This part of the suit forms a clear, skin-like barrier."

Huh? From my perspective she's wearing a two-piece bikini. Her stomach is thin and toned; her breasts are huge and levitating.

"It's actually all one piece."

I can't even believe how good she looks. "How much did that cost?"

She winks at me rather than reveal the price.

"But Jeremy has already seen you in clothes."

She shrugs. "Duh. I wore another figure enhancer for the interview. Bet you didn't even notice."

"No, I didn't. That's neat technology." I wish I had one. "When are they coming to pick you up?"

"Half an hour."

"I bet you'll have a great time." I pace to the window. "The weather is nice, too."

She goes back to her suitcase and slides a sheer black swim cover-up around her hips. The supposed "cover-up" doesn't hide a thing. She might as well be wearing lingerie on her date. The TV audience will probably love her. Is Jeremy the kind of guy to be impressed by big breasts and super suits? I think back to my simple purple bikini. I'd feel more confident about my chances if I had a super suit that would cover any evidence of Fluxem.

From my bed, I can see the door to the room, and if I sit at the very end, I think I'll be able to see Jeremy. Shelley Anne and I watch the clock in the corner of the room. I almost want to tell her about last night out of spite, but I keep my mouth shut.

Finally, the knock comes. Jeremy stands in our doorway wearing a light blue T-shirt for the date. The corner of a camera protrudes from behind him, though this time the focus is on Shelley Anne, not me. When I catch his expression, he's gazing down. Down into her cleavage. He blinks quickly, probably stunned by the gravity-defying effect. He smiles at her, not me.

I should've left the room. And I have this dumb feeling like I'm watching my boyfriend cheat on me... but that isn't the case. But, crap. This is shitty.

He turns his head slightly and our eyes meet. His eyebrows rise in surprise. I guess he didn't know which room was mine. Shelley Anne brushes past him on her way out, and the moment is broken. She shuts the door behind her, harder than necessary. I'm left staring at the white rectangle, fists clenched. I'm trembling with anger and I have no justification for the feeling. Damn Shelley Anne and her miracle bikini.

I give them five minutes to get down the hall before I stalk downstairs to the viewing room. All of us assemble in our usual spots, ready for whatever blows this date will deliver. From the grim expressions, I assume they've already gotten a good look at the swimsuit. Jaime's purple contacts look extra creepy when she's upset. I rub my temples, trying to massage away the stress headache, or maybe it's Jasmine's perfume.

I focus my anger on Jasmine. "Do you have to wear so much damn perfume?"

Jasmine turns on me like a snake. "I've been told Jeremy loves this perfume."

I crack my knuckles. I've already had my chance. There's not much more I can do to win over the viewers now, and the helplessness sucks.

One of her lookalikes wrinkles her nose at me. "Not in the best of moods this morning, are we?"

I want to flip the table onto her. I've got to get a grip. There are more dates to come.

"Want to make a bet?" Brie, a.k.a. clone number two, asks. "Twenty says she jumps him within an hour."

Jasmine leans in. "Jumps him as in, has sex?"

I cringe. Jeremy wouldn't do that. I'm almost sure of it. Brie drums her fingers on the table. "No, no. Makes him kiss her."

Jasmine shakes her head. "I'm not making that bet, even if it is only twenty."

Brie shrugs and goes back to watching the screen. I'd take the bet, but don't have the money.

Shelley Anne sits in the limo at Jeremy's side. They both drink from reusable water bottles with Key West logos.

Praline starts chewing her thumbnail. "Was my date this boring to watch?"

It's Claire that speaks up. "No, there were all those jewels at the exhibit, and the cameraman did a fair amount of panning around." I think she might have meant the bit about the camera as a slam, but since I didn't watch the whole date, I have no idea if she's lying or not.

"How was your date, Praline? I didn't feel all that well and missed the majority of the feed. I did like your dress."

She sits straighter at my compliment. I hope my explanation will make the other girls think I didn't leave yesterday because I was jealous.

"Thank you. I think Jeremy loved it." Looking around the table, I know these girls want to win just as badly as I do.

Jeremy and Shelley Anne are in the canoe now. He's in the back, doing all the work, and she's in the front. He wipes sweat off his brow with his shoulder as his muscles strain to paddle. Then he pauses and removes his shirt.

"Ooh's" go around the table.

His skin glistens in the sun. They must have a camera mounted on the bow of the boat because I'm pretty sure a third person wouldn't fit. Shelley reclines slightly, waving a decorative Japanese fan in front of her face. I hope she doesn't think she's being coy, because with that outfit, it isn't working. Luckily for me the camera is just over her shoulder, so I don't have to stare at all of her assets the whole time. The focus is all on Jeremy as his muscles flex. God, he looks so yummy.

One of the other cameras films from another boat out in the water. Trees surround the lake, and I'm struck by how much money Key West must be spending to preserve their natural resources. Jeremy hands Shelley Anne a bottle of water. She accepts, tipping her head back suggestively and letting the liquid pour down her throat. I'm developing an advanced hatred for my roommate.

She leans forward in the boat. Her lips move, but I'll have to wait 'till the show airs to hear what idiot excuse she comes up with for getting closer to Jeremy. He nods and keeps paddling. From the side camera angle, she's only a foot from his knees. She reaches her hand out to point at something off to the side. The boat rocks. She tumbles head first into Jeremy's legs.

Jasmine pounds her fist on the table. I dig my nails into my hand.

Shelley's throwing herself at him. Literally. Jeremy pulls the paddle into the boat and reaches down to help her back up. He clasps her arm and leans in to steady her, or is that her stretching up to get closer to him?

The camera following alongside zooms in for a better shot of the disaster. Then Jeremy's lips are on hers. They're kissing. Bile surges up my throat. He's having fun. No big deal.

It'll be over in a second. He's going to pull away. Any second now.

They keep kissing. The camera bobs up and down. The cameraman must be standing up to provide this in-depth angle. Jeremy's hand comes up. Thank God, he's going to push her away, but he brushes her breast. Well, he's having a lot of fun. My odds of winning are plummeting.

I'm ready to snap. I want to punch everyone and scream at the top of my lungs. I want to run so fast and far away that I disappear. Erin throws her sandal at the wall. They start fighting about whether the breast brush was an accident or not. I feel sick because he's still frigging kissing her.

The kiss finally breaks. Praline coughs, hacks, and grabs her stomach. I reach over to help her as she staggers out of her chair. Her eyelids flutter shut and she tips headfirst into the wall. I thought she was about to vomit, but this reaction doesn't make sense. Is she unconscious? Did she just ram the wall? I turn her over onto her side in case she pukes.

"Oh, my." Erin fans her face with one hand and flips her hair back and forth with the other. "My, my, my."

Praline murmurs and clutches her heart. Wow. My own anger is diffused by the spectacle of her on the floor. "Should we call Eleanor?" I ask.

Of course it's Jasmine who answers, "Let's wait until the date is over." *Heartless bitch.*

Praline's eyelashes flutter. "Oh, Jeremy. Why, Jeremy, why?" She's lost it.

I offer her my hand. "Come on, I'll help you back to your room." The black bracelet Jeremy gave her slides down and she splays her fingers to keep it on. Her palm is sweaty where our skin meets. It's like Jeremy overloaded her system. I know the feeling. At least she got a bracelet.

I glance back at the screen before I walk out of the room. Jeremy is still paddling along and Shelley Anne is splashing water on her chest. Praline looks back and starts panting. "Don't watch," I tell her and let the door close behind us.

Eleanor meets us in the hall. "You okay, honey?" Praline's head wobbles. She is so not okay. "Let's drop her off at the salon," Eleanor suggests. "That will calm anyone down." Which is a good idea, because she's leaning on me hard, and I don't think I can carry her all the way back to her room.

The masseuse at the front of the salon scans Praline's chip and whisks her off. Eleanor and I walk away.

I lean in quietly to talk to Eleanor. "I don't know how to say this, but is Praline mentally stable enough for this competition?"

Eleanor laughs with a tiny grunt at the end. "You mean you wouldn't normally ram your head into the wall?"

"Does that mean you watch what goes on in the viewing room?"

Eleanor shrugs. But obviously she was watching, or she wouldn't know about Praline.

"I hope they won't show that."

She shrugs again. Of course they will. Everyone will laugh. I feel terrible because Praline really is suffering, and now the world will think she's a joke.

"Don't worry. I'm sure they'll edit the footage into a whole bloopers episode. The cameras will pick up embarrassing moments from all the contestants."

Oh, great. I wonder what idiotic actions they caught me doing. I walk toward the restaurant. I need to be reminded about one of the good things about this contest because right now, after seeing my roommate kiss Jeremy, I feel like getting the hell out of here.

"Have a good lunch," Eleanor tells me. She folds her lips in as she smiles. I wonder if she's secretly on my side and that's why I'm the only contestant who knows the location of Jeremy's room.

I eat a brownie sundae and a piece of apple pie. The flavors are amazing and comforting. But I can't forget the image of Jeremy's hand reaching out to Shelley and her mouth locked onto his face like a sucker-fish.

I trudge back to my room, making sure to scan my hand in at the elevator. As I walk, my hip starts to ache. *Oh, God. What now?* The key card dings and the door opens. As soon as I'm inside the room I slip my pants down to the tops of my thighs. I don't see any new marks. No redness, but when I press my fingers into the skin I get a throbbing pain. I pull my pants back up. I'm either getting worse, or I'm paranoid, and I can't do anything about either one, so I sit on my bed and try to formulate a strategy.

I need a backup plan for getting the money. It will probably have to be illegal. Nothing comes to mind, or at least, nothing I want to contemplate yet. Do I go see Jeremy again? What if he likes Shelley? What an awkward position to put him in. At this moment, he's shared more physical contact with my roommate than he has with me. And Shelley Anne, what do I say when she returns from the date? How can I stand to be in the same room with her after what I saw?

I straighten my back against the headboard of the bed.

I will not run off and question Jeremy.

I will not let Shelley Anne see me upset.

I will not give up.

ELEVEN

I'M TAKING A nap when Shelley Anne comes back from her date. Truly. I'm sound asleep, not just holding my eyes closed listening to her every move. She whistles the tune to a shampoo commercial; I wonder if she realizes.

"Wakey up, roomie. Don't you want to hear about my date?"

Hmmm. Will she go away if I pretend to be dead?

"Helloooo, anyone home over there?"

She'll never leave me alone. "Oh, hi, Shell." *Let's see how she likes her new nickname.* My address makes her pause. I rub my eyes, feigning sleepiness. She puckers her lips at me, sour.

"I actually prefer to use both my full first name and middle name."

"Oh."

"So, did you see when Jeremy leaned in and kissed me?"

Now that's an exaggeration. "From the angle of the camera I couldn't see anything. It looked like you bumped your head on his knee."

"What?" Her eyes are bulging mad. "They didn't get a good shot of us?" She's really not very cute when she's pissed off.

"Maybe they did and I blinked and missed it. But, he kissed you? That must have been nice."

"The camera had to have filmed our kiss. It went on and on and on." She's pacing the room now.

"Well, like I said. I probably just had my eyes closed." I'm not even sure what my point in lying is. I guess I just can't stand to be in the room with her smug attitude. At least now she's not bragging.

"I'm going to go find the cameraman and ask to see the footage," she declares after her tenth circuit around the room.

"Good luck with that. Don't forget to scan in at the elevator if you're leaving the floor."

She huffs at me and slams the door on her way out. I imagine the cameramen are getting ready to shoot Jeremy's date this evening, so they'll be too busy to console her.

I climb out of bed. Now that I've cleared the room, I don't know what to do. I can't go to the restaurant because the other girls might be there, and it's too early to go to the viewing room. Giving in to the little-girl-crying feeling, I sit at the small desk in the corner of the room and click on the phone. The holographic square lights up while I listen to the ringing.

Come on, be home. Mom's shifts at the restaurant change all the time. For once I hope she's on nights. The words *connecting* flash across the screen and then a tiny 3-D image of Mom clarifies. "Honey. I'm so glad you called. I've been missing you so much."

"I miss you, too, Mom." I don't know what to say, I just want her to hug me.

"Is something wrong, Monet?" The beauty of Mom: she figures me out every time. Even with miles between us she knows when something is off. God, I needed to hear her voice. "What is it? Is it those television people, because if they're—"

"No, Mom. It's stupid. I just thought I could win this thing and get all that money. Then I saw Jeremy on a date with one of the other girls."

"Ah, I see. You entered this competition for the money."

Well, shit. "I know that sounds terrible, but we need the money."

"Yeah." Her head shifts down, blocking my view of her face. "I wish you'd just concentrate on being a teenage girl and having fun."

Sure. I'll just have a blast and not notice the open sore on my back. "Jeremy's different than I thought he would be."

Her penetrating look translates even over the video link. "It's okay to like Jeremy and still want the money."

I sigh. "Sounds pretty selfish to me."

"Probably, but I love you anyway." My head snaps up.

"You're not supposed to agree with me."

She shrugs. "I'll have the money for the cure soon. I swear to you. I don't want you to feel like you have to be manipulative to win a prize."

"I don't want you working that hard for me. And I'm just being myself. I'm not that great at pretending."

"Have you had any Fluxem symptoms yet? Do we need to start worrying?"

"No, nothing."

"Good." She exhales heavily. "I worry."

"Don't. I'm having fun. They have great food here and my date was at the beach. It was so beautiful."

"I wish I was there with you." I smile. She didn't notice the lie. If she knew about the mark, she'd probably do something drastic to come up with the money.

"What would you do in my spot?"

"I'd go find that boy and kiss him. Tip the odds in my favor."

"You're right. He's been vaccinated. What am I hesitating over?" It's the one thing I can control right now. "I gotta go."

She laughs. "Hold on a second." Mom sounds serious. "I wanted to ask you about the consent forms you signed."

Uh-oh.

"Were there more papers than what you brought home that one night?" Crap, there were so many papers I don't know what the hell I signed.

"There might have been a few others." Like, twenty.

"Well, I know you're old enough to make your own decisions, but you need to be careful. A man was here earlier to interview me for your segment of the show, and the questions he was asking were not what I had expected at all."

"What do you mean?"

"Did you give them permission to dig into your government files?"

Do I even have government files? Who knows what the hell I signed? "What?" I gnaw on the end of my thumb. "What questions did this guy ask?"

She pauses for a while before answering, and I wonder what she's keeping from me. "Mostly stuff about your birth and our lifestyle now."

I twist my hair into a knot on my head. I don't understand. "Why would they want to know any of that stuff?"

"I don't know. I'm afraid this dating show might not be as straightforward as you think. Probably nothing to worry about. I just want you to know, no matter what they say on the show, I love you more than anything." Her eyes are very serious for a moment, then her expression shifts to her practiced Mom smile, which means she's dropping the subject.

God, every time she tells me not to worry, I worry twice as much. And I thought my only problem was Shelley Anne...

"The interviewer didn't mention what the questions were for?"

"No. Listen, I didn't bring this up to worry you. I just wanted to make sure you didn't sign anything that would take away your rights to confidentiality." I *probably did.* "I'm sure it's nothing, honey. So, are you going to go track down that rockstar and give him a kiss?"

"Maybe I'll go to the restaurant and drink a fruit smoothie first."

"Now I'm jealous. Drink one for me."

"I will. Love you, Mom."

"I love you, too, honey. Good luck."

I click disconnect. I still don't feel good about Shelley's date, but I don't feel quite as miserable as I did.

TWELVE

A T THE RESTAURANT I sit at the bar instead of our usual table. I wave the attendant over and she shows me how to enter my table number into the menu screen so that the studio will pay for my smoothie. I'm so thankful I don't have to sit at table L27. All of the other girls have become my enemies. I don't know when the transition started, but I can't think of them as potential friends anymore. Which really shouldn't be any surprise to me. Not if I want Jeremy. But I can't just go along with this staged dating plan the producers have. No one can form a real connection with an audience and cameraman spying on them. I remember Praline's half-conscious words on the floor. *Why? Oh, Jeremy, why?* Clearly I'm not the only one feeling the effects of this competition.

I watch the attendant deliver drinks and shuffle leftovers into the cleaning rack below the bar. This could be my future. Though her job is probably better than what I'll find in Boston. The girl isn't much older than me and appears happy enough. And if she's not happy, she's at least not miserable.

I punch in a strawberry-blackberry smoothie and pull my scratch pad out of my pocket. I got the pad for Christmas last year and it's almost full. The paper-thin sheets of hardened resin are bound together in a five-inch rectangle. Each piece is coated in black paint that

I scratch away in patterns to reveal the golden yellow below. The girl delivers my drink and I try to forget my possible future by losing myself in pattern and design.

I order another smoothie and flip to another new page. On this one, I scratch in an outline of Jeremy's face and peel away the black to show the curve of his smile. I should take Mom's advice and kiss him, but I'm still so mad.

"Is that me?"

His voice startles me and I almost knock over my drink. "Jeremy," I whisper, sucking in the word. "What are you doing here?"

"Getting a drink, same as you." He punches his selection in and the bottles in front of us rotate around. The machine beeps and the attendant hands him the concoction.

He sniffs the dark and smoky drink.

"What is that?" I ask.

"Double shot of caffeine, one shot green plant liquor, one shot brew, and vitamin medley."

Ew. "Does that taste good?"

"Nope." He shakes his head, laughing, and then downs half the glass. "But it sure as hell wakes you up. I need a boost after that date from hell."

"Didn't you have fun this morning?"

"They had me paddling around a lake for hours. It was exhausting. I think they're trying to make me suffer."

"Yeah, there's been a lot of suffering all around today." I think back to Praline sprawled on the floor, but that image is quickly replaced with the hotness of Jeremy navigating the lake. "You do look damn good paddling without your shirt on." *Ugh, did I just blurt that out?* I take another sip of my drink to hide my discomfort.

He blocks his half-smile with his hand and then raises his eyebrow. "Wait...how do you know I took my shirt off?"

"You know...the viewing room."

"No, I don't know." He pauses and I feel his anger growing. "What is the viewing room?"

Was this a secret? His jaw is set in a firm line.

"Um, they have a room set up where all the girls sit around and watch you when you're on your dates."

He's very still for a moment, hands gripping the bar in fury. "I did not sign up for *that*." The muscles in his neck stand out as he clenches his jaw. I really don't want him to ever be mad at me. This side of him is so intense. I just want to fix the situation. He stands up and his bar stool clatters back. "Everyone has been watching me the entire time?"

"Yeah, I'm sorry." *What can I say to make this better?*

"Why the hell are they doing that?"

"I suspect they're gathering extra footage of us girls being jealous and fighting." He clenches his fists. I can't imagine people trying to manipulate me and make money off of me twenty-four hours a day. "I'm sorry, I thought you knew. I probably shouldn't have said anything."

He slides his stool back in and sits. "I can't believe these asshole producers." His hand around his drink tightens. "So, you saw when Shelley sank her talons into me in the canoe?"

"I did."

"I swear they're making me entertain the craziest girls in the tightest surroundings."

"Does that mean you didn't want to kiss her?" *Please say you didn't.*

"Shelley Anne?" He grumbles deep in his chest and finishes the rest of his drink in one big swallow. "No." The word is firm and final.

I smile down at the bar. "That's good. From my perspective, I thought you were enjoying yourself."

"I'm trying to have fun on these dates, and I don't mind a good kiss, but there has to be some lead up and mutual interest. That one came out of nowhere."

"Maybe she thought her hypnotic swimsuit had already won you over."

"I guess. There are a lot of girls like that who come on to me. Sounds stupid to say, but the lack of skill gets irritating."

"Um, what do you mean by 'skill'?"

He scratches his head and then runs a finger around the rim of his glass, making a haunting sound. "I shouldn't be talking about this with you, huh?"

"I don't mind."

He smiles and then goes quiet for a moment. I wait patiently, absorbing all the physical details of his body. He props his leg on the bottom of the bar stool and bounces one knee. The fabric of his jeans stretches tight over his thighs. And he just noticed me staring. Argh!

"'Skill' is probably the wrong word, but I'm not an animal. I wouldn't mind a bit of intelligent conversation and shared interests. I don't give out kisses like they're autographs."

I sip my drink, caught up in thoughts of kissing Jeremy. "From the outside, it looks like you have such a glamorous, perfect life."

"Ha. If people constantly asking you for money and favors while you have to hide out alone in hotel rooms to keep from getting mauled is considered perfect, sure. I'm so isolated these days. I've got Derek and that's about it."

Crap. That's me. I'm one of those people waiting to ask for money and favors. I want to die of guilt. Except that I'm already diseased, and not wanting to die is what has me in this predicament. But Jeremy is an awesome guy and people shouldn't be taking advantage of him. I'm a hypocrite and now Jeremy's looking at me because I'm probably making a bad face. I swallow. "Derek seems like a good guy."

"He is, but not the most sensitive. It would be nice to have someone to bounce ideas off of. I'm trying to write these deep, emotional songs, and my only friend likes combat and big boobs." He drops his head, looking down at the bar.

"I could help you...or, I mean, I know we just met and won't have much time together, but maybe we could talk online, or—" I take a deep breath trying to pull my thoughts together. I want to be there for him. If he needs someone. "I guess a show like this isn't a great way to meet people, but if you ever need a friend to bounce ideas off of, I'd love that." He doesn't say anything for a minute. Just looks up, appraising me. Is he looking for a friend, or more? Did I phrase that wrong? "I think it's amazing you can be so creative while still touring and traveling around."

He shrugs. "You haven't heard the songs I'm working on now. Maybe my creativity is all used up."

I laugh. "That's never going to happen."

"How can you be so sure? Most musicians get one hit song at best. I've already had more success than most. This might be the end of my career."

"No way. Unless you want it to be. From my perspective, the whole world adores you."

"Bah." He shakes his head and takes another drink. I watch his long eyelashes sweep down across his cheek as he blinks. I rub my sweaty palms on my jeans, trying to work up the nerve to touch his hand.

He perks up and turns to me. "Hey, you live in Boston, right?"

"Yeah?"

"How good of a school is BU? I've heard positive things about their pre-med program."

I let out my breath. The deep conversation is over, and I can't help but feel like I missed an opportunity or should have said more. BU is a college I'll never afford. "I think it's a good school. I haven't attended any classes, but I bet there are a lot of intern opportunities at the Global Skin Cancer Initiative."

"I'll have to look into it." He taps my scratch pad. "Can I see what you're working on?" He leans over. "You didn't answer my first question. Is this a picture of me?"

I tangle my fingers in my hair. "Yeah, but I just started, so it doesn't look very good yet."

"I like it. Can I look through the rest?"

I shrug. *Please, oh please, let him like my designs.*

He starts at the beginning of the pad and slowly flips through, stopping on each page. My heart pounds in my throat and I gulp my drink. He's not saying anything. I punch on my menu screen and try to appear disinterested in his opinion.

He flips back and forth. "This one is my favorite. This whirlpool shape with the sharp lines cutting in and around it reminds me of my song, 'Ocean 65.'"

I choke. "I drew that while listening to your song on repeat."

"The image would make a great T-shirt design for my next concert tour."

"Really?" My stomach is all squirmy and happy. T-shirt design must pay something.

"Absolutely. Make me a copy and I'll make sure the design gets to the right people."

I release the binding of the book and pull out the page. "You can just take the original."

"You sure?" He handles the edges gently and keeps the square safe in his hand rather than placing it on the bar. Then he turns to me, his eyes focusing directly into mine. "You weren't mad about my other date, were you?"

Who, me? Never. "It's a strange situation, knowing you're going on a lot of other dates. All the dates sound like places I'd like to visit, so I'm a little jealous, but really I'm just happy that I've gotten to talk to you."

He rubs his hand over his face. "I feel like I should apologize."

"I know what I signed up for, and if you want to kiss Shelley, or whoever, that's your business."

"Maybe I want to be kissing another girl who keeps turning me down." He leans in slightly, like he's daring me. I keep my eyes on his. *Go ahead, do it.* The smile lines fade from his face and he inches forward. I close my eyes partway–

"Monet? Oh, and Jeremy, too. What luck. And I thought I'd have to sit at the bar all by myself."

Jasmine. I've never wanted to kill anyone as much as I do now. "Hi, Jasmine." She seats herself next to Jeremy. He shifts around, uncomfortable. I wish I had access to a punching bag. A good workout or sparring session would be perfect right about now.

"Jasmine?" Jeremy asks.

She gives him her mega-watt shark smile, which I can see from around her back as he turns to her. Did a shiver just go up his spine?

"The one and only." Or one of three, because of the clone phenomenon in the contestant pool.

"We haven't gotten a chance to spend time together yet," he says, smiling.

"They're saving the best for last." She giggles. *So fake.*

"Well, nice to meet you." He shakes her hand and eases up off his seat, pushing his empty glass toward the attendant.

Jasmine thrusts her jaw out before correcting her expression into a flirtatious grin. "You're going to stay and have a drink with us, aren't you?"

"I wish I could, but I think I'll have to leave you girls to it. They have me recording another monologue for the show before my date this evening."

"Oh, how interesting." Jasmine reaches down to adjust the strap of her sandal and the neckline of her sheath dress falls open.

"Have a good time tonight," I say.

He narrows his eyes at me and I can almost hear him telling me that I'd better not go to the viewing room.

"Thank you for this." He discreetly holds up my drawing, so that Jasmine can't get a good look at the image. "Bye, girls."

We watch him walk away from the bar, his stride long and casual.

Then Jasmine turns on me. "What the hell was that? Are you sneaking around trying to spend extra time with Jeremy?" She's inches from my face. Maybe I'm going to punch someone today, after all.

"No, I just happened to run into him."

She clinks her nails against her glass filled with bright red liquid. "I think you're lying."

What is her deal? "What difference does it make?"

"If you think I'm going to let you get away with cheating, you're wrong."

"I'm not cheating. There's no rule about spending extra time with him. Shit, Jasmine. We're all in the same hotel. Don't you think we might run into each other here and there?"

She flips her hair over her shoulder. "There may not be a rule yet, but there will be, and I'll be watching you."

"Whatever." I slide my stool back and walk out of the restaurant.

THIRTEEN

I PASS SHELLEY in the hallway on the way back to the room. She scowls at me rather than saying hi. I'm not going to the viewing room. Jeremy doesn't think I should be watching, so for once, I'm not going to give in to curiosity. Instead I pace the room, wondering what's happening and imagining the worst. His date is probably perfect. He's in love with Jasmine clone number two. They're eating a fabulous steak dinner overlooking the water and holding hands.

I pound my head on the window, then walk over to the desk and sit down. I can do this. I can survive one night without watching Jeremy's every move. I pull out my scratch pad, but only manage a pattern of jagged gouge lines. Maybe it's better to watch. Then I'll know how bad the date was.

By the time Shelley comes back from the viewing room, I have my mattress flipped up against the wall and I'm practicing kill kicks. I've got a good rhythm. Duck in, kick Jasmine's imaginary head, weave back. Punch her in the gut, dodge her lunge. Spin kick imaginary Shelley when she sneaks up behind me. I breathe in and out, timing my punches.

"What on earth are you doing?" Shelley asks when she sees the state of my bed.

"Working out."

"By attacking your bed?"

"I've eaten a lot of desserts the last few days."

"Oh." She rubs her belly, deeply considering this. I bet she doesn't have a super suit to wear under all of her clothing. "You missed some stuff in the viewing room." *I do not want to hear about the date.*

"Eleanor made an announcement. The dates are going to start broadcasting tomorrow night."

"Right. I can't believe they can get all the footage together in time."

"Jeremy's concert with the final three has been set for the twenty-fifth for months, and Eleanor said the first elimination will be in front of a live studio audience, so the dates are only on a two-day delay to make the timing work." She rubs her belly again self-consciously. I do a final kick combination, then flip my mattress back onto the bed frame.

I clench my jaw and pace to the window. I tap the opening rhythm to "Ocean 65" onto the glass. The idea of standing in front of strangers while they vote on whether or not Jeremy and I make a good couple disturbs me. I don't want to compete, but if I want Jeremy, I have no choice.

I don't watch his morning date, but we're required to watch the first episode with Claire before the evening footage starts. They have us situated in a fake living room. Erin and Jaime have paired up. Funny how those two just don't register as competition to me. They don't have strong memorable personalities like Jasmine and Claire. I glance around the living room and lump Crystal in with the other no-worries girls. Jeremy's a musician and that girl can't carry a tune. Not that I can. Though who knows if my opinion will reflect the audience's? The cameraman works his way around the big, fat couches, filming different angles. A huge viewing wall comes to life in front of us.

"Who will win a date with a rockstar?" the narrator asks as the camera pans over all the girls standing in line. Jeremy's new song plays in the background as the girls yell to family and friends. I see myself, but the camera moves on, and I'm not smiling, or waving, or doing anything else memorable. After a commercial break they begin showing excerpts from the interviews of girls who were not chosen. They select a good mix of heart-breakingly hopeful and painfully embarrassing.

The screen flashes back to the host, Rod Bing. He's wearing a shiny gray suit with a magenta scarf. "Now, let's get a glimpse of the first girl selected." He widens one eye in his signature expression. Every season, he ends up hosting a new reality TV show. I take a deep breath, waiting to see myself. Instead, it's Claire who pops up on the screen.

But she wasn't the first or even second. Okay, so they're just correlating with the order of the dates. No big deal. Still, I was picked first and they've taken that away from me. I feel like I just got stepped on.

Claire's interview continues, and I recognize the interviewer as the same one who spoke to me. She's intelligent. Her laughs are more sexy than giggly and her answers are coy. Red hair falls in choppy layers over her dance outfit. The skirt has a series of ruffles at the bottom.

"What do you enjoy doing in your free time?"

"I love dancing. Latin, formal, pulse, all of it."

The interviewer smiles. "Mind giving us a preview?"

She stands with elegant balance and points her toes into her calf like she might pirouette. Instead, she whips out of the ballet pose into an aggressive circle that throws her skirt up high. Her hand smacks onto the ground and then she leans backward into a slow backbend. The edge of her black panties flash on the screen, then her fingertips touch the floor behind her. With a delicate hop, she flips backward. *Holy shit.*

"Wow." The interviewer, who was unimpressed with me because I had to leave to vomit, smiles wide, and it's obvious how Claire got a spot on the show. I can't really blame Jeremy for being impressed by that. My interview sucked compared to those dance moves.

I sit back on the couch. Claire fidgets with the hem of her shirt. Rod Bing comes back on the screen. He purses his lips and clucks his tongue. "After the commercial break, reality television gets real."

What does that mean? An ad for Shelley's super bikini comes on and I wonder how nervous she is about being found out. I grip on to that idea to keep from dwelling on Claire's backflip. A few more ads and the show comes back on, with Rod Bing's voice booming over images of girls in concerts, girls in line, girls in interviews.

"Now, we wouldn't be responsible producers if we left Jeremy Bane in the clutches of just any girl. So now, the hidden background of contestant one. What does she have to hide? What secrets does she not want us to know? You heard correctly, we've done an in-depth background check. When you decide what girl is right for Jeremy, you WILL know EVERYTHING."

Nervous fidgeting spreads through the group. I start to say something, but close my mouth, uncertain. On the other couch, Praline has the same mouth-gaping expression. Claire's trying to signal Eleanor to come over.

My episode will be airing tomorrow, but I can't think of anything embarrassing in my life. Fluxem was diagnosed through an anonymous test, so they won't be able to tell the world about my disease. I don't have money and we live in a crappy apartment, but I knew they were going to interview Mom, so I figured my poverty would be obvious. I can't think of anything else.

I glance over at Claire. She's biting her nails, staring at the viewing wall. From her expression, I bet the studio dug up real gossip on her. I feel guilty for my curiosity, but I want to know what she has to hide.

A still photo of Claire fills the screen. She's standing in front of a mirrored wall in a dance studio. The colors are muted and dark, but I can make out a tall man with gray hair leaning into her. His hand is...in a rather indecent location and from the blurring they've done to the image, I assume she isn't wearing panties and one of her breasts is exposed. *Oh, la la.* Is Jeremy in a room being filmed as he watches this, or are they keeping him oblivious?

Rod Bing shields his eyes in mock embarrassment. "Our trackers have revealed this man as Claire's forty-year-old dance instructor. Who also happens to be...married." Cue standard one eye widening. The screen changes to the interview with Claire's mother. "Did you know your daughter was involved with her instructor?"

Oh, jeez, poor Claire. I watch her on the other couch. Her jaw is clenched, her fists are clenched. Her whole body tightens, ready to attack the wall, or maybe the producers.

Claire's mom stutters and the interviewer hands her a copy of the photo. "Oh...oh...um..." From the wrinkles and squinting of her face I know she's trying to find an explanation that will make the photo meaningless. But she can't exactly say the guy is just helping her lean into the stretch, because there's the small matter of missing panties. "Whatever mistakes Claire made with her instructor are long over with. She's moved on with her life and dating Jeremy is just the beginning."

Nice cover. She's a good mom. I wonder what my mom would've said if presented with an indecent photo. She'd probably calmly worry, then give me a safe sex lecture. Thankfully, I know I've never been in a compromising situation with a boy, so they won't be able to dig up anything like that in my past.

Claire hasn't said a word and the cameras continue to film her, waiting for her to have a dramatic reaction they can use on the show later. After the big reveal, the actual date footage comes on. There are no more surprises. Claire is playful, Jeremy's having a good time. Even with their mics, it's hard to hear what they're saying in the club, so there are a lot of quick cuts highlighting Claire's dance moves, which have a new color now that we all know what went on while she was learning those *moves*.

Outside of the club Claire hooks her arm inside Jeremy's. "Thank you for taking me out." She leans her body tight against him.

"No problem, I had a good time."

I'm more uncomfortable knowing the kiss is coming now than I was the first time I saw it.

Claire trips herself against him on purpose. I'm sure of it. She whispers in his ear. I can barely understand the words, but I think I get the gist. She's suggesting he come back to her hotel room. Everyone watching now considers Claire a slut. What a shitty reputation to end up with, all for a couple of hours with Jeremy. As the camera captures the way he strides away to the limo, maybe any amount of time with him is worth national embarrassment.

Jeremy opens the limo door with Claire still clinging to his arm. She sits on the edge of the seat with her legs splayed out.

"I'm taking a different car back to the hotel," he says.

"Why not come with me?" Claire asks. The cameraman must be hanging over Jeremy's shoulder, because it looks like Claire is staring directly at the home audience. Is Jeremy bothered by the offer or by being watched?

He tips his head to the side and they share some serious eye contact. What's he thinking? Does he want to go back to her room? I guess I can't blame him, she's an amazing dancer.

Then he kisses her cheek, but lingers a few seconds longer. She turns her head and they kiss. It's delicate, nothing obscene, no visible tongue. And I'm jealous as hell. Shit.

"What a date!" Rod Bing sits behind a console like a weatherman with a big screen of the date behind him. He straightens his scarf and motions to the live studio audience. The camera follows the direction of his hand and pans over the room. I take in the rows of people chanting Jeremy's name with growing unease. Tomorrow night these people will be judging me. I feel sick.

"How do you think she did?"

Cheers and boos answer his question. One girl throws herself into the aisle. "It should have been me!" she screams before security escorts her away.

Rod Bing steps closer to the camera and raises his voice to be heard over the noise. "Voting won't begin until all the dates have been completed, so remember Claire." They flash the indecent photo again. Assholes. Then a still image of her twirling on the dance floor with Jeremy. "She'll be number one if you decide she should continue on to the final three. The decision belongs to you..." He points his finger at the crowd and more cheering erupts. A few credits scroll by so fast I can't even read any names. Then the screen goes black.

I should say something to Claire. I know she's competition, but damn, that was rough. She's sitting still as a statue on the other couch. I approach slowly.

"I, uh, thought the backflip you did in the interview was really awesome. I know everyone must have loved it."

She moves her head a fraction of an inch and I think she's about to freak out on me, but she doesn't. I wait for a snarky comment, but her lip trembles. "I guess I blew my chances before I even got on the show." Her eyes are glossy, but she isn't crying.

"Hey, you don't know that. If they've done background checks on all of us, who knows what the final selection will come down to?"

She nods a little and discreetly brushes away a sniffle. "Your date is tomorrow, huh? Are you nervous?"

"Yeah. Did you see that bright purple bikini I wore? And now the whole world, well, at least anyone bothering to watch, will see me in next to nothing."

Her eyes are less watery when she answers. "For your sake, I hope you don't have anything to hide."

I cringe. I hope to God they didn't find out I have Fluxem. "I'm sure they'll find a few gossip-worthy events," I tell her. She nods in sympathy.

FOURTEEN

JEREMY IS GOING on another date today. I don't want to know, but I do. I shuffle my fantasy into the back of my mind. My back itches. I rush to the bathroom and check the mark. I scoot my butt up onto the sink and inch close to the mirror. Another red patch has appeared next to the old one. I can't believe how quickly the marks change. Are there internal effects that are moving that fast? I scratch the old spot and blood seeps through the skin. Okay, no touching it.

I'm infected. This disease is crawling through my body all the time, ready to announce my contagion to the world. Seriously, the whole world, because I'm on a frigging TV show being watched. How creepy. Like, some guy on the other side of the world might be staring at my butt hard enough to notice the mark tonight. Oh, God. That purple bikini. I'm so cursed. If I asked, could they take me out of the competition and not air my segment tonight? Or do I have enough of a chance with Jeremy to make the public humiliation worth it?

What am I thinking? Like it matters how I look? I could be frigging dying right now! And I don't even know what might happen if I don't get the cure soon enough. I wish one of the contestants did sneak a computer in. I really need to research.

I pull on jeans and a T-shirt and leave the room. I scan my hand at the elevator and exit the hotel. I'm not sure if I'm allowed to leave, but I can't sit in my room any longer.

The air from the hotel whooshes out the door after me, disappearing into the heat. I set off down the sidewalk. I pass people in nice suits with blank gazes as they concentrate on whatever conversations are going on in their ear chips. I doubt I'll ever have a big name job like them—one with a fancy title like corporate marketing engineer protégé. I'll never need to listen to ten people talk as I try to enjoy the world around me. And I'll never have enough money to buy my own flat. I rub my thumb over my bare wrist. If I had money, I'd be in a position to make money.

In history class, I learned the government used to send poor people to college. I can't imagine the politicians doing anything to help the impoverished now. Even if they wanted to, where would they get the money? How would they choose who deserved to go out of so many? A system like that would never work. Still, I wish I could go to college for free.

I search the ground for a rock to kick, but find only white-washed pavement. Key West is scrubbed clean. Even in the distance the sand cutting between the skyscrapers is pristine and white. I walk until I reach the edge, kicking off my sandals, preparing for the soft heat under my feet.

I step forward and a high-pitched noise echoes in my ear. Another step and the volume intensifies. *You've got to be kidding me.* I back up and test the barrier again. I place my fingers in my ears, but that doesn't help. It's like they've figured out a way to pipe the warning noise right into my brain. All that beautiful sand, and I can't touch it. Now that's sad. Why not just use a hologram?

I circle around the skyscraper and try the sand on the other side. The results are the same. I keep going. Tall buildings stretch into the sky in a long line down the beach. Glimpses of water tease me at every corner. There has to be an opening in the boundary somewhere, because Jeremy and I went swimming. On my fifth attempt, I notice a man in a black uniform approaching. I consider running. I'm good at running. The officer walks directly toward me. I'm not sure which branch of the police force he represents, but the star on his chest glints in the sun. They probably didn't appreciate me setting off all of those alarms.

I consider my options as I try to gauge by the speed of his walk how much trouble I'm in. I could run. He might be as fast as me. Or he might zap me from a distance.

Time to be smart. I brighten my face as though I've just realized an officer is near, and jog toward him, my hand outstretched in a wave. "Sir, oh, thank goodness. I'm here on vacation and I've lost my map. I'm trying to find the entrance to the beach, but I keep hearing this weird noise." I twist my finger in my hair like I'm five.

He keeps his hand on his belt, ready to taze me. "Didn't you hear the warning signal?" His voice sounds automatic and monotone.

"Oh, is that what the noise was? But then, how do I get to the beach?" I smile warmly and he takes his hand off his belt.

He shakes his head, not hiding his irritation. "The chamber of commerce sells tickets to the beach and has maps." He points through the buildings. "The water here is kept pure and the city has to maintain that beauty. We can't allow tourists to infect our natural resources without compensation."

I flinch at the word infect, but nod along, pretending to agree. "Oh, of course. I just didn't know where to go."

He tightens his lips and waits for me to start off in the direction of the chamber of commerce. I wonder what he would've done to me if I'd truly been breaking into the beach.

A big glass dome squats on the pavement. Silver-colored letters spell out "Chamber of Commerce." I veer around the welcoming flags and down another street. Electronic banners overhang the sidewalk, flickering on and off to catch attention. The stores are individual, not clumped together in a mall like I'm used to. I wonder how they keep the area secure without a scan system and an entrance.

Window after window show tourist T-shirts spiraling up and down on racks. How many Key West shirts are sold in this city? Weird. I almost want one, but I do have my local bikini to take home thanks to the studio. If I had more money I might buy Jeremy a present. Though, there isn't anything I could buy him that he doesn't already have. I wonder what he's doing on his date today. I try to remember the words scrawled on the date list, but the image blurs in my mind.

I keep walking for a long time, long enough that the sky tinges to pink. Jeremy is probably back from his date; maybe if I'm fast I can catch him at the bar before he leaves for the next one. I think if I jog to the end of the street, turn the corner and hook around, I'll be able to get back to the hotel without repeating any of the scenery.

The banners fade at the end of the street and I assume I'm in a residential district. Square glass tiles climb into the sky. There are probably people living behind every single one. I don't meet anyone else on the street. Maybe the buildings aren't even in use. I quicken my stride, picturing Jeremy chugging another smoky drink.

I like him so much. Damn it. There's no pretending I don't.

A group of guys sits on the front steps of a building up ahead. They're playing a game I don't recognize with smooth gray stones. I try not to make eye contact as I jog around them.

A sharp pain slices across the front of my leg. I pitch forward.

It takes about one second to realize what happened as the pavement rips into my palms. I'm about to get robbed. I jump back to my feet, but they're moving fast. Four of them. I twist away to run, but there's no time. I'm yanked back by my shirt.

"Hold still, bitch!" His pupils are dilated. Face sunken in like one of those anti-drug posters. I throw my elbow, hitting nothing but air. I use the man's grip on my shirt to spin momentum into my right hook. I take him high on the cheek and his grip loosens. He yells some remarkably unflattering swears.

Four of them. No point in fighting. But I can't let it go or stop the adrenaline-fueled response. I rip myself free, trying to get distance from them. Two cut around my backside, while the others approach from the front. No chance.

I rush forward and plant a stomp kick in the groin of the nearest guy. His pal slams into me and we hit the ground. I wrap my leg over his neck, pinning him as I scramble to the top.

Searing pain radiates through my scalp. I'm dragged off by my hair. "Let go of me!"

Then my face is shoved into the street.

"Get her arm, quick!"

I struggle under the weight. One of the guys digs his knee into my backbone. "What the fuck?" I buck my hips off the ground, but I can't knock them off. Through the veil of my hair I see my arm jerked out straight. The man holds a razor blade between his fingers. He cranks my arm over, baring my wrist.

"You've got to be shitting me," he yells.

The weight shifts on my back as one of the other guys leans down to check. "How the hell did you get to Key West without even a chip?"

"Sorry to disappoint, no money for you assholes."

Knuckles hit my upturned face. I blink to clear the tears from my eyes. I start to scream, but it comes out like a wail. Then, all of a sudden, I'm choking out a laugh. I have nothing.

They check my other wrist. My forearms, my ankles.

"Shit, she doesn't have one." The knee on my spine releases and I rip my arm free.

"You don't report this, understand?" One of them grips the back of my hair so hard tears blur my vision.

"Yes," I manage to spit out. He tightens his grip. I don't feel like taking another punch to the face.

"I won't tell anyone," I repeat.

"Just leave her. Let's get out of here."

"Yeah, but the bitch fucking punched me! We should sell her to someone. Get our money that way."

Shit. I push myself up. If it's going to be like that, I'll fight until I'm unconscious and too damaged to be any good to them. One of the guys meets my eyes. He nods like he recognizes my determination. He might even feel sorry for me. That, or I'm having desperate fantasies.

He looks away from me and pats the pissed off guy on the shoulder. "She's not worth anything. We'll get another tourist later on a better street."

He scowls and steps toward me. But one of the others speaks up. "A skinny bitch, and mean, too. Plus she's probably, like, fifteen. I don't want to get caught peddling underage shit." I stand there listening, slowly back-stepping. A few more feet away and I might have enough of a head start to make a run for the hotel.

"Yeah, you're right." He spits in my direction. I wonder if his saliva is contagious, too. Their voices are pissed as they walk away.

I wipe my nose as I walk, noting the blood smeared across my arm. Great, now I've got my contagious blood leaking all over the place. There's another red line of blood across the front of my leg. Frigging razor wire. They cut through my best jeans. I start walking again, faster, faster. Before they come back or change their minds. Or...I don't know. How could this happen? There's security all over this city. I saw an officer earlier today. I tremble as I sprint down the final street, ignoring the throbbing pain in my leg. The hotel in the distance is safety.

I'm running so fast I trip on the strip of carpet leading into the hotel. I crumble to my knees, shaking, sucking in the air. I made it. I'm safe. I want to cry. That could have been the end of my life.

"Monet? Are you okay?"

For a second, I hope I've passed out and I'm having another Jeremy dream, but as I tilt my head up, I see him standing in front of the limo. "Monet." He strides closer and extends his hand. I blink hard, drilling my panic back down.

Mel climbs out of the limo. Her blue-outlined eyebrows draw closer together in challenge. I want to fall into Jeremy's arms. I want him to take me back to his room.

"I'm fine, just an attempted robbery." I hear the words coming out of my mouth and I'm proud of the way my voice doesn't quiver.

He reaches out his hand to touch my face, and then stops inches from making contact. "The person hit you?"

"Damn, does it look really bad?" I've got enough self-image problems to worry about with Fluxem crawling across my back. A black eye would finish me off. Jeremy's arm shakes as he takes in my injuries. He balls his fist and his anger radiates.

"We need medical attention right now!" he yells over his shoulder. No one does anything. I grab his arm. "Jeremy, I'm fine. Nothing a first aid kit won't fix."

"But your nose is bleeding. You could have a concussion." I follow his gaze down my front to the rapidly spreading blood stain. "What the hell happened to your leg?" He kneels at my feet and the brown curve of his hair hangs forward as he pulls the denim out of the slice in my leg.

"Yeah, that's how they got me. If I hadn't gone down, I probably could've outrun them." I shrug. I've almost been mugged many times, but in Boston I know how to escape and keep a low profile better. "Lucky me, no chip to dig out of my arm." I try to laugh, which comes out more like a sob. Then my façade pops and tears slide down my cheeks.

Jeremy grasps my arms and pulls me tight against his chest. "You're okay."

"It was just the stupidest thing. I should've stayed on the main road. I tried to fight back, but there were four of them."

"Four." He pushes me away enough to stare into my face. There's a tremor in his jaw. He's crazy pissed. "Where did this happen? What street were you on?"

"I spent most of the day looking for the beach and then I was on the street with all the T-shirts and I thought if I just kept going, I'd get back to the hotel, but then I—"

"Shh, it's okay. Now, what street were you attacked on?"

I point back in the direction I came. Jeremy runs his thumb under my eye, wiping away my tears. "I'll go check it out."

"No!" I place my hand on his heart, trying to hold him in place.

Mel uses the gap between us to latch onto Jeremy's arm. I forgot she was in the limo, too. Jeremy's date. Though from the amount of attention he's paying her, I'd say Jeremy forgot her as well.

"Those guys need to be taken care of. I can't just let them hurt you. Don't worry, I'll take Derek." His hands stay on my arms even though Mel is not so subtly yanking him away. He twitches his arm like she's a fly.

She thrusts her lower lip out. "Hey, our date's not over."

"Yeah, it is."

Another producer's assistant joins us. He checks his watch. "Officially the date has ended…" He checks his clipboard for her name. "…Mel."

Jeremy focuses on the assistant. "Johnson, we need to report a crime. Notify the police that we'll be waiting in the lobby, and get a staff member with a first aid kit down here now."

Johnson looks sick at the sight of the blood on my jeans and nods his head rapidly. He's probably aware of how many diseases could be in my blood and hurries back inside to call the police. Jeremy ushers me through the hotel doors and onto a white sofa.

"Maybe we shouldn't sit here," I whisper as he kneels by my leg.

"Hmm?"

"The white upholstery. I don't want to ruin it."

"Who the hell cares about the upholstery? I think we're going to need to cut the jeans off."

"No!" They're my silk weave denim jeans. "I can patch the leg. We don't need to make the tear any bigger."

He looks at me in question.

"I didn't pack enough clothes," I say.

Mel clarifies the conversation for me. "She's poor." I bet she wants to add more. Give him a few opinions about how unworthy I am of his time and attention. I can deal with being poor, but I hate being judged. I just wish Jeremy could see me as an equal without our differences being pointed out by the other contestants.

Jeremy still seems more concerned about my injury than anything we're talking about. "I'll get you more pants...if you want."

"Thank you, but these are fine."

He quirks his half smile at my stubbornness and helps me roll the material away from the gash. Thankfully he's no longer focused on rushing down the street to see if those guys are still there. Let the cops do their job.

"They must have had a razor wire line stretched across the entire sidewalk," I say. I'm still in disbelief that the incident happened at all. Statistically, I know the crime rate is high almost everywhere in the world, and I should've taken more steps to be safe.

"I hope you can give the police a good description," Jeremy says. He supports the underside of my leg and stares up at me. I love his concerned expression. It's one I've never seen on TV before.

I told the guys who attacked me that I wouldn't say anything, but it's not like I'm going to be sticking around for them to retaliate. "I'll try and remember every detail I can, but it just happened so fast. I was running back, hoping to catch you before you left this evening, and then I was down on the ground with a knee digging into my back."

Jeremy's jaw stands out as he clenches his teeth, but his hands are still gentle on my leg. "I can't believe they did this to you. I am so sorry."

Mel bumps up against Jeremy's arm, asking whether he wants to go get a drink. He completely ignores her. I gaze down at Jeremy, who still cradles my calf in his hands. My heart is beating so fast from the contact I'm probably bleeding even more, but I don't care. I'm the one he's so worried about.

"We've got to get ice on your cheek. You're already bruising."

A woman from behind the check-in station comes over with a thin case of first aid equipment. She takes out a can of Spray All. Jeremy lets go of my leg to give her room to work. She gives me a two-second blast. The sting fades after an instant of intense pain, and then a barrier of new skin spreads over the slice. "Thank you," I tell her.

"She needs something to keep the swelling down on her face," Jeremy says. Ah, crap. My face is swelling? I need a mirror. Besides what I look like to him, those viewers have to pick me, too.

"Sorry, I don't have anything with me, but there's an ice machine at the end of the hall." Jeremy glares. She packs up the case and hurries off. She must not know who he is, or maybe she just isn't a fan, otherwise she'd try harder to make a good impression.

Derek taps him on the shoulder. "I'll get the ice. Unless you want to just carry her upstairs with us." Jeremy nods like that's a good idea and my heart does a happy flip. He examines my leg one more time and then stands up. "We need to talk to the police first before we can go anywhere."

"Don't get mobbed while I'm gone." Derek jogs down the hall.

I look past Jeremy to see Mel standing with her hand on her hip. "Sorry you got hurt," she says. "At least you already had your date. You'll have enough time to heal up before the finale." She sits on the couch to prevent Jeremy from sitting next to me. I hope she's not going to pretend to be my friend.

Johnson runs across the lobby to us. He lets out a deep breath when he sees the cut is healed. "I hate to break this up, but Jeremy, you need to get ready for this evening. You're having dinner at the Ming Kingsty and the attire is formal."

Jeremy sighs and drives his hands through his hair. The ends curl even more when he pulls his hands back. He is cute even when he's exasperated.

"I'll stay with her until the police arrive to take her statement."

My nose tingles with emotion and I pray my eyes won't water again. I need a nap. I can't control Jeremy's dating schedule and I have no say about who he spends time with. But I wish I did. I need to shake off this hopeless feeling and get back into the game. "I'll be okay, if you need to go."

"I've got time." He settles on my other side so that I'm sandwiched between him and Mel. I can't help grinning. What a slam to her. Not that I moved over to give him room to sit in the middle, but he certainly didn't try.

Derek comes back with ice wrapped in a towel. The whole side of my face feels like it's on fire, but the cold doesn't help. We sit quietly. Jeremy's body presses against the length of mine. I feel shy all of a sudden. I should say something clever, but I just want to curl up against him and go to sleep. I tip my head to his shoulder and his fingers brush my hair. His lips press a kiss onto the top of my head and his voice is very low. "It'll be okay."

I start to nod off, but he nudges my arm. "No sleeping. You might have a concussion."

I yawn. "Okay." I let my eyes go blurry while I relax into Jeremy's warmth.

He brushes my hair back. "The officer is here."

I straighten up, wishing I could spend the rest of the day snuggled up.

"You okay?" He brushes my hair again.

"I'm good." Johnson and Eleanor are yelling at each other a few feet away. "Jeremy, do you need to go?"

He sighs. "No."

He's so lying, which is totally sweet. "I'll be fine." I shove him up as the police officer approaches.

"Will you be okay by yourself?"

"Of course."

"I'll check on you later, okay?"

I nod and sit straighter. He hesitates, staring at me, trying to judge if I really am better. The officer has out a tablet and speaks the date and time into the receiver. He asks me a question that I hardly hear as I watch Jeremy walking away.

FIFTEEN

M Y ATTACKERS DIDN'T have any distinguishing characteristics. Four guys of medium build, medium height. No facial hair, no scars. The officer asks me questions like they're from a memorized list. I think the mood stabilizers they've got law enforcement on are making them into robots. His voice borders on monotone.

"Hold out your arm." He positions a handheld scanner over my wrist. "The one holding you left skin residue, no prints. Fifty percent match rate with that type of data." He puts the scanner away. "Are you staying at the hotel for a while?"

"As long as the show is in town."

He nods once. "I'll contact you if we apprehend any suspects for you to identify." The lack of inflection in his voice makes me doubt they'll find anyone. Which is irritating. The guys had a razor wire on the street. How smart can they be? That's not exactly a low profile crime.

"You're free to go."

Honestly, I'm surprised the officer even came out to the hotel. The assistant show coordinator must have told him I was bleeding to death. I walk down the familiar hotel hallway, stepping in between the geometric square patterns in the carpet. Hypnotic. Jeremy is on another date with another girl. Life sucks.

Jasmine is lying in wait by the elevator. "I saw you trying to interrupt Mel's date."

Great. Just what I need, more of her shit. "I was attacked outside of the hotel. I wasn't intentionally interrupting anything."

"More of your lies."

Maybe this is a good day to punch her. "I'm not lying. I just finished giving my statement to the police. Notice my face and my leg." I point down to the bloody rip in my jeans.

She purses her lips together. "I don't like you."

A laugh bursts out of me. Jasmine is just so...vile. "Yeah, well, feeling's mutual. Have a great day." I lean around her to push the elevator button and scan my hand. She latches onto me, nails practically piercing my skin. I tense my whole body. "Today is not a good day to mess with me." I pronounce the words very slowly in my kill voice.

She drops her hand. "Your show's airing tonight."

"Yeah, so what?"

"I just can't wait to see what secrets you have to hide."

The elevator door slides open and I leave her in the hall. I signed up for Jeremy, not for all this other shit. And now I have to go to the fake living room to watch the studio try to make me look bad. If Jeremy hadn't held me, this day would be the worst ever.

———

I sit on the big, fat couch in my green dress and chew my nails. Five more minutes. Five minutes until millions of people are sitting at home, watching me.

Jasmine and her clones take turns glaring at me from one of the other couches. No one wants to sit next to me. Afraid of what will be revealed, like I might be contagious—which, technically, I am. Shelley Anne finally takes the seat next to me and I'm almost relieved not to be alone, even though I know she hates me, too.

Who will win a date with a rockstar and thirty thousand dollars? flashes across the screen to the opening song from Jeremy's ocean collection. Rod Bing is back behind his desk. He's wearing a purple scarf. I wonder if he was trying to match my bikini. I feel like puking.

"This week, contestant number two vies for Jeremy Bane's attention, but you will decide whether she deserves him or not." Drums crescendo in the background. I can't believe Rod Bing is talking about me.

They show the line footage again and then the camera cuts to me entering the interview room. My face fills half the wall. I look nervous, meek. Wet hair tangles around my shoulders and I appear washed out from all the rain.

I shiver, remembering the three days in line. What misery. It's hard to judge myself. Shelley Anne called me pretty. But what will the TV audience think?

The interviewer asks the question about Jeremy's music—probably the only answer I gave that makes me seem somewhat intelligent. I'm staring at the one-way glass, but the camera must have been right below because it seems like I'm staring directly into the camera. My eyes meet my own on the screen and the sensation brings a wave of nausea. Creepy. They only show my answer to the one question. I let out my breath in relief. After the Claire exposé I wouldn't have been surprised to find they filmed me puking in the bathroom.

Rod Bing leans over the desk and raises his eyebrows. "Now, before we get to the juicy details, let's take a look at their date."

Juicy details? I'm pretty sure my life doesn't have any of those, unless they fabricated something. Did I sign anything giving them the right to lie about me? There's no way they could know about Fluxem. I shift around on the couch. My legs bounce continuously. Shelley Anne narrows her eyes and I try to sit still. I have no control and I hate it.

On screen, I step out of the limo and the camera slides up my leg and over my T-shirt. How the hell did they get that angle? I would've had to have been standing on top of the cameraman. Maybe there were lenses on the limo door. Jeremy climbs out after me and brushes against my arm. Our heads tip together. I remember the conversation, the feel of him next to me. I want to go back to the beach all over again. Well, without the cameras.

When the show gets to the part where we wade out into the water, I hold my breath, praying my mark won't be visible. Jeremy blocks the view and once we hit deep water the footage turns boring. Our heads bob up and down in the distance for a few seconds, then they cut back to us walking out. They missed all the romantic stuff when Jeremy was teaching me how to swim. Instead, they zoom in on the front of my dripping wet body. I'm so embarrassed. But at least my breasts are keeping the attention off my back.

Crystal makes a guttural noise from the other couch. I catch Claire's attention and she smiles sympathetically. She and I are now in the already-traumatized-on-TV club.

Rod Bing comes back on the screen. "Stick around. After this commercial break we'll find out what contestant number two has to hide." They montage tribal drums over song eight of Jeremy's new release, building a sense of doom. I'm offended on his behalf that they messed with his work and pissed that they're not showing more of our date. I guess since we didn't wear our microphones during lunch they're not showing any of that footage. Still, they could've showed a few clips of us walking in the woods.

I gnaw the end of my fingernail. I guess there's no chance the juicy details about me will be positive. I think I'd rather be jumped again than watch whatever they are going to reveal. I prepare myself for slams about my lack of direction in life, my inability to get a good job, maybe a few panoramas of my shitty apartment building.

The show's back on. Here we go. Okay. How bad will it be?

Mom sits on our tiny couch. An interviewer squeezes in next to her. The close proximity looks silly, but I know there's nowhere else in our apartment to sit.

"Why did you choose to have a female child, Ms. O'Neal?"

The question surprises me.

Mom sits up straight and she looks both beautiful and frazzled. "Monet has always been the biggest joy in my life."

He taps a pen on the tablet in his lap. "Yes, of course. But why did you choose to have a girl rather than a boy?"

"That's a very personal question, sir. I'm not sure I feel comfortable answering." She holds her head high and I'm so proud of her.

"Actually, according to your fertility records, you and your husband did in fact choose to have a boy."

WHAT? Husband? This is all news to me. My mother was married when she conceived? My father. I have a father? Not just a DNA donor. I've never even seen pictures. I've never received birthday presents. As long as I can remember it's only been Mom and me. My head spins.

"How did you get that information?" Mom is pissed.

"Your daughter has given us full rights to explore her background. Now, let's get back to the question. Isn't it true that you were supposed to be inseminated with a male embryo?"

"I have never regretted a single second that Monet has been my daughter."

"But the initial procedure?" he prompts.

"Yes, we selected to have a male." My heart drops through my stomach. She wanted a boy? I never knew.

Mom presses her lips in a tight line. From the way she leans forward and clenches her fists, I think she's close to violence.

"A technician made an error and we got a girl. Honestly, I'm surprised there aren't more errors."

The asshole on our couch raises his eyebrow and shrugs. Like maybe I'm a girl or maybe my mom is lying. "What I'm interested in," he pauses dramatically, "is whether or not your husband left you because of the error.

"We managed to track down your ex-husband. Do you want to hear what he had to say?"

Mom looks grim. She should have told me. When we were on the phone, she should've told me. Tears glint in the corners of her eyes as a man's body fills the screen.

Oh my God! He's fiftyish. Graying hair, slightly overweight. Strong jaw, expensive suit. I'm taking in as many details as I can before I pass out. I'm sure my brain can't handle the strain.

Then he speaks. Perfect white teeth. The man has money. "Of course for my one child I selected to have a boy to carry on the family business." His title scrawls along the bottom of the screen. Walter O'Neal, CEO of Fission Cooperative.

"And when the female result was reported?"

"I told Katherine to have the fetus removed." A commercial pops up on the screen. I glance at Jasmine and she's smiling. My teeth clack together as I fight the urge to mess her up. Praline grimaces when I look at her. I need to call Mom. I need to throw up. I need to hear the rest of what my father has to say immediately. How can they screw with my life like this?

The show comes back on. The interviewer does another intro, then my father...holy shit...my father... is back on the screen.

"She refused, claiming some attachment already, and I left her. No law against me having another child with a different woman."

I have a father and he's an asshole. This is why Mom never told me. He didn't want me. The screen switches back to Mom.

"Monet, if you're watching this, I just want you to know that I love you and I have absolutely no regrets in my life." *Oh, Mom. I love you, too.*

"Really?" The interviewer taunts. "Even if your choice means living in poverty?" Now they do the pan of our apartment building. Then they show the full hundred square feet of our apartment. "Monet doesn't have a lot of options for her future."

"Sir, my daughter is brilliant and she will succeed in anything she sets out to do in this life." Tears roll down my face.

The screen switches back to showing me in my bikini. I hope it's my imagination and they're not intentionally zeroing in on my crotch. I'm speechless over the fact that they actually tried to cast doubt as to whether or not I'm a girl. That's insulting. I think I'd rather be labeled a slut like Claire. I hope Jeremy never sees this. He's on his date now, but I'm probably doomed to be immortalized in reruns. Hell, Jasmine will probably be hanging out by the elevator, waiting to tell him as soon as he comes back from his date tonight.

Rod Bing rubs his chin. "Remember, voting won't begin until all the contestants have had a chance." A still image of me fills the screen. My one breast says "Key" and the other says "West." Better that than the sore on my back. After finding out I have a living father who never wanted me, the words on my chest are nothing.

"Vote number two at the end of the competition if you think Monet deserves a chance to be in the final three. The choice is yours..."

I'm too shocked to even cry. What did my mother give up by choosing to have me? How long did she live in wealth with that man? I don't remember her ever having money. I race through every fact. If he never wanted to meet me or know anything about me, then screw him.

Claire sits down next to me. "Wow, I'm sorry. I didn't think they could do anything worse than what they did to me. They were really stretching with that one. Digging into your conception files is low."

"I didn't know."

"Yeah, I didn't read all those papers we signed, either."

"I mean, I really never knew I had a father. I thought my mom just wanted to have a baby. I've never known her to have a permanent relationship with any man."

Claire stands up and wipes her palms on her jeans. "I'm going to the restaurant for a coffee. Wanna come?"

"No. I need to talk to my mother."

She nods in understanding and leaves me. Jasmine takes the opportunity to sashay over. "I really enjoyed your episode," she says, deadpan.

I don't even bother to respond to her, and after a few seconds she walks away. I sit for a long time on the couch, staring at the blank wall. I eventually make my way back to the room. I hear the phone ringing before I open the door.

I know it's Mom before I even hit the button. Her tiny 3-D shape materializes. She fades in and out, smoothing her hair over and over again.

"Honey, I didn't know they were going to show all of that." She twists her fingers together. "I never wanted you to find out like this."

"Mom, you have to sit still or the display can't get a good lock on you."

"Oh." She tries to stop fidgeting, but I can still tell how upset she is. "Monet, talk to me. Are you furious?"

Am I? "I'm shocked. I feel like I should've known about this."

"There was just never a good time to tell you. It's been so long. I hadn't even thought of that man in years."

"My father, you mean."

"That man has never been your father."

I don't argue. That point we can agree on. "Why didn't..." I trail off, not knowing what to ask. I heard the man's own words. He didn't want me. He said it on camera. I am not a boy. "Did he ever come to see me?"

"After you were born?" She's already shaking her head no as she speaks. "I didn't think he deserved to spend time with you."

"Did he try?"

"No—honey, I'm so sorry about all of this." The image of her fades out.

"Mom, you're moving again. And I'm not mad at you." Okay, maybe a little, but I can't stand to see her so upset. "Did you miss him after he left?"

"No, I didn't. I had you, and after I realized what kind of person he was—I was glad he wasn't around."

"But the money?"

"Oh, Monet. There are a million things in this world more important than money."

I think about disagreeing with her and starting our old argument, but I let it go.

She pauses, smoothing her hair obsessively. "Are we still okay?"

"Yeah, Mom. I love you."

"I love you, too." Her tone is relieved. I wish I could hug her. "I've worried about this for so many years." The tears in the 3-D image of her are hard to see, but I recognize the gestures. She wipes at her nose and eyes.

I want to get off the phone before she makes me cry, too. "I've got to go. But I'll talk to you soon. They don't have too many more days of filming."

She nods and wipes her eyes again, trying to smile for me. "Good luck with Jeremy."

"Thanks, Mom." I hit disconnect. I feel like I've been run over. I retreat to the bathroom and sit in the tub. I don't even bother with the lights or water. I just sit.

SIXTEEN

I WAKE UP to pounding on the bathroom door. Ouch. I'm still in the tub and my neck is killing me. I stumble to my feet.

"Are you okay in there? How's your leg?" That sounds like Jeremy. "Monet, are you dressed?"

Holy shit, that is Jeremy! "I'll be right out." I take a quick swig of mouthwash and glance in the mirror. I run my fingers through my hair. There's a bit of purple bruising under my eye and across my cheek. Not too bad, just makes me look more dramatic. I shrug and open the door.

Jeremy leans against the doorframe, radiating sexiness. "I was afraid I was going to have to barge in on you again." His eyes widen when he sees my clingy green dress. He blows out a breath, looking me up and down. "Oh, your face." He brushes my hair back and his fingertips skim the bruise.

I shiver. "It doesn't hurt anymore. The swelling went away."

"Shit, and your leg, too." He kneels at my feet. My legs are bare from the knees down and his face is inches away. "Does it still hurt?" He pokes the edge of the tender, healing skin.

"Only when you poke at it," I say jokingly.

Shelley Anne sits on her bed, glaring at us.

He glances over at her. "Uh, Shelley was kind enough to let me in." I bet she was. Probably almost died of happiness until he asked where I was.

Wait. Is Jeremy here because he saw the show? Please, let him not be here because of that. "How was your date?"

"It was good, not much to tell." He drops his head and shifts against the wall. His jeans hang off his hips perfectly. I'm way too tuned in to his body.

I tip my head slightly in Shelley's direction because I know she's listening to our every word.

"You want to get out of here?" he asks.

"Absolutely."

"Monet, can I speak to you for a second before you leave?" Shelley doesn't bother to disguise the anger in her voice.

I turn to Jeremy and give him my exasperated dealing-with-Shell eye roll. "Sure, I'll just be a minute," I say over my shoulder. Jeremy quirks a half smile and waits by the door.

Shelley walks to the other side of the room and I follow her. "You're not allowed to go out with him," she says under her breath.

A laugh bursts out of me. First Jasmine and now her. "Are you serious? You really think you can tell me what to do?"

"We all saw you interrupting Mel's date this morning, hanging all over Jeremy with your supposed injury."

Interrupting? Like I chose to get attacked. "What the f–? I was jumped. They cut my leg with razor wire–"

"Monet, is everything okay over there?" Jeremy's voice has this don't-mess-with-my-girl tone and my anger melts back a little.

"Yeah, let's go."

Shelley grabs my arm. "I'm not kidding. Jasmine already told Eleanor you were cheating. And if you try to leave this room with him tonight, I'm going to report you." It's not cheating if it's not a rule. Unless this was in more of the paperwork I didn't read.

"Go ahead." I stride toward Jeremy and let the door slam shut behind us.

We walk down the hall. Jeremy leans his head closer to mine. "You're beautiful in that dress," he says under his breath as we approach the elevator. Derek is waiting for us. His arms are crossed, displaying prominent biceps. He still has his half-restrained grin. I wonder what Jeremy has said about me.

Derek nods to Jeremy and then to me. Jeremy claps him on the back. Derek punches his shoulder. Very manly.

Jeremy raises his eyebrows. "What was with the claws back there in the room?"

"Nothing. She tried to tell me I'm not allowed to go anywhere with you. Apparently, I'm cheating."

Derek chuckles. "Uh-oh, cat fight."

"Whatever. I can take any of them."

Jeremy takes a few steps back and holds up his hands. I pretend to punch him and he dodges away, laughing. "I'm serious," I say.

"Hit me, I can take a punch." Derek tightens his gut. "You sure?"

"What's a girl punch going to do to me?"

I whip my fist back and punch from the hip, throwing my body behind it.

"Ouch, shit. Okay. I won't question you again." He rubs his belly in pain, and I feel satisfied as the elevator door pings open. It's then that I realize we've been in the elevator longer than usual. We step out into a gray, narrow hallway.

"Where are we?"

"I have a surprise for you," Jeremy says. "I figured you needed cheering up after getting attacked earlier."

I think I might cry. I don't know what to say. I sigh. I don't have many friends and the idea of being cheered up by anyone other than Mom leaves me awed. The gray hallway stretches out as far as I can see. "Are we underground?"

"Yup."

"Are we supposed to be down here?" I ask.

"Nope."

"Where are we going?"

He smiles. "I told you, it's a surprise. Derek will keep guard so that we don't get in trouble."

"Do I have to be blindfolded or something?"

"Do you want to be?" He lowers his voice and raises an eyebrow. I almost trip on my own foot.

"I, uh, if you want me to be."

His eyes meet mine in question. Then he grips my hand and keeps walking. He's so seriously sexy. I think this qualifies as a second date. My nerves tingle in anticipation. We pass under a vent blowing warm, moist air onto our heads.

There's a massive door set in the wall and Jeremy stops in front of the scan pad. Derek comes forward and scans a card that releases the door. He winks at me.

"How'd you get that?" I ask.

"Affectionate kitchen staff," Derek says.

I shake my head. How much trouble has Derek helped Jeremy get into in the past? Jeremy pushes the door open and I forget everything. Warm air billows out. Derek takes a position outside of the room and I follow Jeremy inside.

Plants climb up mesh cylinders to the ceiling. They're packed in, hanging with ripe fruit and vegetables. Nutrients and water drip down from tanks along the ceiling. The walls are covered with clumps of healthy lettuce. I know what a hydro garden is, but I've never been in one. It's like another world or a foreign planet.

"Cool, huh?" Jeremy stands in front of me and I'm not sure how long I've been staring at the place.

"I love it." The tanks above my head are a golden yellow like a false sun. Bright grow lights hang from the top of each line of veggies. When I close my eyes the heat radiates through my eyelids and into my limbs.

His fingers lace with mine and he pulls me forward, deeper into the mini jungle. "I thought you might." He picks a cherry tomato off the vine and holds the little red sphere out to me.

"Won't they notice if we eat anything?"

"Nah, the restaurant staff come down here to harvest and maintain the space every day. A few tomatoes are no big deal."

"Did you learn all that from Derek's reconnaissance?" I bite into the tomato, careful to avoid an explosion of precious juice. So sweet and fresh.

"Maybe," he says, laughing. "Back here there's a spot where we can sit." He leads me down the narrow path to a stack of wooden pallets. There's a hotel room blanket spread out on top. He shrugs. "I sent Derek down earlier." Partners in crime.

"You didn't have to do this for me."

He tips his head. "Eh, I thought we could both use a break from all the cameras, and I felt so bad when I had to leave you alone with the officer earlier. I should've stayed."

"You didn't miss much. I gave him a description, but I don't think he'll find the guys." I sneak a tomato off the plant by the pallets and sit down on the blanket.

He sits down next to me. I'm alone-*alone* with Jeremy. "How is your leg?"

I lift my leg up slightly, and the slinky dress slides up with it. I pull the hem down a bit. "The cut doesn't hurt anymore."

"When I saw the blood on your pants...man. I really don't like seeing you hurt. I wanted to kill those guys."

My heart pounds. What do I say? "It was probably my own fault for thinking I could circle around the block and walk back to the hotel a different way. I didn't know anything about the neighborhood. I'm usually not that stupid."

"Don't be so hard on yourself. I just wish I'd been with you instead of on that stupid date."

"I wish you'd been there, too." He takes my hand in his. "How was your evening date?" I ask. "Do anything exciting?"

"I guess. The studio sent us on one of those sunset hover tours of the city. The area's nice, cool beaches. Jaime was interesting to talk to, but too forward." Hmm. So she probably at least kissed him. Comparatively, my date didn't have much action. I wonder what the viewers will prefer.

I try and smile. "Are the girls what you expected?"

"I don't know. Every time I think I've got women all figured out, something happens to knock me on my ass. It's hard to really talk on TV. I hesitate a lot, thinking about how my words will be perceived by the audience. These girls are intense with their fascination, but I think it almost blinds them to who I really am."

"Struck deaf and dumb by your amazing powers of attraction?"

"Ha, ha. I recognize that line. So, you watched the documentary on my face, huh?"

"What dutiful fangirl wouldn't?"

"Is that what you are, Monet?"

Why do I feel light-headed all of a sudden? "I'll always be one of your biggest fans."

He drops his head. *What did I do?* "I guess I'm hoping to find more than a fan." He runs his fingers through his hair and the wave flops over his eyes. "In your interview I felt like we already had this connection. I know it sounds stupid. I just, uh, thought you got me."

"I do. Or at least, I hope I do. But there's so much depth to your music, I'm sure it would take a long time to truly understand you."

"I feel the same way about your art. Like all those lines are connected to thoughts that I'm trying to unstring."

My heart thumps fast and my face is hot. All of a sudden this conversation is too much. Too much hope for my brain to function. I need distance, before I start believing Jeremy and I could have a future.

I take another tomato off the stem and sit back down. "They made us watch the second episode of the show. The one with our date." I shift around nervously.

"That must have been fun to watch."

"Not really."

"Oh?"

"Have you seen any of the episodes yet?"

"No. I think they want me to stay out of the loop so that my reactions are more believable. But who the hell knows with these assholes?" He trails his fingers over the back of my hand and onto my forearm. I can barely remember what I was talking about.

"Yeah, they're definitely not endearing themselves to me. They did background checks on all of the girls and they expose the results on the show."

"The ol' reality TV gets real bit. I can't believe that still brings in the ratings. So, what did they find out about you? Wait, let me guess." He's smiling like he can't imagine they could ever dig up anything on me. Then he leans away enough to see my face. "I'm betting extremely high scores on all standardized tests and... you once got drunk and puked in a public place...and, oh wait, you're an artist, so you've been picked up for graffiti before. How did I do?"

"I wish that was what they revealed. I have done graffiti, but I've never gotten caught, and no drunk puking."

"What's the matter? It can't have been that bad. Do I need to yell for Derek? You're not a killer, are you?" He nudges my shoulder.

"No, I'm not a killer."

"Okay, so what was so bad?" he asks.

Jasmine will tell him if I don't, and that will be much worse. "They said my mom wanted a boy, and the in-vitro got messed up. Then they had an interview with my father. He said he never wanted a girl, so he left. I never even knew I had a father."

Jeremy doesn't say anything for a long time. "Man, that's some heavy shit."

"Surprised the hell out of me. What about your dad?"

"He's a great guy. Married to some other woman now."

"Do you get to see your sister a lot?"

"Not as much as I'd like. She's nine now. Cute kid."

"You're so lucky to have a sibling. I really think they should change that stupid law."

He laughs. "Which one?" He stands up and picks a cluster of grapes from near the ceiling. As he stretches his T-shirt lifts up, flashing a narrow trail of belly hair. So distracting.

Right, laws. "Limiting women to only being able to have one child, but not placing any restrictions on men. Seems like some guys just keep getting divorced and remarried so they can have bigger families."

"You'd have to be a pretty big stud to convince more than one woman to use her only child pass on you. Especially with the imbalance between the number of men and women. What is it, three men to every one woman?"

I nod in agreement, though thinking about the sperm donor—my father—as being a stud is kind of weird, but I guess he is rich. I realize I'm scowling and try to relax my jaw. "All this family crap is messing with my mood. I don't mean to be so depressing." I finger comb my hair back away from my face and he sits back down next to me, offering his grapes.

"Don't worry, you're not. And even if you were, that's okay, too. That's a lot of crap to be bombarded with just for a TV show." He looks apologetic, like he might take back being the star of the show if he could. Or maybe that's just what I would feel like in his place. His hand runs down the center of my back in a comforting gesture. I lean into him.

"Ouch." I flinch back. He pulls his hand away. *Crap.* He hit one of my Fluxem sores. *Please don't let it be seeping through my dress.*

"Are you okay?"

"Oh, sorry. I think I just have a tender spot on my ribs from where I fell."

"Do you want me to look at it?" He climbs onto the pallet, looking behind me.

"No, no. It's fine." I grab his arm and pull him back to face me before he sees anything. "Please. I don't want to think about the attack."

"But if you're hurt—"

I run my fingers over his lips. They're so soft. He takes my hand, lightly folding it into his. "Bet you regret coming on the show after everything you've been through."

I tip my head up so that I'm staring into his eyes. "I think getting to meet you was worth it." I drop my head and run my fingers over the hotel room bedspread.

"I think so, too...although maybe I should wait and see how awful the rest of the girls are before I decide." His eyes crinkle at the corners and so does his mouth.

"Hey." I punch him lightly on the arm. He was joking, right?

"You're aggressive tonight."

"Hmmm, is that a good thing or a bad thing?"

"A sexy thing, for sure." He turns to face me and slowly looks me over, smiling. He flips my palm up and traces a circle in the center of my hand; jitters swarm through my arm. His touch makes me so tingly and sensitive.

There's a single short beep. "What's that noi—" Then the room fades to black.

His voice sounds disconnected in the dark. "Even plants need cycles of light and dark to grow properly."

I did not know that. Without my vision, the smell of ripe fruit and vegetables fills the air. There must be herbs near us. The scent of lemon, mint and lavender fills my senses. Jeremy keeps his hand over mine, barely touching since the lights went out. I wonder if Derek will come and get us, but then I remember there's no window in the door.

"You're quiet. Not afraid of the dark, are you?"

I take a deep breath and weave my fingers with his. "I'm not afraid." And in the dark, I can be absolutely certain we're finally alone. That no one is secretly filming me.

He exhales heavily and his fingers squeeze mine. His other hand reaches around me and lifts my hair away from my face and over my shoulder. I turn my head to him. *Do I lean in? Do I open my mouth?*

"I can't even see you." His hand touches my neck and then cups my cheek. I'm hot all over. The humidity in the room is steaming me to death. Dizziness hits me and I have to remind myself to take a breath. Any second. He knows I have Fluxem and there's no way I can infect him. Breathe, I have to breathe. Any second now.

His lips brush my cheek. More of a touch then a kiss. My lips part in anticipation as he lightly brushes another kiss across my mouth. Then the touch is gone. I lick my lips, lean forward. The warmth of his breath heats my face.

Kiss me all the way.

His hair tickles my nose, and I tilt my head to the side. There's a long pause and my heart thumps all over the place. Then, finally, he presses his lips against mine. Adrenaline zaps through me. Pins and needles of sensation tingle through my mouth, making me whirl with desire. I rise up on my knees and fall against him. I'm exploding. His arms wrap around me, keeping me close and we kiss and kiss and kiss. I'm lost in the sensation. Warmth builds in my chest and I want to dance around.

There's another beep and then warm mist rains down on us. Jeremy pulls back slightly. His lips still touch mine as he talks into my mouth. "We're getting wet, do you want to go?"

I brush my lips back and forth against his. "No," I whisper and lean back in to kiss him. I'm in another world of kissing. Every caress makes me needy and hot. Hours are probably passing, maybe even days.

Jeremy slides his hand up my back and pulls my dress off my shoulder.

"Don't." The lights will come back on and that's where my mark is. I feel him nod against my face as he traces circles on my shoulder.

His breathing increases and I know he's excited, too.

"Hey, you guys okay?" I jump back at Derek's voice. "Did you know it's raining in here?"

Jeremy clears his throat. "Yeah, we did notice that."

I straighten my dress, glad that the lights are out. I feel like I just got caught doing something very naughty. Jeremy slides his hand down my arm until he can find my hand. We stumble our way toward the door, trying not to knock over any of the plant stands.

"You guys were in there a looong time." Derek raises his eyebrows suggestively as he opens the door.

The light from the hallway blinds me, creating floating spots of color in my vision. Cool air hits my chest. I look down to see the material clinging to my breasts. I shiver. When I glance back up both Jeremy and Derek are staring at me.

"Sorry," Derek mutters and takes the lead down the hallway.

Jeremy kissed me. My grin encompasses my entire head. An intentional kiss, not one of those I-latched-onto-him-and-he-couldn't-get-away types. This is the best night of my life. He holds my hand as we get back on the elevator. I feel shy and quiet. Does this mean anything? Does he want to be my boyfriend now? Do musicians even have real girlfriends? He doesn't live in Boston, so how would we be able to see each other? Deep breath. You're not going to freak out and act possessive. It was just a kiss. Okay, a glorious, perfect, absolutely mind-boggling first kiss. I press my top lip flat, but the smile is permanent.

"I'll walk you back to your room," Jeremy says. Isn't he going to invite me to his room to play video games at least? "I don't want to get you in too much trouble since you're not 'allowed' to be out with me tonight."

"I don't care what my roommate thinks." I wait for him to change direction, but unfortunately we arrive at my room.

"Goodnight, Monet." He leans in and kisses my cheek. His lips are a soft brush and then he and Derek are off. I sigh and unlock the door.

Shelley sits on the edge of her bed, staring at the door. She takes in my wet dress and her face twists up into a monstrous expression. Has she been sitting there the entire time?

She narrows her eyes. "You are so dead."

SEVENTEEN

I LAY IN bed, staring at the ceiling and listening for any movement from Shelley's side of the room. Does she have it in her to try and suffocate me in my sleep? Jeremy's kiss feels fresh on my face, like the imprint of his lips marked me. The hydro garden was so perfect.

I roll onto my side and face Shelley's bed. "Why do you want to win this contest so bad, anyway?"

She takes a long time to answer and I begin to think she might be asleep. "From the first time I heard his music, I got this feeling he was meant for me."

I got that feeling, too.

Her bedspread rustles and she turns on the parrot lamp on the nightstand. "Then when I got diagnosed with skin cancer right after his little sister got cured, I thought, I don't know...that we were meant to be together."

"I'm sorry. I didn't know you had cancer."

"Ah, it's okay now. I got treated at the facility in Boston. They grew a new patch of skin for me." She taps the end of her nose. "Can't even tell, no matter how close you look."

"I never would've guessed." I'm silent for a while, feeling guilty about being so happy over a kiss.

"I wish we had more dates." I feel like shit. I did have more dates. She sounds so sad, and I get it. One date makes you want more dates—a whole lifetime of dates that end with a big happily ever after.

"Are you worried about your show tomorrow?"

"No." Her answer surprises me. They sure did enough digging on me. She smiles at me like she has a secret and won't tell. Has she already seen the show? They'll probably focus on the cancer angle to play up how charitable the producers are, which will definitely not help my chances of winning.

I let out my breath. "So, are you going to smother me if I fall asleep?"

"As if. I'm not a killer."

Phew. "Just checking. Goodnight, then." I stay awake until her breathing regulates and I'm pretty sure she's asleep, just to be safe. Am I really in trouble with the date coordinators? Worry filters into my dreams and I spend more time flipping back and forth than actually sleeping.

———

There's a knock on the door at ten a.m. Shelley narrows her eyes and then answers. Absurdly, I think Jeremy might have come to say good morning to me. I imagine him with sleep-ruffled hair and sparkly, warm eyes. His lips soft on my neck—

"We're having a group meeting with all the girls in the viewing room in ten minutes to discuss the rules of the show. Everyone is required to attend." I don't recognize the guy at the door.

"That's hardly enough time to get ready," Shelley huffs.

I don't hear his reply. She slams the door. "Can you believe that? He just walked off like he didn't even hear me. Ten minutes. Who can make themselves presentable in ten minutes?"

I can. I brush my hair, slide on my jeans, and throw on a clean T-shirt. "Let's go."

Shelley makes a high-pitched growly noise. "We're only having this meeting because of you and your cheating."

Oh, shit. I wait the extra five minutes she takes to get ready so that we can walk down to the meeting together. I'm not exactly eager to get in trouble.

Eleanor waits with her clipboard in front of the conference table and we sit quietly while the other girls file in.

"All right, everyone help yourself to the donuts the restaurant has provided."

No one moves and I kind of want a donut, but I don't want to stand out if I'm already in trouble.

"It has come to my attention that a few of you are trying to spend extra time with Jeremy." Jasmine glares at me from across the table. Eleanor stares directly at one of the clones until she looks up. What does that mean? Is one of the other girls spending extra time with Jeremy, too? Then Eleanor shifts her focus to me. "While there are no prior rules forbidding this kind of activity, the producers have decided it is unfair. They want the TV audience to be able to see everything that transpires between Jeremy and the contestants, otherwise they won't be able to make informed votes."

Sounds like a lot of crap. If they wanted the audience to have all the info, they should've showed us at the café.

Eleanor takes a deep breath. "Which is why we are changing all of your room numbers and mixing up the pairs. I also don't want to find any of you hanging about the elevator trying to follow Jeremy around." She sets down the clipboard and the click echoes through the silent room. I bet the elevator comment referred to Jasmine. "Hand in your room keys now." I scramble in my back pocket for the disc that has been paired with my thumbprint.

"But our clothes and stuff are in our rooms," Shelley squeals.

"Weren't you told to move your suitcases out?"

"No," we mumble.

"All right, then turn in your current cards within an hour and pick up your new assignments at the front desk. After today's dates there will only be one more day. Jasmine, you have the last date tomorrow afternoon. We'll be staying here at the hotel until after the show at seven p.m. After that we're departing to New York City for the live studio broadcast of the first round of voting, followed by Jeremy's benefit concert."

I can't believe the dates are almost over.

"Now, I know you're all probably nervous about being up in front of so many people, but..." she pauses, a smile like a muted drum roll surrounding her words, "you'll all receive two hours with a professional makeup and clothing specialist."

Phew. One less thing to worry about. Across the table, Jasmine nods. I suppose that's the sort of treatment she expects.

"You're excused."

I hurry back to the elevator. Oh God, what if I get paired with Jasmine? I'll have to stay awake until we leave for New York.

Shelley packs her suitcase in silence, and I stuff my few belongings back into my tote bag. She has to wait for a bellboy to come help her carry her stuff, so I wave goodbye. We're not really friends, so I don't bother with anything more.

The receptionist gives me a new key. I don't see any of the other girls yet, so I assume they have more luggage and are waiting for help. I'm the first one into my new room. I wonder if Jeremy will be able to find me, and if they moved his room, too. I choose the bed by the window, which has a view of an apartment building. Not nearly as nice as my former sliver-of-water view.

I can't believe I'm only going to be in Key West for one more day. I wish I could've gone to the beach again. I wish I could've spent more time in that forest with Jeremy. How can I go back to plain old Boston and its stuffy, polluted air after this?

The door cracks open.

"Hello?" Praline pokes her head in. Our eyes meet. "Oh, thank God."

"Hey." I wave in greeting. Praline's not so bad. Probably not a killer.

"I'm so relieved it's you. I don't think I could deal with Jasmine and her friends. They're so...intimidating."

"I'm glad it's you and not Jasmine as well."

Praline makes a beeline for the open bed and flops forward, clutching the bedspread. She's speaking into the mattress.

"I can't understand anything you're saying."

She turns her head slightly. Hair is caught in her mouth. "My date is on tonight," she sobs.

"Oh, I'm sorry. All of us have something to hide, even if we don't know about it." I sit down on the bed across from hers.

"Yeah, but..." She breaks off, hiccupping and sobbing. "My secrets are *really* bad."

"I can't believe that. They tried to suggest I'm a boy."

"Right. Which no one in their right mind would ever believe, so they might as well have said nothing about you."

"I never thought of it that way. Thanks."

"Well, don't get used to me. I won't be in the final three."

"Come on now, you can't be sure of that."

"Monet, I'm a mental patient."

I laugh.

"I'm serious." She doesn't laugh.

"Oh."

"I was only in for six months. But during that time, I was pretty fat, too. I bet they've got horrendous videos from when I was committed."

"Shit, that sucks." I feel awkward asking, but... "What were you in for?"

She flops onto her back and blows her bangs out of her face. Then she pulls up her sleeve, holding her arm straight out for me. The long scar running from wrist to elbow is easy to make out. "I tried to kill myself over a boy." She drops the arm. "That, and I'm bi-polar, and I have an eating disorder."

I don't know what to say. I shift my legs underneath me. "It would be shitty of the producers to bring up any of that stuff."

She shrugs. "Who do you think was trying to spend extra time with Jeremy?"

Me. I'm sick to my stomach. I already feel bad for Praline, and I do not want to admit to secretly kissing Jeremy. She'll probably find out sooner or later. "I think they were referring to me. I, uh, Jeremy ran into me at the bar and he likes my drawings. Nothing big. He thinks one of them might work for a T-shirt design, so we were talking about that and then Jasmine showed up. You know how she can be."

"Oh, so you guys have stuff in common." She's not crying now, and I don't know if that's a good or bad sign.

"I guess."

"That's nice." Her voice cracks.

"Look, I'm really sorry." *Sorry about this whole contest.* "I'm so sick of being manipulated by this TV show." *I just want to be with Jeremy.* I pace to the window and back to the door. I try staring out the peephole into the hall. I haven't seen Jeremy all day. Not that we made any plans after last night, but I kind of thought he'd be around, or that we'd run into each other. Something. Anything.

"Are you going to the viewing room to watch the date?"

I almost want to tell her Jeremy doesn't appreciate us all watching his every move. But I don't. "I'm going to see if the hotel has a gym instead." I dip into the bathroom to splash water on my face before I go. Praline repetitively straightens her shirt at the door. I suddenly can't stand the curiosity. "Do you know what Jeremy's doing today?"

"Touring the coconut liquor plant this afternoon, and in the evening I think he's going on a gambling cruise."

I wish I hadn't asked. I want to do those things with him. I feel like a fist has slammed me in the chest, crunching my ribs in so that they press sharply on my heart. "Have a good day," I tell her.

She forces a smile and closes the door softly behind her. I'm not sure if I'm brave enough to go for another walk outside of the hotel. I scan in at the elevator and then grab a grilled veggie wrap to go. I eat in the hotel lobby, gazing out at the street. What are the chances that I'd get attacked twice? Slim, right?

"Monet."

"Oh, hey, Derek."

He shakes his head and laughs at me. "I hope you're not going out. These streets are apparently dangerous."

"I was just looking. I thought I might see if the hotel had a gym."

"They do. I can show you where, or if you still want to go out, I can tag along."

"I'd definitely rather be outside. Suck in all the clean air I can get before the show ends."

I finish my last bite of sandwich and place a hand on the wall to steady me while I stretch my quads.

"Running has got to be better than watching Jeremy make out with other girls."

Derek shrugs. "I'm sure he's not making out with them all." *Very comforting, thanks.*

"Do you run?"

He narrows his eyes and grins wide. "What do you have in mind?"

"A race. Flat out. We jog for one hour and then we race back."

His face gets serious. "That's a lot of running."

"Not up for it?"

He comes over to the wall and starts his own stretching exercises. "I take winning very seriously."

"So do I."

He sets his watch for one hour and we set off down the sidewalk, dodging pedestrians until the tourists thin out. Pounding my feet to the ground and focusing helps block out the idea of Jeremy drinking coconut liquor with another girl. I keep my head up, pulling the clean air deep into my lungs. We pass blank offices and apartments all towering in the clean air dome. I can't stop watching for the four guys who attacked me, wondering if they're waiting down another street corner. Derek would kick their asses. He has military numbers stamped on his arm, and even though he can't be much older than Jeremy, I bet he's frighteningly lethal.

"What branch of the military?" I pant out.

"Army, reserves right now." His voice shakes less than mine.

I wipe the sweat off my forehead. "Specialty?"

"Shooting things, ordering people around, kicking ass." He pauses between words as his feet hit the ground.

I nod, impressed. I wonder if Jeremy sent him down to the lobby to check on me.

"That's an hour." Derek grabs his knees, gasping for breath. "I think you're trying to kill me."

"Nope. I'm hoping you'll say nice things to Jeremy about me."

He chuckles in between pants. "Like you need it. He's obviously into you."

Joy skitters through my limbs and my exhaustion melts away. I could run forever—high on the confirmation that Jeremy likes me. I sprint back toward the hotel.

"Hey!" Derek's feet pound the pavement behind me, but he doesn't have enough breath to argue. I touch the hotel wall a good five seconds before he does, and, amazingly, don't throw up.

We stumble into the hotel bar, breathless. Fifteen minutes pass before my heart rate slows to normal again.

"I can't believe I won." A hostess ushers a well-dressed couple past us. The girl narrows her eyes at my sweaty appearance, but I take a seat at the bar.

Derek wipes his forehead on his arm. The attendant brings us water. "Nice, rub it in some more, why don't you?"

"I won. Woo-hoo!" I wiggle back and forth on the barstool.

Derek spits water around a startled laugh. "You're an easy person to like. I hope Jeremy picks you."

"What about the other girls, who do you think is doing the best?" *Ooh. Insider information.*

"I liked the one with the levitating boobs." He pushes a few buttons on the menu screen. "After you, Jeremy probably likes one of the brunette lookalikes. That's his usual type. Oh, but not that one that leaped into the elevator with him the other night. She's a bitch with a capital B." *He must mean Jasmine.* "He said something about the girl he's going out with tonight.

Saw her interview and wants to see how lucky she is at cards."

"Oh, does Jeremy play?"

"Eh, you know how it is. What rich guy doesn't like to gamble? It's like saying f-you to the money gods."

Huh. I can't imagine ever wasting money. So that's one bad thing about Jeremy. Not the having money, but the taking it for granted. So this other girl is rich, too, and they have shared interests. They'll have a great time at the floating casino. I nod casually. Not like I'm fuming with jealousy. Three brunette clones and me, guess that's what he likes, but finding Jeremy has a type and that I fit the mold isn't as reassuring as I thought it would be. Having a type means he's dated a lot. Hopefully I'm special enough to stand out.

"It must be hard watching Jeremy get all the girls."

Derek raises his eyebrows high. "I actually don't do too bad myself."

"I bet the two of you are trouble."

"Nah, Jeremy's a softie."

I take another drink. As the adrenaline from our run fades, I start to worry more and more about Praline. "I should probably go comfort my roomie before the show starts tonight. Thanks for the run."

"I can *almost* say it was a pleasure."

I shake my head and smile as I walk away. How much fun will Jeremy have at the casino tonight? Only a few more days to go and then the final three will be selected.

I find Praline camped out on one of the big couches. Her eyes and face are a puffy red and she's gripping a bag of gummy candy in her fist.

"Want company?" I ask. She sniffles and I take a seat next to her. "It'll be okay. Jeremy's a good guy, he's not going to care about whatever they dredge up."

"What about the audience? They're the ones voting on us."

"I'm sure Jeremy has a way to influence the votes."

She nods, but looks doubtful. My logic's not crazy, right? I'll ask Jeremy when I see him again, just to be safe. The other girls show up a few minutes before the show starts. The atmosphere has all the joy of an open casket funeral, with Praline starring as the soon-to-be corpse.

Her expectations are not wrong. Midway through the show an image of her is blown up. She's thirty pounds heavier, her hair dry and tangled, but the biggest shocker is the crazed look in her eyes. I saw a show once with a horse and a burning barn. Praline's eyes have that desperate, white-edged appearance. She squeezes my arm as the image stays on. I count silently in my head, willing them to move on. Thirty seconds pass before they start talking about her time in the institution. It's an awkward amount of time for the picture to be seared into our heads.

When they show an interview with the guy Praline tried to kill herself over, I begin to think my episode wasn't so bad. The old love, Aaron, starts talking about whichever girl he's with now and the tears pour out of Praline so fast a wet patch forms down the entire front of her shirt.

I grab Praline's elbow and haul her up. "We're leaving."

"But, but, the show isn't over yet."

"You don't need to see this crap. You're over him, right? It's in the past?" She nods and I stand in front of the TV to block her view. "Good, then let's go." Jasmine gives me a parting smirk and I notice Shelley on the other couch with one of the clones.

"If y'all are going, I'm not staying, either." Erin smiles up at us in solidarity.

"All of us should leave," I say.

Claire straightens up in her chair. "I, uh, I get what you're saying, but I still want to try to get to the end."

Most of the others shift around, watching the TV and hoping I won't single them out.

"Whatever." I head for the door. They're idiots if they think following the rules of the producers will endear them to Jeremy.

"I think we're required to watch," Praline says as I yank her away.

"You had a date with Jeremy. You already won." If I keep telling other people that, maybe I'll start to believe it myself.

Praline and I spend the rest of the night in our room listening to Jeremy's music. I wait and wait for Jeremy to show up at the door, but he never does.

EIGHTEEN

THE NEXT MORNING when I arrive at the viewing room, a sign hangs from the door panel. CLOSED FOR CLEANING. I try scanning my card, but the knob doesn't turn. Eleanor arrives after me.

"I was just going to put up a sign for you girls. No more viewing room: the timeline has moved up because of a tropical cyclone off the coast of Haiti. So head on back to your room and pack your bags."

"But what about Jasmine's date?"

"She's on it right now. Don't worry, you'll see the footage when the show airs."

"They're not letting Jeremy snorkel in severe weather, are they?"

"The people running the underwater tour assured us that it's fine to swim in the rain. They'll pull him out if the lightning starts."

Real comforting. "When are we leaving?"

She shoos me away with her hand. "One hour. Hurry, hurry. Tell your roommate, too, and anyone else you see in the hall. We need to be on that plane and out of here."

I trudge back to the room. What a letdown.

Praline is still in the bathroom when I get back and I tell her the situation through the door. She starts packing furiously. I've never seen a tropical cyclone before. I know they're dangerous and life threatening and all of that, but the idea of truly severe weather fascinates me. No matter how much control I think I have over my life, a cyclone of wind and rain could rip it all away in seconds. I feel like if I looked into the center of a storm, I'd understand all the chaos of life. Boston doesn't get much for severe weather, and so far freezing my ass off in the snow hasn't led to any snippets of enlightenment.

I offer to help Praline with her stuff, but she waves me off, and I go sit in the hall with my tote bag. I hope Jeremy's safe. I take out my purple bikini and trace my finger over the words "Key West." I savor the memory of Jeremy's face when he floated me on his hands in the water. Now that I know what his lips feel like, I add kissing to the memory, and try hard to forget the part where I slammed my butt into the ocean bottom.

The other girls trickle out in a frantic mess. Shelley has her luggage tied together, so that she can drag all the bags at once. Jaime whines about not having had enough time in the bathroom. One of her eyes is brown, so I assume the other purple lens is still in her contact lens solution. Claire's the most composed, except for the tiny tick in her jaw. I can only imagine how much worse it would be if they all still had their phones. At least this way they can only complain to each other. I hate having to listen to other people's calls, especially when as soon as they hang up they call someone else so that they can have the exact same conversation all over again. No matter how high schools change the rules to limit interruptions, technology advancements are always faster, and I'm so honestly sick of it all, I'll probably never make any close female friends. Or date.

I wait for Praline to emerge, and then we all scan in one final time at the elevator. The process moves quickly. There's a drop box for room keys, and as soon as I place my disc in the slot, Eleanor screams at us to load onto the shuttle. I want to ask about Jasmine, but maybe if I keep my mouth shut, we'll leave her behind.

Outside, rain falls in heavy diagonal lines. Gray haze eats at the top of the storm clouds and the air is oddly stinky. Mildewed. "Ew," Praline mumbles, "I hate when they take down the dome."

Oh. "Why do they do that?" I ask her.

"Budget cuts. I guess it costs a ton to maintain a barrier like that with all the wind and rain disrupting the signal. Besides, they always claim everyone is inside during major storms, so it serves no purpose."

"I know this sounds stupid, but I kind of thought the dome was a permanent, physical structure."

"Hey, that's not stupid. I used to think that, too, but I read a lot while I was in the institution." She forces a laugh. "I find civil engineering fascinating."

"Now that *is* insane." I nudge her arm so she knows I'm joking. We dash from the overhang entrance to the shuttle. Eleanor checks off our names as we take our seats. No Jasmine. I expect Jeremy to be in a separate vehicle from us, but Jasmine...

The wind rocks the shuttle back and forth. Is it safe to fly in this weather? I press my fingers hard into the seat bottom as the shuttle revs. I need to see Jeremy. Even for a second, just a glimpse so that I know he's okay. I watch the hotel entrance, waiting. *Please be okay.*

Derek slips out with a pile of luggage and hugs the wall to keep under the awning. I recognize the signature black box that Jeremy's gaming system was in. A moment later, a limo pulls to the curb. Jasmine pops out and runs to the shuttle. She has a sleek black raincoat over her shoulders. Underneath, she's wearing a bikini made of shells. I'm not close enough to check, but I'm fairly sure her breasts are encased in perfect clamshells like in a Renaissance painting. She looks like a goddess. Eleanor hands her a blanket from the overhead compartment and I go back to watching the limo.

Jeremy's hair is plastered to his forehead as he emerges. He grabs the top two suitcases from Derek and they both run to the open trunk. His hair and skin are even brighter next to the gray weather. I press the palm of my hand against the window, wishing I could hug him, kiss him, just once more. Then we're off. The driver speeds down the street Derek and I ran along, and then we turn off and zip toward the airport.

We load onto the plane with Eleanor yelling constantly about hurrying and staying in line. The white leather couches Jeremy sat on during the first flight are empty, but he left after us, so he'll probably arrive in a second. "Buckle in. It doesn't matter where you sit." A flight attendant goes over how to use the life vests and oxygen masks, which is very unsettling since we didn't receive those instructions the first time.

I keep waiting in my seat for another glimpse of Jeremy, but the world is not cooperating with me. He must be on the plane by now. I know he's not avoiding me. I mean, he couldn't be.

The plane bounces through the sky in a series of jerks and drops. Jaime pukes into a bag and Mel complains constantly. Well, if the plane crashes I won't have to worry about the Fluxem cure anymore. Though it would be nice to kiss Jeremy again before I die. When we land in Newark, New Jersey, I'm still expecting Jeremy to open the curtain between his part of the plane and ours. Even when we climb down the stairs and onto the tarmac, I'm sure he'll be right there waiting.

He isn't.

When we pull into the Blue Finn Inn, I start to feel particularly desperate. Even I know the difference between a nice hotel like the last one, and a cheap-ass inn like this one. The whole place feels abandoned. Jeremy isn't here and I'm pretty sure he won't be staying at this establishment.

Mel stands in the open door of the hotel transport. "Are they sticking us somewhere cheap to cut costs, or what?"

Jasmine pushes past her. "Why aren't we in New York City?" I shrug. With the final show and concert being in the city, it would have made sense for us to stay close by.

"Maybe the ratings suck," Jaime says, hunching into her jacket.

I wait next to the vehicle, appraising the one-story, flat-roofed inn. No one builds single-story buildings anymore, so the place has to be at least fifty years old. To preserve what's left of the green space, the government started really limiting building permits. Boston was already too built up to notice the difference. In the suburbs however, residents were pissed. Many were making money subdividing their lots and letting people build in what had been their backyards. The idea makes sense to me. There's all that empty space in the sky, might as well go up.

Around the inn, puddles are slick with oil on the pavement. Rain mists down on us, destined to get worse as the storm works its way up the coast. Across the street, a twelve-foot, barbed-wire fence cuts through the industrial landscape. An Air Force sign hangs at an angle from the post closest to us. Behind the fence, weeds sprout through the concrete in tall patches. Well, it could be worse. The place isn't that bad, a little old, but plenty big enough.

Eleanor exits the transport last and wrinkles her nose. "Okay, then. Welcome to Newark." She doesn't conceal the inadvertent grunt that escapes her throat. "We're here for six days, girls, while the rest of the world watches the dates. The studio thought it best for you not to be recognized on the street by anyone. So, in their infinite wisdom, here we are."

Jasmine narrows her eyes. "This location was not in the paperwork I signed. My lawyer read through those documents and he wouldn't have let me come *here*."

"Look, Jasmine, I don't have control over the show. Either you want to be in this or you don't. By all means, have your lawyer come pick you up if you'd like to withdraw from the competition." Eleanor straightens her rain jacket. "Anyone else have a problem?"

Everyone stays silent.

"We'll keep the same room assignments, since Jeremy won't be here for you to worry about." She takes a look at us and then at the motel, shaking her head.

Great. Having Jeremy nearby is the only thing that makes living with these girls tolerable. Well, that and the hotel restaurant, because I bet the food here isn't going to be anything like Key West.

Checking into the inn takes a while. They don't have a modern scan system and the person in charge is about one hundred and fifteen. The old lady types in each of our names with shaking fingers and provides a plastic card. I feel like I'm in an old movie.

Six days. I bet this was in the producers' plan from the beginning. This is the twenty-five percent they're donating to cancer research. They didn't take it out of their own paychecks; they just downsized our comfort level. I shrug. I've lived in worse places.

I wiggle the key in the lock of our door and push it open. The door catches on burnt orange carpet. I press harder, until the opening is wide enough for Praline to drag in her suitcase. Floral bedspreads contrast sharply with the wall art—abstract paintings from China.

I leave the door open, letting the stale, mildewy air out. Praline sits on her bed in a serious depressive funk. She slips the bracelet Jeremy gave her from one wrist to the other. Her head tips back against the glued-up headboard, and her entire face droops like weights are attached to every feature. "Your show wasn't that bad," I tell her.

She doesn't move. A wired phone in the corner gives two buzzes. I pick up the antique device and fit it against my head. So weird. *Eleanor*, I mouth to Praline.

She sounds irritated. "This is the situation. The hotel doesn't even have room service, so in a half-hour we're taking a field trip to the local supermarket to get enough supplies for the week." The phone clicks off.

"What'd she want?" Praline asks in a monotone voice.

"We're going to the market. There's nothing to eat here."

When Praline nods, her head bangs against the headboard.

"Come on, get out of bed." The carpet squishes as I walk over and prop her upright.

Praline nods slightly.

"Up. Up. You want to eat, don't you?"

"Not really."

Oh, man. Suck it up. This is a competition. "Too bad. And if you don't cheer up, I'll trade rooms and make you stay with Jasmine." That finally motivates her.

"Hold on, I gotta get my shoes."

We climb onto the shuttle with the other girls. I shift in my seat, checking out the landscape as we cruise down an empty road. I had no idea there were parts of the country largely uninhabited. The news always focuses on the over-population problem. I've seen tons of footage of clusters of people and buildings, plus all the warnings about scarcity of food and skin-eroding pollution. But I've never heard about abandoned parts of the country. There's probably a reason there aren't many permanent residents here, leaking nuclear waste buried underground giving everyone cancer, or something even worse. Boston is looking pretty good.

Kreeger's Market has a glass front and three stories. I'm a little excited. I wonder what sort of budget they gave Eleanor for us. I can't imagine the other girls would be content with a diet of veggie-spread sandwiches. I bet the producers are trying to protect themselves from getting sued by bringing us all to the supermarket. No one can say they weren't fed if we have the opportunity to pick out our own food.

The ten of us, tromping through the aisles, don't look like we belong, except for me. They're more like misplaced fashion models. We end up with a lot of prepared food. Vitamin bars, bread, and chips—all of the essential nutrients, no need for cooking. Eleanor picks out these ready-heat mac and cheese containers. When you rip away the metal wire on the bottom there's a short burst of heat that cooks the pasta. I've never had one, but I've seen the commercial on TV. I'm surprised when she scans three bags of oranges into the cart. I watch the dollar increment on the handle shoot up.

And so begins six days of hell.

Jeremy doesn't call. No one knows where he's staying. Presumably in New York. The Fluxem splotch on my back spreads. A third one starts on my hip, right on the side I usually sleep on, so I spend half the night trying to get comfortable and then sleep like crap. The room smells weird, and I can't tell if it's just the hotel or if I'm starting to smell like a basement, too. The weather gets worse as the storm moves up the coast. Horizontal rain pelts the roof of the inn, destroying my sleep even more.

Every night another contestant gets knocked down in front of the world. The Blue Finn Inn isn't equipped with a viewing room, so we all crowd together in Eleanor's room for the show. A single camera films us, but I doubt the footage will be usable. Shelley Anne has weight issues, but the majority of her episode focuses on her battle with skin cancer. Mel is a pill addict. Brie drinks, smokes, and plays in an underground gambling ring. I try to gauge Jeremy's reaction to her after what Derek said about their shared interest in throwing away money. Jeremy flashes his devilish half-smile throughout the date, but I can't tell if he's flirting or just pleased with his cards. With the amount of chips he lays down on the table, I assume he's being dealt killer hands. I never thought of one vice being more attractive than another. Maybe I should have been picking out more glamorous, slightly illegal hobbies other than scratching. Brie is far cooler than me. After her show, I almost want to talk to her and find out more. Her dirty secrets are so much more exciting than mine.

The studio couldn't have planned a better mix of messed up girls—but then, they probably *did* plan them. Bastards. As the days pass, I start to obsess about Jasmine's secret. She still doesn't seem worried. Every night she watches the episodes with a detached calm, smirking and silently passing judgment. On day four, I'm convinced she's managed to bribe a producer. All my missing Jeremy energy is devoted to fantasies of her downfall.

Then her show airs.

The familiar words flash across the screen—*Who will win a date with a rockstar?*

Rod Bing sits down behind the desk and the audience claps. His scarf is black and white stripes. "Tonight, the last contestant's date and secret will be revealed."

Here we go. What I've been waiting for. Jasmine slammed down a notch.

"Meet contestant number ten, Jasmine." She enters the interview room with calm poise. She's polished. Dictionary perfect.

Get on with it, bring out the dirt. Praline's hands are balled like she's thinking the same thing. Even the clones eagerly lean forward, waiting for the gossip. The show continues. Blah, blah. Jasmine loves Jeremy's music and is overwhelmed by his attractiveness. She only hopes she can be "worthy of his attention."

Rod Bing widens one eye. Here we go. "Now, we didn't know this at the time Jasmine was selected, and her modesty does her credit..." A picture of a little boy and girl fills the screen. Their arms are linked and the boy has mud up to his knees. I guess their age to be around five, the boy is missing a front tooth and smiles a familiar smile. I fill with dread. A big hand flips the photo over and then the camera pans up to show a woman who's an exact older replica of Jasmine. The focus shifts back to the writing on the back of the photo.

Jasmine and Jeremy age five, Whisper Creek.

There's a collective gasp in the room. My ears are ringing, but the noise does nothing to block out the TV.

"Jeremy was always hanging around our house when he and Jasmine were little." Jasmine's mom leans in like she's going to tell the camera a secret. "I think he had a bit of a crush on her." My knuckles crack as my hands tighten into fists. I want to cry. Please let them have actual bad stuff about her. This can't be it. "When he moved away, I know we all missed him. I think it's a blessing that the two can be reunited on the show." The picture fills the screen again. Jeremy as a little boy. What a cutie. And Jasmine...she was beautiful even then. Tears prickle my eyes.

The screen shifts to Jasmine at the hotel. No wonder she's been so smug. They filmed her while we were all going through hell, wondering what was going to be revealed. I'm furious. I'm beyond furious. She has the nerve to accuse me of cheating. The footage only gets worse.

"Why didn't you reveal you knew Jeremy in the initial interview?"

"I didn't want him to feel obligated to pick me. I wanted him to see me for who I've become these long years we've been apart." She drops her gaze modestly. What an actress.

"That was taking a bit of a chance," the interviewer says.

"I'm a fairly confident person, and I had faith there'd still be a spark between us."

Rod Bing turns away from the viewing screen behind the desk. "After the commercial break, witness whether or not there's still that spark."

I stare at Jasmine. She flicks her black hair over her shoulder with perfectly manicured fingers. Mel crosses her arms and slides to the other end of the bed. Jasmine doesn't need friends, she's apparently got Jeremy.

On screen, a boat cuts through choppy water, heading away from a dock. Jeremy and Jasmine stand at the back, looking worried. Cut to the onboard camera. "Is it safe to snorkel in this weather?" Jasmine asks, yelling over the noise of the engine and wind.

"Oh, sure, sure. No worries." The tour guide hands her a lifejacket and goggles. Jeremy shrugs and takes his set with a smile. The camera zooms in on Jasmine's perfect bottom as she pushes off the edge of the boat into the water. The tour guide follows them in and motions them away from the boat. This time it looks like Jeremy has a camera mounted to his shoulder. They do quick cuts of the waves rising and falling around him, with Jasmine's scared face looking back at him. It would've been nice if they'd spent as much time on the production of my date. Then maybe they wouldn't have missed every romantic thing Jeremy said.

"Keep swimming!" the tour guide yells, pointing into the distance. "The turtles are this way." Jeremy ducks underwater. A turtle swims close and then angles away. Jasmine's legs are long and slender under the water as Jeremy swims forward. The rain picks up, and from Jeremy's camera I can't see the guide anymore. He slips below the surface again, and it's easier to make out where Jasmine is in the water from underneath. Her legs spiral around, kicking furiously. I can sense her panic from the rapid flailing of her legs.

Jeremy gurgles as a wave crashes over his head.

This can't be safe.

He swims hard for her. From the boat, his dark brown hair is barely visible as he bobs toward Jasmine. He ducks under again as a turtle skims Jasmine's leg. When he comes up, even at a distance, I hear her screams.

Then he's there. He takes her in his arms. Her lips are trembling and she's gulping for air. "Calm down, calm down," Jeremy says over and over again as he pushes her hair out of her face. The goggles are hanging loosely around her neck. She's scared, and she's beautiful, and I want to die. The waves knock them back and forth. Then the guide shouts to swim back to the boat. Jasmine shakes her head no.

"It's too dangerous for the boat to get any closer!" Jeremy yells. She shakes her head no again, eyes wide with terror. He takes her arms and hooks them around his neck so that she's on top of his back. Then he swims, towing her behind. At the boat, the guide climbs in first and Jeremy hands Jasmine to him before climbing in himself. In the last scene, Jasmine huddles in a towel with Jeremy's arm around her.

There goes the end of the competition.

Jasmine wins.

She wins the whole damn thing. How can the audience not vote for her? I imagine the show playing out in the studio execs' minds—childhood sweethearts reunited, a gut-wrenching date, romance in every second. Then, during the final three show, she reveals to Jeremy who she really is. A teary embrace and the end of Jeremy and me. The rest of the contestants— nothing but gossip-worthy distractions. I can't even see how the audience would vote me into the final three with all the kissing that's been happening on the different dates.

"Congratulations, Jasmine," I say, and leave the room.

NINETEEN

THE REST OF the night passes in a blur. I'm depressed. Not even the promise of getting a mini makeover can cushion the blow of Jasmine's date. In my dreams, turtles nibble my legs and I sink to the bottom of the ocean. Over my head, Jasmine and Jeremy embrace while I struggle for air.

I wake up and sling my tote bag over my shoulder. I'm ready to get the hell out of here. The ten of us are taking a shuttle all the way to New York. I press my forehead against the cool window as the landscape wizzes by. Outside of the city, a huge growth dome towers next to the highway. A line of tractor trailer trucks wait to take the exit ramp. The circular building has clear plastic panels held in place by a large steel grid overlaying the whole thing. Solar cells pop off the top like big vents. The dome probably supplies enough produce for the whole state. A pod skims the outside of the structure and drops out of sight, another ride for the tourists. If I ever visited outside of the show, I'd save my money and watch the virtual version.

The shuttle slows for the upcoming brake lights. A digital sign flashes about accidents up ahead. I overhear the driver talking about flooding. Jasmine's quiet, smug smiles grate on my nerves.

The entrance into New York is jammed solid. We're in the outer lane and I can see the lower branches of the bridge, with cars so close together they might as well be a magnetic train. Below the cars, grayish-brown water sloshes back and forth. I wonder if the politicians ever thought about trying to put a clean air dome over New York or just decided that the city was too far gone. From the advertisements flashing along the bridge supports, I'd guess they've sunk all the taxpayer dollars into building up their entertainment infrastructure.

Once we're inside the city, I'm reminded of Boston. Tall buildings, stained black from exhaust, are framed by the mass of people moving along the sidewalk like one giant wave. No pigeon traps, though. We round the corner and dead in front of us there's a fifty-foot forest—or at least, the likeness of one. A Bank One banner hangs off one of the projected trees.

Another turn and we arrive at the Sheridan Luxury Deluxe and check into paradise. This hotel is even more amazing than the one in Key West. The reservation counter occupies the middle of a vast open space. Clear elevators slide silently up and down the twenty-story interior walls. Maybe the show's ratings have improved and they've decided we're worth more money.

When we get upstairs, there are fruit baskets on our beds and notes containing our stylist's name and appointment time for tomorrow. I have Monique. I bet she'll make a joke about the similarity of our names. I look over at Praline, who's been practically catatonic since the Jasmine episode. She repeatedly pokes her finger into the cellophane covering her basket. The hopeful momentum of the show has been replaced by the uneasy feeling we've been set up to fail. I can't even fantasize about punching Jasmine anymore if Jeremy truly likes her.

A 3-D image comes to life on the desk. "Hotel reception. Is there a Monet available for a phone call?" *Jeremy?*

"Oh, hi, Mom."

"Don't sound so excited. The contestant coordinator called and gave me your new room number. Are you too busy?"

"No. It's fine."

"What's wrong this time?"

"You saw the show."

"Ah, Jasmine's her name, right?"

"Yeah." I want to cry again.

"Here's the thing, honey. That was more than ten years ago. Do you still want to date Fritz Schneckle?"

"Mom, you know how bad that kid turned out."

"Exactly. The kid you hold hands with in first grade isn't the one you marry."

"But the date. You saw how he saved her."

"All I saw was a young man who's conscientious enough not to let some girl drown. That tour guide should be brought up on charges. Really, who would push those kids off a boat in that weather?"

"The show coordinator probably paid him to."

"I can't say I think much of these people."

Yeah, me neither. "I gotta go, Mom. I've got an early appointment with a stylist and I need to try to sleep." Or search the halls for Jeremy.

"Good luck tomorrow, honey."

I take the elevator to the first floor and begin walking. The hotel is laid out in one big circle. I stride down corridor after corridor, slowly circling my way up. I've probably covered three miles by the time I find Derek in the hallway.

"Monet." He tucks his handheld screen back into his pocket. "I heard they sent you to New Jersey. Jeremy had me asking everyone where they'd hidden you girls away."

"Blue Finn Inn." Which girls specifically was he trying to find? That almost implies that he has a relationship going with more than one of us.

Derek cracks his knuckles and then stretches his back. He's totally oblivious to how worried he just made me. "Never heard of it. Nice place?"

"I wouldn't say that." I twist my hair into a knot. Once I see Jeremy, I'm sure he'll clear this up. Maybe he's friends with another one of the girls, but still likes me.

He laughs, but makes no move to invite me into the room.

"So, uh, can I see Jeremy for a minute?"

Derek scratches his fingers through his buzzed hair. When he tips down, I notice a lightning strike shaved into the top. "The thing is, the studio is paying me to sit out here and make sure none of the girls get a chance to see him before the show tomorrow night."

"Don't you work for Jeremy, though?"

"They offered a BIG bonus." He holds his large hands wide apart in the air. "They wouldn't even let him go to his New York apartment yet. Said there was something in his contract."

Damn, that's motivation I can understand. "Any idea why it's so important for him to be in lockdown?" The long hotel corridor looks safe enough. No loiterers except me.

"They didn't tell me." He shrugs. "Escape prevention?"

"Why, you think he wants to get out of doing the show?"

"Absolutely. It's no fun dumping girls, and tomorrow night he has to watch seven girls get eliminated all at once. You'd have to be a cold bastard not to be affected by that." It never occurred to me how shitty the process would be for Jeremy. All my thoughts have been about making it to the next round. Now I feel selfish.

Derek shifts his legs out straight and digs in his pocket. "Here, before I forget." He hands me a bank chip. "Jeremy said to tell you since the production people didn't have a tax form filled out for you, you'll be responsible for reporting the income yourself. Let me think...what was the rest of the message?" I hold the little metal disc carefully in my hand. I have no idea how much it's worth. "Oh, right. And the merchandise guy loved the design, blah, blah, and wants to meet with you after this is all over."

"Do you know how much is on the chip?"

Derek shrugs. "How should I know?"

I give a last, longing look at the closed door. Derek shakes his head seriously. "Don't even try."

I backtrack down the hallway to find the ATM I noticed on the first floor. My steps are bouncy and strong. I sold a design! The Metal Society has presumably sold my art in the past, but I've never known anything about those deals. This feels more like I'm an adult making my own money. Plus, since I'm dirt poor, no matter what the amount on the chip is, I'll feel successful. Maybe it'll get me closer to having enough for the cure.

I take the glass elevator to the bottom floor. I'm holding money in my hand and I don't even know how much it is. Like a winning lottery ticket that I haven't scratched yet. The elevator can't slide through the floors fast enough. When the door dings open I want to run to the machine, but I'm afraid I'll look like a criminal if I do. Instead, I take normal-sized steps and maintain slow breaths.

I slide my chip through the scanner at the bottom of the machine and wait. My balance isn't shown on the screen as a safety precaution. *Withdraw funds.* I punch in enough to buy a present for Mom and wait to see how much the receipt says I have left.

I hold my fifty dollars and the slip of paper in my hand.

Remaining balance, 24,450.

I stagger to one of the couches in the lobby and collapse. I hold the cure for Fluxem in my hand. I just earned enough money to cure myself. In all my fantasies, I never cast myself with the ability to solve my own problems. Maybe I had this strength all along.

I skip all the way back to the room. I'll get the series of shots when I return to Boston. That should be soon enough. I rub the spot on my back. Ouch. Okay, it's only a few more days. Suddenly, my life is filling up with possibilities. I don't have to betray my feelings for Jeremy by asking him for money. He solved my problems after all, and not just by feeling sorry for me. Actually, in a way, I solved my own problems. I worked for this and I succeeded. I love the world. I'm bursting with happiness.

I have the chip in my hand, and that one thing has made all of this worthwhile. And Jeremy. If this ends badly, I still have the money for a cure. I can't stop smiling. Now, if only I could be Fluxem free and have Jeremy.

Back in the room, Praline takes in my bouncy temperament and slams a chocolate-covered strawberry into her mouth. "What made you so cheery?"

I can't explain any of this to her. But for me, for my life, this little chip in my hand solves everything.

That night, I dream Jeremy and I are at one of his houses. I have a huge sheet of metal painted black. I sit in the center, scratching a design. "Is that me?" Jeremy asks. "It's us," I reply. He crawls across the marks and kisses up my arm, neck, and finally face. "I love it."

"Wake up call for room 4013." The 3-D receptionist materializes on the desk next to me.

"I'm up." I yawn as the receptionist fades away.

Praline is face-down in bed, sheets and candy wrappers twisted around her legs. "When is your appointment?" I ask loudly.

No response.

"If you miss your appointment, Eleanor will be pissed."

Still no response. I climb out of bed, stretch, and walk over to Praline's bed. I place my hand on her shoulder and shake her back and forth. "Get–"

Her arm flops lifelessly over the edge of the bed.

"Praline!" I flip her onto her back, fumbling along her neck for a pulse.

"Medical Aid Emergency," I scream into the room. The sensor in the corner picks up the words and automatically contacts the EMTs. Praline's holding a bottle of pills in her other hand. Her skin's still warm.

"Praline?" I slap her cheeks over and over again.

A pre-recorded voice echoes through the room. "If the person is not breathing, begin chest compressions now. Help is on the way."

I do as I'm told, compressing her sternum and pausing as the voice counts for me.

"If you're alone in the room, do not panic. Help is coming."

I breathe air into her, watching her chest rise and hoping like crazy my saliva stays in my own mouth.

"Average response time is four minutes. Three have passed. Hold on." The recorded voice sounds so calm. I should have said more to her last night. I should've comforted her better after the show. My arms shake as I try desperately to fix her. *Please, just breathe.*

"EMTs. Open up." The door busts open before I take my hands off Praline's chest. "Step back, ma'am. We'll take it from here."

"There's a pill bottle." I point to the spot on the bed where the bottle rolled when I flipped her over. One of them grabs the bottle while the other fits a mask over Praline's face. The tech reads the pill bottle into her headset. I don't recognize the name of the drug. Electrodes are stuck to Praline's temples and chest, monitoring her vitals.

"Delivering level two shock."

The other tech has a panel strapped to his arm. Numbers and lines flash across the screen as the electrodes report out Praline's vital statistics. Her chest rises once.

"We've got a beat."

Two more techs come in with a hover bed. Praline's shifted from the bed to the cot. They tuck her limp arms in along her sides and then they're gone, running down the hallway while I stand at the door. I slide to the floor and cry. None of this is worth dying for.

Claire opens a door down the hallway and looks out. "Monet? What's going on? I heard a bunch of yelling."

"Praline...she...she... Praline tried to kill herself." I mash my palms into my eyes, pressing the tears away. "I woke up and she was unconscious."

"Oh, no!" Claire crosses the hall and sits at my side, gripping my hand. "Is she still alive?"

"I don't know." We sit in silence. When Eleanor and the others show up, I let Claire tell the story. In my mind, Praline's arm hangs off the edge of the bed, the black bracelet Jeremy gave her still locked on her wrist. A candy wrapper flutters to the ground, over and over.

TWENTY

ELEANOR LEADS ME down the hall to meet with my stylist. "Praline will be fine. Just a minor incident."

I tighten my jaw.

"Really," Eleanor insists. "I'm sure she'll be back on her feet in no time. She'd want you to go on with the show."

I know her words are bullshit, so I don't bother to respond. I'm pretty sure if Praline had the choice, the other nine of us would drop out of the contest and she'd win. I'm also pretty sure Eleanor hasn't received any information on Praline's condition, because she just showed up. So much for Eleanor being a secret ally. The only side she's on is the producers'. I was a fool to think otherwise.

The salon has a black and white marble floor. Monique's red leather heels clip clop when she walks closer. "What's wrong with her?" she asks Eleanor.

"Oh, rough morning." She nudges me forward. Rough morning? That so doesn't cover it.

"Well, then, let's get started. Do you need coffee, honey?"

"Why not?" I mumble.

"That's the spirit." She hands me a white porcelain cup that matches the décor. I gulp the too hot liquid and the burn makes me feel better. Eleanor waves goodbye and Monique gives me a once over. "Where to start?" she says under her breath. "Skin pigment? Hair?"

"No," I tell her. "I'm fine with my current coloring."

"All right, go ahead and put on this robe and we'll start with a mud wrap."

I gulp and glance around, making sure we're alone. "I have some open Fluxem sores. I don't want to contaminate anything."

She takes a step back from me. I hold my hand out to take the fluffy white robe. *That's my condition, deal with it.*

"Uh, most everything is disinfected. I just need to check with my boss." She backs away, taking the robe with her. If I wasn't so numb I might actually care.

I wait.

There's a big, steaming basin of mud on the other side of the room. Presumably the mud wrap that I won't be receiving. I walk over and stick my finger into the sludge. Something rubs up against it. Yikes!

A small fish surfaces and dives back under. Nasty. I don't even know what the fish are supposed to do to your skin. For once I think being contagious works in my favor.

Monique returns, all smiling like there's nothing wrong. "Okay, let's get you off to hair and makeup." I convince her not to attack my long brown hair with shears. She looks very disappointed as she tucks them away. Theoretically, I know synthetic hair feels the same, but I'd just as soon keep mine real and not plastic. When she pulls out a little needle tool and closes in on my eyebrows, I have to duck to the side to avoid a permanent makeup tattoo.

The selection in wardrobe is more fun to sort through. With a few clicks, Monique has the rack displaying fifteen different outfits in my size. All of them are designer and TV appropriate. My mind wanders. Are they going to take Praline off the show?

If she's alive, will she still be able to compete tonight? Did anyone tell Jeremy what happened?

I feel different than I did standing in that line for three days. The reality of being on TV, of touching Jeremy, of real people's lives being messed up...I don't know.

"Don't look so glum! Try this one on." Monique hands me a mint green gown and I shake my head no. "This one?" It's purple. Maybe that's my new signature color. Though this shade isn't neon purple—more of a subdued plum, fading to black at the floor-length hem. I wiggle the dress over my head and straighten the middle, which is very form fitting.

Monique smiles wide. "Gorgeous. This is the one."

I look older and elegant. Sexy. I smile before I remember Praline won't be trying on any dresses tonight.

"Do you have any jewelry with you that'll match the dress?" she asks.

I run my fingers through my hair. It's never felt so soft and slippery. I shake my head no, loving the way the strands brush against my back.

"We have a box of fake stuff, if you want to dig through."

I nod and she presents me with a plastic bin. The colorful beads and metal bits create a mosaic of color, like found art. I pull out a black disc with a raised silver spiral. I bet I can mar the surface with my drawing knife to create a new pattern around the silver.

I can't face going back to my room with the kicked-in door and signs of Praline. All those candy wrappers. I hope housekeeping comes by and clears away the evidence. I wait in the lobby for the others. At the front desk, I ask about Praline, but they won't give me any information because I'm not a relative.

I didn't get a chance to eat this morning and I don't want anything now. The folds of the dress hide

SARAH GAGNON

a pocket, which now contains my soon-to-be cure for Fluxem. I rub my thumb over the bank chip for comfort.

Seven of us are being eliminated tonight, unless Praline isn't considered part of the competition anymore. Damn, that's depressing. At this point, I think Shelley has a better chance at the sympathy vote, or maybe Praline. My date wasn't visually romantic. I don't see how the viewers would vote me into the final three.

At least I'll see Jeremy tonight, even if we won't have a moment alone. It's been days since I got a glimpse of him climbing into the limo outside the hotel. I tried watching the documentary about Jeremy's face with Praline in the dirt motel, but the Jeremy on TV didn't feel like my Jeremy anymore. I don't know when my fantasy musician got replaced with a real man, but the image of him on the screen just felt so far removed from our time together. For that one night, I felt like his girlfriend, but then I spent a week without a single word. Does that change things? And the date with Jasmine...my kiss was before that. And the date with Brie. The kiss with Claire, the making out with Shelley and Jaime. My neck twitches.

I tap the leather pumps Monique gave me on the lobby tiles, white to black in a diamond pattern. Finally, Eleanor arrives. Her hair frizzes out in a halo, but she's wearing a classy, high-neck black dress.

I jump up to meet her. "Have you heard anything?"

She takes a deep breath. "She's alive, but not awake. Her brain may need time to regenerate." She tucks a stray hair behind her ear. "Her parents are flying in to take care of her. But she won't be able to continue with the competition."

Like she gives a shit about the show after what they revealed in her episode. "The producers should cover her medical bills," I say. "If they hadn't screwed her life up with that segment, she wouldn't have been pushed over the edge."

"We can't know what caused this," Eleanor states formally, like she's already testifying at the trial.

"Yeah, we can. And when she wakes up, I'm sure she'll be able to accuse them herself." *I'll testify on her behalf.*

"I'm sure they'll cover her bills, regardless of fault." Eleanor waves her hand in the air, catching Claire's attention as she walks into the lobby. A shimmery turquoise dress hugs her curves.

"You look great," I tell her.

"You too." I wonder if she'll make the cut. As the others arrive, I'm overwhelmed by how different we all look away from the viewing room. We might as well be lined up for the Miss USA pageant. Eleanor repeats the story about Praline, and everyone is respectfully somber. At least on this one point we can all agree on appropriate behavior.

"We're all here. Into the limo." Eleanor pushes us along. I slide in next to Claire. Jasmine keeps her eyes on her own lap, but I can still see the curve of her smile. I guess she doesn't have any worries about making it to the final three. Once Eleanor climbs in the back, she snatches the bottle of champagne off the center table. "Really, I told them no alcohol." She struggles to find a spot in the mini-fridge.

Eleanor clears her throat. "When we arrive, we'll all walk in together. You can expect media and press outside of the studio. Now that Bill is done with the background research, he'll be here to take the lead as we enter. Walk directly into the building and follow him onto the stage. There are chairs numbered one through ten. Um, or rather one through nine with Praline out. Don't fidget while you walk, keep your heads up, and don't do anything you wouldn't want a million people to see. Turn to your neighbor and check her teeth. If you have any bits of vegetables stuck in your smile, now is the time to find out."

I wasn't that nervous before, but the instructions make this event real. I'm about to be judged by the world. "Your teeth are fine," I whisper to Claire.

"Yours, too."

"After the selection, we'll all meet back stage and go to the benefit concert together."

The bubbly murmurs of excitement halt as the limo pulls to a stop. Eleanor reaches into her purse and quickly applies hair product over her frizz. Cameras flash through the tinted glass, and as the door opens the lights blind me. I hold my head high and keep my arms at my side—even though I want to hug myself around the middle and hide as much of my body as I can. Bill stands at the top of the red carpet leading into the building. Claire goes first, which is great since she's the most poised and least likely to topple over. Or maybe she should've gone behind me so she could grab hold of me if I start to fall.

I concentrate on smiling and not clenching my fists. Every time a reporter screams a question, I want to cover my face and run. I don't know how Jeremy stands so much media attention.

We wind through the building and a big open arch leading down to the stage. The studio audience stands and cheers for us as we walk by. One girl holds out a sign with Jasmine's name painted in glitter letters. Ugh. After that, I try to keep my gaze on the back of Claire's head. She sits in the number one chair and I sit next to her in number two. Jasmine waves at the audience before she takes her seat. The front row chants her name. This isn't fair. But three girls are being selected, so even if the producers have skewed Jasmine to be the favorite, there's room for me in the final three.

"Now the moment you've all been waiting for... Jeremy Bane!" His music blasts over the loudspeakers and he jogs down the aisle. Everyone stands, including me. He waves to his right and then left as he jogs, flipping his hair out of his eyes with a quick head's up. He takes the steps onto the stage two at a time. The cheering is mind numbing. There's a special red leather couch for him across the stage from us. It's in the shape of a heart. How cheesy.

Rod Bing strolls out in a rainbow suit, blowing kisses to the audience as he passes. This time his scarf is a tame white. He holds both hands up and motions for the crowd to calm down. Other than a few lingering whistles, they comply.

"You've watched the episodes. Now, tonight, you vote. Under your seats you'll find a numeric pad. When the time comes, you'll cast your vote for the girl you think deserves the most eligible rockstar on the planet!" More cheers and drums. "For those of you watching at home, text your vote to D-A-T-E-5-5-5. Those votes will be added to the ones from our studio audience for the total score. I do have some sad news to report amidst all this excitement." He drops his head and the crowd quiets. "Praline has had a minor accident and won't be attending the selection tonight. If you would like to vote for her, just enter in the number three. But before all of that, let's see some behind-the-scenes footage." Praline's name whispers through the audience as the lights around us dim. Please don't let it be more secrets.

They have an overhead screen for the audience to watch, which I have to crane my neck to see. The screen flickers to life and shows the viewing room. *I knew it.*

"Now let's get a glimpse of the girls watching Jeremy on his other dates." Oh great, the Shelley Anne in a canoe footage. I can't believe how angry I look.

Praline's the worst; her face starts to turn red and puffy when Shelley throws herself into Jeremy's lap. Oh, God. How can they show her like this while she's in the hospital, unconscious? Didn't they have time to edit her out? They had enough time to make sure there were only nine chairs on the stage.

I cringe and look away before Praline rams the wall. It's not at all funny after seeing her half dead. Her sprawled out on the floor just reminds me how pissed off I am at the producers. I glance over at Jeremy and our eyes meet. He raises his eyebrows in question and I almost hear him asking me what's wrong. I give him a tight smile and close my eyes for a count of ten. I wish he could hold me. I wish we were anywhere but here.

The footage rolls on. Apparently, there was a fight between the clones at the restaurant that I missed. There are surprisingly few shots of me and I'm extra glad I avoided the viewing room. Though at this rate, I'm not making much of an impact on the viewers. Jeremy is staring at me again and I think he's trying to communicate something with his eyes, but I have no idea what. He mouths a full sentence. I shrug.

Then I pop up on the screen. The camera films me sprinting down the sidewalk and falling to my knees outside of the limo. Jeremy helps me up and there's a close-up of my blood-soaked leg, and then they zoom in on my swollen face. The skin underneath my eye bloats out, making my whole head look lopsided. Oh, God. Could this be any worse? The studio audience "oohs" when Jeremy holds me close. I glance at him again and he's smiling at the screen. This is driving me nuts. I want to sit with him on that couch.

Rod Bing narrates over all the footage, making jokes and describing the fun of the week. After the montage of bloopers fades, the lights come back up. "Now it's time to review contestant number one. Go ahead and grab your pad from underneath your seat."

There's a strange grinding noise above my head, and when I look up, rectangles are dropping down from the ceiling. I watch a series of red zerocs illuminate over me. We've all got them. My heart starts pounding furiously. This is awful. "For those of you at home, start casting your votes. Remember audience members, only one vote per controller. You'll be locked out once you enter a number, so choose carefully."

Immediately, Jasmine's counter starts ticking upward. I guess that means viewers at home are already dialing in their favorites. My counter is silent. Highlights from Claire's date play on the screen. She's up to ten votes. "Punch in number one now if you think Claire deserves a second date." There's a flurry of beeps and Claire's number stops at 2,633. I'm next. I think I'm gonna puke. I can't stand to twist my head around to see Jasmine's count.

Scenes from my date unfold on the screen.

I'm going to be sick.

I'm going to die.

I shift in my seat. The purple dress sticks to my butt. I need to stand up. I need to run. I look across the stage. Jeremy is watching me with sad eyes. Then Rod Bing says the dreaded words.

"If you think contestant number two deserves a second date..." He pauses. I squeeze my eyes shut. "... vote now." The whole world wobbles. I clamp my teeth down on my tongue and force a polite smile as my number rises. How many people are at home, judging me? I can't believe I ever thought this was a good idea.

4,310. That's my number. So few, but still more than Claire's. That's something, I guess.

One was my mother, and I don't have any other relatives that would vote. In fact, I'm surprised I got more than one vote. What was I thinking? This is humiliating. My eyes water and I have to widen my lids to keep the moisture in place.

The show moves on to Praline's footage. They cut her date down to less than thirty seconds and she only gets a few votes. Occasionally I get a small ding over my head. Can I just go home now? I have the strongest desire to be in my tiny foldout bed at home. Pull my blanket over my head and forget this dream. None of this is real. Jeremy's a dream and this voting thing is a nightmare.

Except that when I look across the stage, Jeremy is still watching me, and I think he wants to run over and scoop me up. Part of my brain might be shutting down. For a split second I envy Praline and her coma. "Vote for number four now..."

I twist in my seat to watch Shelley Anne's number soar. A guy in the audience screams out "boobs!" He holds his touchpad over his head and hits Shelley's number. That damn super suit is getting Shelley more votes than any of us. After her number climbs into the six digits, I look away. I'm still number three and there has to be a twist to the voting. Six more girls to go.

A few drops of water slip down my face. Sweat from the lights. Just sweat. I don't wipe it away because I don't want to draw attention to it. Number five and number six have small numbers. I'm neck and neck with Mel, but I'm holding onto the third place slot. Then comes Brie, the gambling clone. In seconds, she beats out Shelley.

Which means...she beat out me. Which means...I'm not in the final three.

I wait for the twist that will change the numbers around. Jasmine's counter is recording six-digit numbers. Wait, now seven. Please make it stop. The hurricane is edging up the coast, maybe there'll be an electrical storm and the system will short out. Maybe Jasmine's counter will explode and set her hair on fire. I dig my nails into my palms and pray for that.

"All right, last chance. Anyone who hasn't decided, now is your last chance to record your opinion." Rod Bing pauses for a dramatic ten seconds of silence. But on stage the tiny clicking of the boxes overhead is deafening.

"That's it, folks." The audience stands and cheers. No one chants my name. "Numbers four, eight, and ten, please stand up." Balloons and confetti release from the ceiling and the mess rains down on me. Spotlights illuminate the final three and I'm left sitting in the dark, stunned.

I lost.

"For the rest of you, it's time to say goodbye."

The lights flicker. Jeremy stands up. "What about this?" He pulls a big red card from behind the loveseat and holds it over his head.

Rod Bing opens his arms wide and walks across the stage as the audience quiets. Lights flash over his shiny suit. "You know these opinionated musicians are hard to please." The crowd snickers. "We've given Jeremy a save card."

My pulse thuds in my throat. I can barely breathe. Claire reaches over and grasps my hand.

"What do you think, Jeremy? Did the audience do a good job picking, or is there someone left behind that you want to use your save card on?"

"I'll use the card." No hesitation. My belly flips. Please, no puking this time. He crosses the stage, hazel eyes set on me.

The audience shouts out different names, but he stops in front of me. "Monet, this is for you."

I take the red paper. He quirks a half smile and offers his hand. I stand on the stage next to him. So shocked to be chosen.

Only a few people clap. Most are still trying to convince him to pick one of the other girls.

I'm frozen.

Black clouds spot my vision. Jeremy grips my arm so that I don't slump to the floor. I can't make out any one voice, but I get the gist. "Not her."

Why? What's so bad about me?

Then the crowd starts cheering again. Jasmine, Shelley, and the gambling clone stand next to us. I kick the confetti away from my feet. I wanted to be chosen, but I wanted the viewers to think I'm good enough for Jeremy, too.

Rod Bing motions for Claire to stand up. "Go ahead and say goodbye to Jeremy on your way off stage." He points to the door at the back of the living room setup.

Jeremy shakes Claire's hand and gives her a brief hug. I watch as the rest of the girls embrace Jeremy and walk off. Then it's my turn. Our cheeks brush together as I lean into him. "It's almost over," he whispers as he gives my hands a final squeeze when I pull away. I cross the stage and walk through the door.

Back stage is dark. I stand there blinking, waiting for my eyes to adjust.

Jasmine bumps into me from behind. "What the hell is this?"

Then the lights slowly come on. The ten of us stand there, blinking at the scene. There are people in front of us. It takes a minute to register. They're the people from our episodes. We exited the stage only to find ourselves on another mirror image of the first, only this one is populated with people we don't want to see.

There's a grating sound and the stage vibrates. The whole floor beneath our feet starts to rotate around. I'm almost knocked down as we start moving. Shelley grabs hold of me for balance. The whole stage moves until we're back in front of the audience again.

Then chaos breaks out. My father, sperm donor, whatever the hell he is, stands on the other side of a yellow line. I recognize Claire's dance instructor.

Everyone talks over each other. I can't hear anything. I thought the show was over. There's even a guy in a white lab coat over there. What are we supposed to do, brawl?

Two guys in security uniforms wait along the side. Rod Bing stands behind them, pretending to cower. A woman screams in Spanish and steps up to the yellow plastic tape. Security tells her to move back, and then she launches herself at Claire. I stumble to the side as the two crash to the ground. I catch the Spanish word for slut and I'm guessing this is Claire's dance instructor's wife. Security strolls over, nice and casual, letting them get into it.

I look across to where my father stands, wondering what he thinks of all the theatrics. He shakes his head in disgust. The white lab coat guy approaches Shelley. I want to get closer to hear. Then—bam—I hear his voice over the loud speaker. A screen over our heads flashes to each zoomed-in conflict. The new guests are all wearing personal mics and the producers switch between broadcasts.

Lab coat says, "I want to offer the studio audience a discount of twenty percent for utilizing my plastic surgery services. Just look at Shelley Anne, and tell me you wouldn't like curves like that for yourself."

Shelley tries to shush him. "He doesn't mean that I've had work done."

"What? But you had an appointment just last month."

She makes a chopping motion at her neck. "Patient confidentiality," she whispers.

He shrugs. Then the view shifts. I glance back at Claire, who's finally pinned the wife. Her dress is up around her waist, flashing lace panties. Security carries them both off stage while the dance instructor follows behind, asking them to "Please be calm."

Then my father walks toward me. How did they even get him to show up here?

"Monet," he says as he walks closer. The gray hair around his temples makes him appear more distinguished and I understand why he hasn't had it colored. I take a step back, but he hugs me anyway. Or at least, tries to. His body stays stiff. This is too weird. As soon as he's close to my head he says, "Smile for the fucking cameras, daughter. Company stock already dropped after your episode." He squeezes my arms. Okay. I get it. I step back from his embrace. His mouth lifts in a half circle. It's supposed to be a smile, but it doesn't look like one. He narrows his eyes. Oh, right. I'm not smiling. I start, but no. What the hell am I doing? I don't even know this man. He's never done anything for me.

"So, where have you been my whole life?" I ask.

"Oh, I wanted to see you. Of course I did. Your mom kept us apart." He gestures his arms out wide in frustration. A show for the audience.

"That's bullshit."

"You're my daughter. Family is of utmost importance to me."

I get it, he's got a high profile job. Makes a lot of money. Being outed as a deadbeat dad on national TV didn't do much for public relations and company stock, apparently. I glance around, trying to see if Mom is over there, too. I'd rather let her deal with this asshole. Sadly, I'm on my own.

I sigh. "Just get out of here. You've never been there for me, you don't know me, and don't bother trying to say that you do." I take a deep breath. I never fantasized about having a father and I don't need to start any what-ifs now. He looks up at the screen to see if the cameras are still focused on us. They're not. Purple contacts is busy crying while some guy screams at her.

"Looks like our moment is over," he says. "If you'd cooperated, I could've gotten in a plug for Global Fission. That doctor managed to get his ad in."

I gulp down my anger. "Aren't you at all curious about me?"

"Why would I be? You're lucky enough to get my DNA. You know I didn't get to have another kid. Leaving your mother was supposed to provide me with opportunities. Then I find out some food additive has made me sterile."

I swallow the bile back. Our first in person conversation and this is what he chooses to say.

"Speaking of that, how do I even know you're my real daughter? They messed up your sex. Maybe they messed up whose sperm they used."

Wow. I'm almost going to cry. I clench my jaw. He does not deserve that much of a reaction. I turn away. He doesn't need my response. He has his own ideas, nothing I say will make any difference. I search the audience for Jeremy, but he must have left to get ready for the concert.

"No answer for that?"

I look back at him. My poor mother was married to that. "Honestly, I didn't know you existed, and now that I do, I don't even care."

I walk across the stage to a raised seating area where Jasmine's watching the battle below. I can't believe they still haven't found anything in her past to bombard her with.

"Enjoying the show?" she taunts.

All this rage swirls around in the front of my skull. My asshole father, and now Jasmine. I take one look at her smug ass expression and my fist connects with her jaw.

There's a big thwack and her head tips back.

"You punched me. You fucking punched me?"

Huh. I look down at my burning knuckles and shake out my fingers. "Uh, yeah. I guess I did." The audience is screaming and pointing at us. Finally someone cheers my name. My happiness lasts all of two minutes. One of the cameras picked us up and there it is on replay right in front of me.

"I want her arrested!" Jasmine screams to the security people. Instead, they smile at me.

How could I have lost it like that? Now I'm immortalized on TV for this. Shit. Then FBI agents swarm in from the back entrance. I freeze.

"She's right here!"

Jasmine points at me, but they run past me to the brawl.

"Brie Logan?"

The gambling clone looks up, takes in the approaching officers and sprints toward the audience. They chase after her. She's almost out of the room, but then more feds emerge from the door right in front of her.

She's down on the ground with her arms twisted behind her in seconds. "Brie Logan, you are under arrest for criminal tax evasion. You have the right to an attorney..."

The rest of the contestants still on the stage stare at the officers as they drag her away. Rod Bing steps out to the center of the stage, shaking his head and clapping his hands. "And that is a wrap."

I should've known the show would go this far. Eleanor talks with Claire against the back wall and I make my way over.

"Can we just go home now?" Claire asks.

"Hey, did you forget about the concert?" Eleanor asks in an excited voice. Yeah, like that's going to make us feel better.

"And then in the following days those of you who aren't part of the final three will be giving opinions about who Jeremy should select." Eleanor smiles like we didn't just go through hell. "That way, if one of the girls has been a real bitch to the other contestants, they'll get a chance to return the favor." I wonder if Eleanor knows how much we all hate Jasmine. She must have seen me punch her. No one in the room missed that replay.

Shelley joins us. "Final three? Isn't it four with Monet?"

"Nope. Since Brie will be in prison, she's out."

I stare at Eleanor, waiting for a bit of remorse. "This feels awfully planned."

She shrugs and points us toward the back exit of the studio. "Either way, the numbers work out."

I can't believe these people. This time, when we leave the stage, we'd better actually get out of here.

"Jasmine! Come on." I turn around and see Jasmine talking to a lady from the audience. Her jaw has a big red mark from where I hit her. I cringe. I'm more upset about losing my control than actually hurting her. Jasmine is borrowing the lady's phone and is bitching at someone on the other end. Probably her lawyer. Once again, I don't have any assets, so she should save herself the effort and not sue me.

We file out the back of the studio door. Artificial light from the city illuminates the dark gray clouds. Wind frizzes Jasmine's hair around the edges of her face. She catches me looking and glares.

We drive to Madison Square Garden. Fans line the sidewalk, screaming Jeremy's name. They press against the glass, vying for a glimpse of who's inside. I turn away from the smooshed noses and flip my hands over, flexing each finger. I'm an artist. I made my own money. I'm good enough to win this competition. Jeremy and I get along, we care about the same things, and I want him like crazy. The audience just didn't witness all the time Jeremy and I spent together.

The rain picked up while we were inside getting humiliated. I feel like the hurricane is chasing me down. I let the rain soak my beautiful dress as we step out of the limo in the back parking lot.

"Hurry up!" Claire grabs my wrist and drags me toward the door. Maybe she's worried I'll end up like Praline. The wind whips my hair back and forth, yanking out my misery.

4,310 votes. Hardly anyone believes I'm good enough to date Jeremy.

Red carpet, black tile, white tile. One foot in front of another. "You're all a sorry bunch," Eleanor says. "I'm taking you to a concert, front row seats, not a funeral."

I think her comment is particularly shitty after what happened to Praline, but I lift my head and try to take in the distant domed ceiling. Fake gold paint outlines the edges. The real metal would've been scraped off years ago. Once the government managed to pass a law giving them the right to use precious metal for expenses, they started harvesting everything. I bet The Metal Society would love to restore the room. My seat squeaks as I sit. I shiver and my teeth knock together. With my luck I'll be trampled to death when Jeremy arrives. I'll get one last glimpse of him before feet cover my head.

Claire nudges my arm. "Look at that." She points to a man at the back of the stage talking into his earpiece. "He's holding a weather track pad."

"So what?"

"Do you think they're going to cancel the concert?"

"That would suck. I mean, we should at least get our consolation prize." The girl behind me kicks the back of my seat and I turn around to glare at her. She scrunches down and pulls her legs close.

On stage there's a raised platform with computer screens all plugged into a central mixer. All the different colored wires coil on the ground, making Jeremy's spot look like a nest, or maybe an engine.

The general lighting dims and the central walkway illuminates from underneath with pinpoints of light. Screams fill the room as Jeremy jogs down the path. Red and blue beams of light hit under his jaw, accentuating the angles of his face. He's a god walking on top of a universe of stars. He raises his hands above his head when he reaches the stage. The shouting rings in my ears. A rainbow flickers over him as he removes a button-up shirt to reveal a very tight T-shirt underneath. I bite my lip. He's so perfect.

The arena goes into absolute darkness and the noise dies out in anticipation. In the black, the sound of a wave rushes over us and fills in with clear tings of notes. Individual, different, sad. His voice fills the space. "I found you in the sea / Beauty cutting through me." The lyrics are new.

When the lights come on, he's glowing in the center of his instruments, concentrating on the screens, flipping buttons and punching in code. He's so intense. I close my eyes for a minute and let the music transport me to his ocean. I'm the girl in the sea.

Jasmine leans forward in her seat at the end of the row. "Psst, Eleanor. I thought I was getting a special seat on stage for having the most votes." I focus only on Jeremy's face and his rapidly moving hands. Eleanor doesn't acknowledge Jasmine's request.

After the song ends, an official-looking guy in a suit walks on stage. "Sorry to break the bad news, but the mayor has just posted a state of emergency for the entire city. So we're being forced to cut the concert short. The box office will be offering partial refunds of your tickets."

"But we only heard one song!" a guy from behind yells.

Jeremy wants to keep playing. His lips move rapidly as he talks into his headset and he pushes buttons like he's getting ready to start the next song.

"Unfortunately, the storm is beyond my control. Have a good night, everyone."

The electricity cuts off and Jeremy's screens go out. He strides across the stage and takes the mic. "I promise you this concert will be rescheduled for the next available time slot after the storm. All the proceeds will still be donated to the Global Skin Cancer Initiative." The man motions him off the stage and his fists clench as he walks. I know how much he cares about getting money for the cause.

Claire turns to me as we stand. "At least we heard one song."

I nod as the crowd behind us rushes to leave. Jeremy is exiting at the back of the stage. Derek notices me and jogs over as Jeremy steps through the curtain. "Monet, here." He hands me a folded-up piece of paper and heads back toward the door Jeremy disappeared through.

I have to wait for the rest of the fans to file out before I can leave. I discreetly open the paper. A phone number and nothing else. I hope it's Jeremy's.

Eleanor stands under an umbrella, wide-eyed. "Hurry up. We're not supposed to be on the streets."

The concert venue is only a few blocks from the hotel. They should've just made us walk. I leave a dripping trail into the hotel and up to my room. The door has been replaced. The candy wrappers have been removed. I sit on my bed and wait. I can't stop analyzing the show. My father being there, not caring about me. Jeremy did use his save card on me. That's something, but what does he want me for? The competition is ending and he has his whole rockstar lifestyle.

I'll give him an hour and then I'll call.

TWENTY-ONE

THE CLOCK ON the wall slowly counts down the time. I break at fifty-five minutes.

Ringing. Derek materializes on the desk. "Hey, Derek, is Jeremy there?"

"Monet!"

"Is Jeremy back from the concert yet?"

"Yeah, he's just getting in the door now. Hold on a sec."

Derek fades out of range and Jeremy replaces him. Wet hair sticks to his forehead and he's breathing hard like he just ran in. "Are you okay?" His voice sounds anxious. "You looked so sad on the show. I swear to you, I had no idea they were setting all you girls up for a confrontation at the end."

I tuck my hair behind my ears. "I'm okay. Just humiliated, you know? Not many people thought I would be very good for you."

"That's not true." Now he sounds pissed. "They don't know anything about you."

I massage my shoulder and do a slow neck roll. "Maybe."

"I'm coming to pick you up. Can you get away?"

"Yeah, with Praline in the hospital, no one will notice."

"They told me. I still can't believe it." He fades in and out. I only hear bits of the conversation he's having with Derek.

"Where are you?" I ask. Every few seconds the background of the image picks up his surroundings, and it doesn't look like the hotel.

"I have an apartment in New York. They finally let me go home."

"Oh."

"Do you want to come over for a few hours?"

I feel like shit but... "Yeah."

"Meet me in front of the hotel in ten minutes. I'll be in a brown car. Just come right over, okay? I don't want anyone else to see me."

"Okay."

He clicks off.

I'm sick. Overloaded. Up one minute, down the next. I pull out a change of clothes from my tote bag, but decide to just take the whole thing with me. It's not like I have a lot of possessions, anyway.

I wait on the sidewalk, still in the purple dress, letting the storm coat me. I'll probably have to return it in the morning. A gust of wind knocks me to one knee. When the brown car pulls up, I almost don't believe it.

"Shit, Monet. You could've waited inside." He reaches across the seat and rubs the goose bumps on my arm. With his hands off the steering wheel, the car slips into a low idle.

"The rain felt nice."

He shakes his head. "It's a frigging hurricane out there. State of emergency, remember? The eye should be over New York by morning."

"Yeah." I should ask about the other girls. Find out if he wants to be in a relationship with one of us, or if this is all for fun. Even if he said he did want me, that wouldn't even be possible if I'm in Boston and he's traveling all over. Maybe he knows that there can't be anything long-term between us.

"Come here." He pulls me over the center console and rubs his hands up and down my back, creating friction. I try not to flinch when he rubs over the Fluxem marks. I'm shaking in his arms, but I think it's proximity and shock rather than cold. I need to accept this moment with him and not worry so much.

"Shhh, it's okay." He runs his fingers along a strand of wet hair, then pulls my head tight against his chest. "You're so cold." His heart beats into my ear and I don't feel cold anymore. He kisses the top of my head, and when he sighs the noise vibrates in his chest.

"Oh, Monet." He holds my head in his hands and pulls back enough to look at me. His brow crinkles with worry. He softly kisses my eyelids and then releases me. He punches in coordinates on the steering wheel and the car slides out into traffic. The car drives itself, but you're supposed to monitor the vehicle the entire time. Occasionally, there are glitches in the system. The rain hits the windshield, cutting visibility down to nothing, but the car continues on without being affected. *If this is the end, I'll be so sad. Don't think about it.*

"My apartment here in New York isn't much. I have nicer places, but housing is hard to find in the city." He drums his fingers on the top of the steering wheel nervously, which is silly considering I live in a hundred-square-foot apartment.

"I'm sure it's the height of luxury compared to my house." He raises his eyebrows like he doesn't quite believe me and then glances back at the road.

"This is it." He pulls to a stop in front of a skeletal steel building. Sections of metal and glass reflect the ambient light trapped in gray clouds. He climbs out of the car first and I pat the door, trying to find the touch panel that will release me. He opens the door from the outside before I can figure it out. God, I hope he doesn't think I was waiting, expecting him to open the door for me. Rain drips off his nose as he offers me his hand climbing out. My tote bag drips water down the side of my leg. So much for dry clothes. We hustle to the canopy overhanging the front entrance of the building. The air swirling around me feels aggressive.

"I wonder if the hurricane will spark tornados?" I ask.

"I think we're safe in this area."

I nod. Derek comes out of the building and tips his head up at the sky. "Hey, Monet, I, uh, watched the competition. Bummer about your dad." He jogs off to the idling car and takes Jeremy's place behind the navigation panel, presumably to bring the car underground to park. *Bummer, yeah, that about covers it.*

I shiver as the wind whips up my skirt. The rain slides down the center of my spine. "Let's get you inside." Jeremy's hand is burning hot when he laces his fingers with mine. He scans his hand and then retina at the door. High security. Then he scans in again at the elevator. "I live on the top floor," he explains as the minutes pass and the door doesn't ding. "Hundredth floor."

"Does Derek live with you?"

"He has an apartment down the hall, with cameras that monitor the entrance to mine. Another one of my guards lives with him, so they can switch shifts."

I bite my lip, unsure of what to say. How weird to be important enough to need protection. Even weirder that the one point of contact between our two hands heats up my whole body. I have these few hours with Jeremy. If they're my last, I'm going to enjoy them. Now that I can afford the cure, I have a future. Jeremy was never a part of that. I lean into him. *Jeremy as a boyfriend was never part of the plan.* And now I'm lying to myself in my own head. Ugh. Why do I always want more? I should be content.

He keeps hold of me. I feel like I might faint if he lets go. I nuzzle against his chest while he presses his palm against the door. The light turns green and the handle swings down. "Monet," he mumbles softly. I look up into his face and his lips press into mine. Life floods back into my body from the point where our bodies touch. His kiss is hot and delicate.

He pushes the door open with his foot and we back into the apartment. He kisses down my neck and along my collarbone. "You're so cold. Let me find you dry clothes to change into."

"No." I drag my fingers through his hair, and he works his way back up my throat.

"You taste nice."

I dissolve into the kiss. I don't want to remember anything else from this night—just the warmth of Jeremy's arms and the growing sensation of his lips. It doesn't matter if the world doesn't think I'm good enough. All that matters is that he wants me.

I want to say every slushy romantic thought that flits through my mind, but instead I channel the desire into our kiss. "I'll get those clothes," Jeremy says. Though when he goes to pull away he's back in an instant, like I'm magnetic. I wish I didn't have the Fluxem sore. I glance at the bed, but there's no way I want him to see me naked. Not yet.

Jeremy's apartment is one big room. A thousand square feet, at least. There's a pile of dirty laundry next to the bed, which makes me smile. I take a step forward.

"Hold on. I'll find you something." He runs his fingers through his hair and takes a deep breath. Drawers line the underside of his bed. I sit on the edge, sinking into the foam while he digs through the clothes. "Do you think these will fit?" He holds the sweatpants up in the air. I recline slightly on the bed. My wet purple dress accentuates everything. He presses his lips tight.

"I think with the drawstring they'll be okay," he says when I don't answer. He goes back to the drawer and I pull my hair forward, so that the dark strands frame my face. My chest pounds with anticipation. Then he stands up and hands me a concert sweatshirt.

I sigh. He's being a respectful gentleman. "I'll go change." The bathroom is off to the side of the bedroom. His towels are forest green. I take one off the rack and squeeze the water out of my hair before peeling the dress off and hanging it on the bar. I slide my legs into the sweats and take a quick peek behind the shower curtain. His shampoo is Jaher. I repeat the name in my head. Maybe when all this is over I can buy his shampoo at home and remember how he smelled. I press my hands to my face. I don't want this to be our last date.

I finish getting dressed. Once I roll the pants at the top they only drag on the floor a few inches. The sweatshirt is warm and cuddly, but definitely not sexy.

I step out of the bathroom. He's sitting on the bed, but jumps to his feet when I come out. "Do you want to watch a movie?" he asks.

"Okay." *Do not overthink it. Cheer the hell up.* We walk away from the bed to the other side of the room, where the TV is. Two sides of his apartment are glass and I press close, staring down. Cars on the street below appear no bigger than my thumb. Rain slams into the glass wall in sheets. I sit on the couch while Jeremy clicks through his digital library.

"When is the hurricane hitting?" I ask.

Jeremy straightens up and looks at the rain on the other side of the wall. "This is the leading edge of the storm. It'll probably get worse before it gets better."

"I guess I should stay here tonight."

He gulps. "Probably safest. What types of movies do you like? I have everything."

"Tonight, I'll take anything that is as far away from reality TV as possible."

"*Skunk Fu Takes Tokyo?*"

I laugh. "Perfect."

There's a thudding on the door. "Be right back. It's probably just Derek with the car keys."

I turn on the couch so that I can watch him stride across the room. Perfect posture, hurried steps.

Derek drips water on the floor and holds up a paper. "This was in the mailbox. Mandatory evacuation notice."

"No shit." Jeremy takes the paper. "Is the building clearing out?"

"I stopped and asked the attendant, but he said only a few old ladies from the lower floors left."

"What do you think, Monet, should we get out of here?"

"It's up to you guys. I'm not afraid of the storm." Plus, I don't want to cut the date short.

Derek shrugs. "It's your call, man. But for your safety, we should probably get out of here."

Jeremy looks at me. "We'll stay."

Derek takes in our silent eye contact. "Okay, then. I'll be next door if you need me. Oh, wait. Is that the *Skunk Fu Tokyo* movie?"

"You are not watching a movie with me and my date." Jeremy shoves him out the door.

"Goodbye, Monet," Derek yells through the closing door.

Jeremy shakes his head and turns back to me. "Can I get you anything to eat?" he asks. "I have a cake. It's pretty good. I got it at this bakeshop down the street yesterday."

"Sure," I say since he obviously wants cake.

"Cool." He comes back with two matching pewter plates and sinks down into the couch next to me. "This is delicious," he says around a mouthful of yellow cake with coconut frosting. He rests one leg on the coffee table. I've never seen him in such a casual pose. I just want to climb on top of him.

"Pewter, huh? That's one of the few the government hasn't tried to reclaim."

"I know, right? They're trying to squeeze money out of every corner of the world. Poor Brie. I swear the only reason they ever arrest anyone is tax evasion, and it's like a ransom demand. This other musician I know got busted for not reporting second party T-shirt sales."

I nod. He's so in-tune with the world and everything that's important to me. If only our lives didn't keep us separate. I take my plate and eat my slice as the movie plays. He turns the volume down low so that we can talk. The whole set-up seems so normal. Not how I imagined rockstars to be at home, but then, he's always been that way with me.

He scrapes up the last bite. "Tell me about what happened to Praline."

I describe what happened and he snuggles me against him as I talk. The movie finishes and I'm so warm and comfortable I just want to sleep. He kisses the top of my head and I close my eyes.

The pounding rain and wind wake me.

We're still in the same position. Jeremy's head rests on the back of the sofa. There's a tiny piece of coconut on his cheek. I wiggle out from under his arm to kiss the spot. He smiles and grumbles, stretching out his back. "I think we fell asleep," I say.

He rubs his eyes and pulls me closer so that I'm straddling his lap. "Did I tell you that you're adorable in my clothes?"

I kiss his jaw. "You taste like coconut," I say.

He massages my back with both hands.

"Uh, Jeremy, don't touch my back too much. That's where I have marks."

"Oh, shit!" He leans back fast. "Did I hurt you?"

"No, I'm okay." *Way to ruin the moment.* I run my tongue along his lips.

"You taste good, too," he says. He relaxes against me. "But Monet, about Fluxem—"

I press my mouth against his. Fluxem is the last thing I want to think about right now. I have the money from my design and I'm almost as good as cured. Soon. I just have to forget about the marks enough to enjoy this. He deepens the kiss. I feel so safe and relaxed in his arms. And completely turned on. My knees tremble. *I want you.*

I dip my hand under his T-shirt and over his abs, exploring each muscle. He groans against my chest and slips his hand under my sweatshirt. His hands trail up and down my belly. I'm tingling and shivering all over.

I kiss his neck and the stubble on his chin rubs my face. He drags me tight against his chest. The combination of his soft sweatshirt moving against my skin and his gentle fingertips makes me squirm.

"Monet," he whispers. I lean back enough so that his hands can glide over my front. "I love the way you kiss," he says.

I smile against his lips and draw back. His eyes open, staring into mine. "I think you're an amazing kisser, too." I run my fingers through his hair, flipping the wave to the other side.

The wind whistles against the glass and the pounding rain sounds like my heart in my ears. He strips off his shirt. Being with him in his apartment, just us and no cameras, is the most perfect date ever.

The whistling grows louder. I wish I could turn the volume of the world down so that I could hear his contented sighs better.

I kiss his chest and run my tongue lightly over his skin. He smells like the shampoo from the bathroom. I can't believe I get to touch him. That it's just me here in his apartment.

The noise is so loud I pause and look up. He doesn't seem to hear anything. "Jeremy, is that—"

Boom!

A twenty-foot chunk of iron slams through the glass and spears the couch right next to me. Fluff from the cushions flies up in a swirl. Chunks of rust cover my borrowed sweats. I stare out the gaping hole in the window in front of us. Rain pours in sheets onto his carpeted floor.

I grip the edge of the couch and hoist myself to my feet. The wind tries to blow me back down. "What the hell is that thing?" I yell over the pounding. A siren blares on the street below.

The big iron rod is still attached to something outside of the window. Criss-crossing supports cover the sides. "A crane?" I yell to Jeremy.

He's on the floor, scrambling to get back on his feet. He flips the coffee table out of the way. There's a grating metal sound. The side of the couch snaps off.

Jeremy grabs my arm. "Get down!" he screams.

I drop to my knees, still trying to see the storm outside.

Derek bursts into the room. "Jeremy, over here! Hallway. No windows."

Jeremy tries to pull me.

"Wait!" I yell back, but the rushing wind eats my words. "My pants are stuck." I struggle to unhook the material from the rusted metal spear.

"Damn it! On the ground, now!" Derek screams as he runs toward us.

Jeremy rips me free. He stares back, frantic. Like I might blow away if he lets go of my arm. The other side of the glass wall is hanging on. Then there's a loud pop. We duck our heads. Jeremy's hand slides down my arm, grasping my hand.

Derek starts to crabwalk toward the door and we follow. Then the metal wrenches away from the couch and swings across the room. The crane slams into the other half of the window. Wind whips my hair back. I turn toward the noise.

"Shit." I watch the glass shatter and come at me.

Jeremy pulls me against him.

I feel weird. "I think something hit me."

"Oh, my God! Monet! Stay with me!" I hear him scream. His voice is muffled in my head, then everything gets dark.

TWENTY-TWO

I WAKE UP in the hospital. There's a pint of blood hanging above me and a tube in my arm. I pat my free hand over my body. Everything hurts. My skin pulls tight around my middle and I loosen my hospital gown with one hand and look down. A huge line stretches from under my breast across my stomach and down my hip. New fake skin holds me all together. Thank goodness I wasn't conscious when they put on that stuff.

"Oh good, you're awake." The nurse stands by my bedside, monitoring the screen displaying my vitals.

"Is Jeremy okay?"

"He's fine. A gash on his forehead, but nothing too bad."

I half expect him to be sitting in the empty chair in the corner of the room. I try to sit up a little to be sure he isn't. The nurse rests her hand on my shoulder. "He left a bag with a change of clothes for you. But don't even think about trying to move yet. You need to be very still for another day. New skin only works so well on a cut that long and deep. That glass just about cut you in half."

"But I'm okay now?"

"Yeah, you'll heal up fine. You might have a small scar. The doctor on duty can answer more of your questions when he makes rounds later."

"Okay, good." I try to think this through. I'm in the hospital. Did anyone tell Mom? How the hell am I going to pay for this? "Can you just hand me the bag for a minute?"

The nurse shakes her head at me, but grabs my bag. I reach my hand inside. Aw, Jeremy packed his own sweatshirt for me. I reach deeper. Thank God. My bank chip is still in the bottom of the bag and not stuck in the wreckage of his apartment. I pull out the chip.

"Um, how soon can I get out of here?"

"Well, the doctor will need to approve your release."

"I don't have health insurance."

"Ah, well, you don't need to worry about any of that. Mr. Bane scanned his chip in when you arrived. He said he'd cover any charges and impressed upon us that we were to provide you with top notch care."

"Wow." *Like, holy shit, WOW.* "I also want to get the cure for Fluxem while I'm here. I have enough money, so you don't have to charge Jeremy for that."

"Oh, he scheduled that yesterday. You've had the first two shots already. One more later today and you'll be all set."

I'm already two-thirds cured! I slept through it. All this time and my problems were being fixed while I was unconscious. "Oh." That's just incredible. I can't believe Jeremy did this for me.

The nurse winks at me. "He's quite the keeper." She moves around the room, checking the monitors. "He stayed with you all day yesterday." She points at the enormous bouquet of roses on the other side of my bed. "Those are from him."

"Oh. Do you know when he'll be back?"

"I'm not sure, honey. A few guys came by in suits. I didn't listen in, but I take it he had a prior obligation."

The show. They came to pick him up for his final dates. I should've had one more date. I ruined my last moment with him by not ducking down. Stupid.

"Do you want me to tell your friend you're awake?"

"Friend?"

"A Miss Praline is in a room just down the hall. She said you guys lived together."

"She's awake?"

"Yup, she came around about the time they were bringing you in. I'll send her over." The nurse leaves me with a glass of water.

Praline's okay. I am so thankful. She walks in beaming with excitement. "You missed it."

"Missed what?"

"The show last night. It was so awesome." I *doubt that.* "Jeremy finished the benefit concert. From the footage there was still debris all over the road in front. But, oh, my, Jeremy was so dreamy."

"Wow. I wish I could have seen the rest." *The one time the show isn't berating the contestants and I sleep through it.* "What did he wear?"

"He had on this tight gray T-shirt with waves printed on it, totally cool. And of course his usual frayed jeans."

"What were the waves like?"

Praline curls her hand through the air, mimicking the shirt. I'm not positive, but I think it might be mine. I sigh. "I can't believe I missed the show. I love his concerts. I was so bummed we only got to see one song after the selection."

"I was unconscious for that, but they've been replaying the show all morning on the re-run channel." Praline flops down in the chair. "So, I hear you're the one who really won the other night. The nurses have been gossiping about how Jeremy Bane carried you through the front door of the hospital himself. You were all drenched in blood and he was pale as death." She pauses and fans her face. "So romantic."

"Did they say anything else?"

"Not much, just that Jeremy was totally worried about you and so cute about it."

My heart rate on the screen by my bed increases.

Praline bites her nails. "Are you going to turn on the TV, or what?"

"Huh?"

"Duh, seven-thirty. Tonight they're letting the other contestants give Jeremy their opinions on who he should pick. They even filmed a segment with me in my hospital bed earlier today." Praline cracks an evil smirk. "They had me act extra sick and recline like I was near death. Guess it adds to the drama. Too bad you weren't awake. I bet you had some stuff to say about that ho, Jasmine. Oh, I should warn you, after they left my room I heard them asking the nurse about taking a few pictures of you."

"Ugh. While I was unconscious? That can't be legal." I fumble for the button on the side of my hospital bed and the show pops up on the wall. The nurse's checkboard blocks a corner of the projection. The final two sit in another fake living room setup, with the other girls on couches surrounding them.

"—one thing and then she'd do the opposite. She was all like, 'I'll be in the restaurant or I'm going for a walk,' when I know for a fact she was just lurking out by the elevator, waiting for Jeremy." Mel finishes and the camera pans back. Ooh, I bet she's talking about Jasmine. Jeremy sits off to the side, watching the proceedings. He rubs his hand across his mouth and down his neck. I wonder what he's thinking.

The screen switches back to Rod Bing. "How about you, Claire, do you have any recommendations for Jeremy?"

"Yeah, don't pick that bitch Jasmine. I don't care what she was like when you were kids. She's a pit viper now." Jeremy shakes his head and the camera focuses back on the host.

"Wow, harsh words." The crinkle of Rod Bing's eyes gives away his joy. He's loving the drama and probably fantasizing about his ratings zipping up. "Jasmine, do you have anything to say to her accusations?"

"I honestly have no idea why the other girls would be so mean. I can only assume that they are upset about my prior relationship with Jeremy."

They flash back to Claire, who narrows her eyes in challenge.

"Well Jasmine, there's one contestant who won't be saying anything negative about you tonight." A picture of me fills the screen behind Rod Bing's desk. I don't even look like me. I'm deathly pale and expressionless. "Monet was struck by debris during the hurricane, but don't worry the doctors have said she'll be just fine." He straightens the scarf around his neck. Jasmine shrugs. Then the footage shifts to Praline in her hospital bed. "That's me!" I shush her so that I can hear what she said.

"I think Jeremy should pick whoever he likes the most. Jasmine doesn't deserve him. She's been trying to manipulate the competition the entire time, and just because the television audience has been fooled, doesn't mean Jeremy should be, too." Praline reclines back in the hospital bed, like she's out of breath and that was her dying sentence. Very good acting. I smile over at her and give her a thumb's up. The microphone picks up a weird popping noise, and I imagine Jasmine clenching her jaw.

One of the other clones starts talking. "At first I thought Jasmine was my friend, but she never even told me that she knew Jeremy."

Praline sits up straight. "Oh, and I forgot to tell you, Shelley has cancer again."

"That's terrible."

She hangs her head. "It's possible she doesn't, but after they got done with the concert, they had that doctor come back, which is kind of convenient drama for the show." She shrugs. "Who knows? It's TV, but that's what they said." What an awful thing to joke about if it isn't true. Jeremy comes back on the screen and we both go silent.

"Jeremy, what do you think about all of these revelations? I'm getting the impression that none of these girls want you to pick your childhood sweetheart."

Jeremy cringes at the word sweetheart. "I take their opinions very seriously. There are a lot of wonderful girls here, and I had a great time getting to know every one of them. But in the end, the choice is mine." That sounded a little scripted.

Rod Bing turns to Shelley Anne. "Well, you must feel pretty good right now. Your fellow contestants haven't said a thing about you."

"Well, Rod, in one way that kind of means I'm not memorable enough to form strong emotions about. But I hope Jeremy will remember *our* kiss."

The show goes around the living room, giving each girl a chance to talk. Jasmine gets nailed so bad, I'm not even sad that I missed my opportunity to get in a few digs. I wanted Jasmine taken down, but it doesn't show the other girls in a very flattering way.

"Tune in tomorrow night for the grand finale." Big drum roll. "When Jeremy finally picks the girl of his dreams." Fade to commercial.

I turn to Praline. "What do you think? Is Jasmine out of the running now?"

"Who knows? Claire had her description right, she's like a pit snake."

"Even if Jeremy does pick her, I can't imagine that he truly has feelings for her." I try to shift myself up, and wince when my skin pulls funny. Praline's full of color and life again. "You look so much better. Are you really okay?" I ask seriously.

She hangs her head. "Death by candy binge." Her laugh sounds forced. "Oh, I'm okay. The producers have managed to convince everyone that the overdose was accidental. Apparently, they don't want anyone suing them, which works out perfect for me. My parents would probably send me back to the institution if they thought I'd tried to kill myself again."

"I'm glad you're okay. But even if everyone thinks it was an accident, you should still get some counseling. Trying to kill yourself is serious."

She sighs. "I know."

"So don't ever do that to me or anyone else again. Finding you like that was terrifying."

"I'm sorry."

I reach out my hand and she squeezes it. "Never again."

"I have to tell you one more thing. When you were unconscious I gave you CPR. I have Fluxem and I wanted you to be aware that there's a small chance some of my saliva could've transferred." It feels so weird to finally just admit to having the disease.

"Oh. Ew." She grimaces. I look down at the bed.

"No, I didn't mean that you're gross. Just the idea of drool going in my mouth. My parents sprang for every vaccine known before I was admitted to the institution. Their way of trying to fix me." The nurse pops her head in.

"Sorry to interrupt, girls, but I have to give Monet her final shot."

"Sorry, this one has to go in your hip," the nurse says. "But then you'll be Fluxem free."

Praline nods. "Guess that answers my next question. I'm glad you're getting the cure. I'll stop by again later."

I relax on the bed and shift so that my one hip is up. The shot is instant.

Bam. I'm cured. The sores will take a few days to heal up, but the disease is out of my system.

After all this time. Just like that. I feel like it should hurt more or take longer. Such a simple procedure. I'm done. Fluxem free. Which means, since Jeremy already paid, I'll be able to go to college. At least for the first semester. My nose tingles, and since there's no one else in the room, I don't even wipe away the happy tears that run down my cheeks.

TWENTY-THREE

PRALINE TRUDGES BACK to my room in time for the finale with her dinner tray. "You're in a good mood," she says.

"Pain medicine."

She glances at the clock. "Almost time. I can't believe the show's ending."

"It's strange, I feel so different from who I was standing in that line," I tell her.

"I know what you mean." She laughs. "Maybe it's our near death experiences. Or maybe Jeremy's star power has rubbed off on us."

I shake my head. "Who do you think he's going to pick?"

She smiles big. "You."

"No, really. I'm not even there."

"Come on. He gave you the red save card. Of course you're his choice."

I *wish*. The familiar black screen shows on the hospital wall and then the words scroll across with Rod Bing's voice. *Who will win Jeremy Bane's heart and 30,000 dollars?*

Jeremy sits on the heart couch facing Rod Bing. He has a red line on his forehead, presumably from where a shard of glass hit him. A huge red curtain cuts the stage in half. Jeremy and Rod Bing are on one side, and on the other, each of the finalists stand in a soundproof glass box. They look like huge porcelain dolls.

"So, are you ready to make your final selection tonight?" Rod Bing asks. He's wearing a red scarf tonight and the extra makeup around his eyes only intensifies his exaggerated expression. "I notice we're a few girls short here. Brie will be tied up with the court system until she can arrange payments for those back taxes, and Monet is still in the hospital. Do you know anything about that?" He winks.

Jeremy drops his head. "No, but I hope she's better soon. I want to offer my condolences to anyone affected by this catastrophic weather." Ah. I guess he can't say we were hanging out. That would be against the show rules. Still, that just sucks.

Rod Bing nods along. "Well, despite all of that, a decision must be made. Are you ready?"

"I think I am. I've met a lot of great girls this week and it's a shame I can only pick one." His words sound rehearsed to me. But Praline "oohs."

"Can you give us a hint about what qualities impressed you most about the girl you've selected."

"Her sense of fearlessness and her beauty, obviously."

"Before you choose, we have a few highlights from the week." There's a musical montage of romantic moments from the dates.

Rod Bing asks Jeremy more questions. I can't take the answers seriously when Jeremy sounds like he's reading. Then the drums begin. Faster and faster. "Which girl do you want to speak with first?" He does his signature eye-widen.

"Shelley Anne." Rod Bing pulls back the curtain and releases her from the glass booth. She teeters slowly across the stage on high heels. Rod Bing links his arm with hers and pats her hand as they walk. She stops in front of Jeremy and gazes up at him.

"I was sorry to hear about your recent medical news. I hope the money this show is generating for research will help them find a cure for you."

She keeps her chin up, nodding and waiting for his decision.

"I'll talk to Jasmine first before I make my choice."

Rod Bing releases Jasmine from the soundproof box. She struts across the stage and Bing has to hustle to keep up with her. Judging from her smile, she's sure she's won. She thinks because she's last, Jeremy picked her.

"All right, time to talk to the last contestant."

"Jasmine, I've really enjoyed being reunited with you, and while our date wasn't exactly fun, it was certainly memorable. I remember all the times we had when we were kids and you have turned into a beautiful woman, but...I still think of you as just a friend, which is why I didn't choose you."

"Wait. Does that mean you pick me?" Shelley bounces up and down. Her boobs follow.

Jasmine's mouth gapes open and shut. "Her?"

I'm thinking the same thing. It has to be a sympathy pick. Ugh. That makes me sound so shallow, but Shelley?

Jeremy yells over them. "Sorry, girls! I pick Monet!"

ME?

I can't breathe. My heart stops. I glance at my vitals, surprised that it didn't truly fail.

Shelley stops bouncing.

Then Jasmine turns to Jeremy and slaps him. Right across the face.

I'm staring in disbelief when the door to my hospital room bangs open. A camera lens focuses on me. I look back at the TV and there my image is on the screen above the stage. On the display, money rains down around my head. Bells and whistles go off. There's a number on the bottom of the screen symbolizing my bank account inflating. Holy shit! I just won 30K, and Jeremy picked me. The camera records my shocked and crazy grin. Praline waves to the at-home viewers.

"How does it feel to be chosen by Jeremy Bane, the most wanted rockstar in the country?"

I gulp and cough. "Good." I cough some more and try to recover. "Jeremy is an amazing guy, whether he is a rockstar or not." I push my hair away from my face. *How do I feel?* "I'm happy."

"What will you do with the money?" he asks.

"I'm going to go to college for art." I sit up straighter. Right now, I'm awesome. I accomplished all of this. My life will change.

The cameras keep filming, but I turn back to the TV. Jasmine stalks off the stage. Shelley moves closer to Jeremy, and all of a sudden, she jumps him.

He tips his head back and away, but she climbs him. Then she has him by the back of the head. My reaction shows on the screen above them, but all I can do is watch in horror while she kisses him.

Praline starts laughing. Security helps Jeremy untangle himself. Rod Bing stands next to him. "I guess that one was going to get the last say no matter what."

Jeremy shakes his head and then smiles at the screen. "I'll be over right after this," he says to my picture.

I smile and wave back at him. "I'll be here waiting for you."

He blows me a kiss and the audience cheers. End credits roll and the cameras back out of the room.

Praline wraps her arm around me, squeezing.

"Ouch, ouch. New skin, remember?"

"He picked you. I knew he would."

A new nurse sticks her head in. "Monet, you have a phone call, should I transfer it in?"

"Yes, please."

My mom materializes on the bedside table. "You're in the hospital? I saw you on the show in a hospital bed. Please tell me it was just a stunt for ratings."

Praline picks up her tray. "I'll leave you alone to talk to your mom."

3-D Mom fades in and out. She can't sit still again. "No, it wasn't a lie, but I'm okay. It was the hurricane. I got cut by a piece of glass. No big deal."

"Well, if you're in the hospital it is a big deal. Someone should've contacted me immediately. How bad is this cut?"

I smile and shake my head. "It's already healed."

"Does it still hurt?"

I sit up straight, trying to exude healthiness. "No, I'm fine. It wasn't that bad. And I got the cure for Fluxem."

She fades in and out, bouncing around. "Already? But you just won the money a few seconds ago."

"No, Jeremy took care of it."

"I'm so proud. And he picked you! I knew he would. Are you sure you're okay?"

"Yes, I'm fine."

"Your father called. I assume he feels bad about being such a selfish ass on TV. He wants to talk to you again sometime...if you want to. We might be able to sue him for back child support if you want to go through the testing."

"Uh, I don't know about all that. Can't we just leave it?"

"Why? That bastard deserves to pay."

"Yeah, maybe. But I've got to go, now. I'm expecting Jeremy."

"Ooh la la," she says before clicking off.

I can't get out of the bed to go to the bathroom and fix my hair. I do my best to finger comb out the snarls. I can't stop grinning. He chose me! But what does that mean? I missed the final date, and he's still a musician and I'm still me.

The nurse pokes her head back in. "You have another visitor. Let me remind you that it is after hours." Jeremy walks in and the nurse shakes her finger at him. He drops his head submissively.

Jeremy pauses at my bedside. "Can I sit, or will it hurt?"

I wiggle over to make room, careful not to sit up and pull the new skin. Jeremy squeezes my hand. "I am so relieved you're awake." He hangs his head low and shakes it back and forth. "God. In the apartment, I didn't know if you'd ever open your eyes again."

I squeeze his hand back and smile. "I'm okay now. I hear you saved me. And you got me the cure for Fluxem. Thank you for that."

He shrugs. "If I hadn't brought you up to my apartment none of this would've happened." He slouches low. "It's all my fault. I knew there was a hurricane coming and I didn't even think twice about it."

I touch my fingers to his lips, lifting his face up to mine. "It's not your fault."

"But I suggested the movie. We would've been safer on the bed."

I laugh. Hard to imagine climbing in bed with Jeremy as the safe option. "Will they be able to fix your apartment?"

"Who cares about that? I'm just worried about you."

My chest tightens as our eyes meet. All the breath whooshes out of me. He's so cute and my heart has been trapped in a week-long whirl spin. "So, you picked me, huh?"

"I did." He takes my hand and kisses my knuckles, one after another.

"I think you know I'm crazy about you, but we need to talk first. I saw most of the dates, and I know you were having a good time, which is cool, but not if you and I are starting a relationship."

He looks down at the bed. He just picked me to win a ton of money, and gave me a 20K gift for the Fluxem cure, and I'm getting picky about how many girls he makes out with. I suck in my saliva. My non-contagious saliva. Holy crap. *I'm worth it, I don't need to compromise.*

He looks up and holds my eye contact for a moment. "I don't know what to say about those dates. A lot of the time, I don't want to disappoint people. I'm out with these girls, and they think that they love me so much. It doesn't hurt to give them something back." He flattens his lips. "Okay, wait, that sounds like I'm giving charity kisses." He drops his head and runs his hand over his face. "Let me start over. The kisses are nice, but I prefer yours. If you want me, that's that."

"I want you."

"Yeah?"

"Oh, totally. But how am I ever going to see you again?" I flip his hand over and trace the lines on his palm. "We don't exactly live next door to each other."

"Yeah, I've been doing some thinking about that. Touring full-time drives me crazy. When you were sleeping yesterday and I was sitting here, I kept thinking about med school. I might try to take a few classes."

That doesn't answer my question, but... "That's great. I think you should."

"I did some research on my tablet about BU, and it really is a great school."

"It is."

"How would you feel about me moving closer to you? I mean, I couldn't be around all the time. I'll still need to tour some, and the cameras will still follow me, but I'd like to give this relationship a chance."

I grin so wide. "That would be the most awesome thing ever. I was thinking of taking a few classes at BU, too."

His smile matches mine and he takes my hand in his. "I know this is crazy, but during your interview, there was this one moment when you were staring right through the glass at me, and I felt like I got punched in the gut. If I could've ended the competition right then, I would have. I let the producers choose the rest of the girls. You were the only one I picked for me."

My face heats and the machine by the bed beeps rapidly. There's nothing I can say to top that. So I lean in and gently kiss his lips. He brushes my hair back from my face and pulls away. He takes in my expression and gives me his full smile. I melt.

"Does the smile mean you'll be my girlfriend?"

"Oh, Jeremy."

"Is that a yes?"

"Absolutely. I'm crazy about you!" I grab his T-shirt and pull him back in for another kiss. My boyfriend, Jeremy Bane.

ACKNOWLEDGMENTS

Thanks to: Carla and Angie for your unwavering support and emergency pep talks. To my husband for tolerating writerly mood swings. My daughters for occasionally playing nicely. My mom and sister for buying me all those books. My editor, Danielle Ellison, and all the hardworking people at Spencer Hill Press. My agent, Nicole Resciniti, and all the helpful people at the Seymour Agency. I couldn't have done this without any of you.

ABOUT THE AUTHOR

Sarah Gagnon grew up in the frigid woods of Maine amidst snow and animal skins. As a small child she wrote ship-wrecked romances all while being stared down by a taxidermied duck. She has a BFA in photography and a minor in writing from the University of Southern Maine. She's the mother of two tiny, feral children and two ill-behaved dogs. For fun she's taken up construction and interior design. Her first project: moving into a dilapidated farmhouse with her computer-genius husband.